IT'S TIME

COULD YOU RISK YOUR SANITY

TO SAVE YOURSELF?

The Hebrides Series

Book 1

Rachael Dytor

To Paul, this book would not have been possible
without your love and support.
And to Kyle, Lauren and Lucy -
may you always shine brightly!

CONTENTS

CHAPTER 1

February 12ᵗʰ 2018

Thomas

An unexpected ring of the bell. That's what jolted me awake from my slumber that night. It had been bitterly cold that day, the day that my life changed forevermore - the kind of cold that penetrates your skin and bones and is unshakeable even as you curl up into a foetal position in the wee hours of the night. It gnaws at your stomach and no amount of food will be sustenance enough to tame the icy cold fingers sending shockwaves throughout the entire body. Perhaps that ice-cold, all-consuming feeling should have woken me even before the ring of the bell. The feeling that I had admitted to myself was not only a result of the cold but also had its origins in a long-forgotten memory, something I had hidden in the deep recesses of my subconscious.

I figured that if I kept the memory hidden for long enough it would cease to exist. I didn't need months of therapy, all I needed was to find a little hiding place in my mind, a compartment to store this particular ill away and there we go, gone! In theory, a brilliant idea, but, of course, fatally flawed. Flawed, because everyone knows even those carefully compartmentalised boxes have a way of un-ravelling. Not just un-ravelling but creating a domino effect. As one box opens there's a crescendo effect and like a set of dominos when that first box opens all the other boxes open, their sides torn apart, falling just like a set of dominos at an ever-increasing speed until I can't take it anymore. I am becoming undone; I am having to face a reality I tried so hard to resist but it is my reality and it is my truth and the ring of the bell at 2 a.m. on that frosty February morning has finally made me face up to it.

His face should be strange to me. But of course, it's not. He doesn't fit into this façade I've created here to fit in and normalise myself. I have spun a very intricate web of lies and deceit. With the glossy exterior of tailored clothing, just the right car sat on the driveway, and very satisfying bank balance, I had fooled myself (and everyone else) into thinking this was me. But he knows who I am and where I've came from. He can see the pile of dominos laid out before me on the icy path. We need no introduction. Yes, he hasn't seen me since I was a boy but without a single word passing between us, he looks me in the eye, and he knows.

He doesn't look like a vagrant or someone you would necessarily cross the street to avoid (although I very much felt at that moment I'd love to bolt across the street). He did, however, have an un-nerving, knowing look which penetrated beyond the subtle aspect. He was communicating with me though his stare without a spoken word. He knew my truth and there was no escaping from this. Although I willed beyond anything to remove myself from this frozen nightmare, there was no movement to be had. My legs and feet betrayed me; they were frozen, motionless. They told my conscious mind you must stay here and listen, just stay put!

We both stood there, unsure who should start the conversation first. There was so much to be said but how do you form the words? How do you put sound and form to something which has lain dormant for so many years? Once the words are spoken there is no way back. This mask I have hidden behind will crumble.

How do I contemplate the enormity of de-masking myself, of being laid bare? I not only risk exposing myself but there's Janey and Michael to think of. They only know the masked version of me, the one I have carefully cultivated over the years.

In singing my solemn song, my truth, my life, and that of my family, will be set on a new trajectory. Right there at 2 a.m. on that Sunday morning I had a choice to make. Do I close the door and hope and pray that I can somehow shut the Pandora's box? Or do I form the words which in some distant part of my soul feel as though they're already forming on my tongue?

"Hello George, it's been a long time."

There, the words are out there before thought or process interject. I have acknowledged his presence before me and there is no going back now. I have started the conversation and the door will remain open. He acknowledges simply with "Thomas."

He doesn't need to add "you know why I'm here." Without any spoken word we both know why he's here. He says it anyway …

"It's time."

Of course it's time. I had been waiting for this moment. Subconsciously waiting. Waiting on this ring of the bell for him to tell me 'it's time.'

"It's time." Two words; two simple words but profoundly powerful. I knew exactly what 'it's time' for. It's time to go back. To go back to the place of my boyhood, to face up to the dark places. Had I not (almost) mastered the art of illusion, I would have realised the date. Not just the date February 12th but the significance of the timeframe, February 12th 2018, some 20 years since that fateful day.

To the onlooker I am Thomas, a 34-year-old man. Well thought of locally; well-presented and affluent; the epitome of normality. In all honesty I was someone who was to be respected and looked up to. Many co-workers aspired to be like me so tangled and expertly woven was the web I'd weaved. There was not a crack to be seen in the picture-perfect façade; even down to the beautiful wife I had chosen and of course the naturally gifted and handsome son I'd fathered.

Not until that day. This was distinctly out of character. A strange visitor in the middle of the night. However, there was no on-looker and, had there been, he wouldn't have understood the scene for what it was. Yes, I stood there, but only in form for I wasn't there, I had been transported back to February 12th 1998.

A tidal wave of emotions overcame me and no longer was I self-assured 34-year-old Thomas. I was a 14-year-old boy lost in time and space dealing with a situation, its magnitude way too huge to comprehend.

CHAPTER 2

I barely registered the hand pressing on my shoulder. In some distant place I heard my name being called. I was still lost in thought, but the sound of my name was becoming more urgent, piercing the black.

My eyes opened and took in the scene. There was no figure before me. He had disappeared. All I could see was my frozen garden; it was breathtakingly beautiful this frozen scene. However, the cold cut through my throat and lungs and rendered me speechless.

"Thomas; Thomas, are you OK?"

Janey was calling my name, not George, her voice full of tenderness and concern. Still I was unable to respond but I turned around and gradually I began to pull myself back to present day.

She was speaking very quickly, too quickly for me to understand and form any kind of response.

Why was I at the door in the middle of the night in the freezing cold?

When was I coming back to bed?

I remained silent and eventually she took in the scene; how ridged my body was and how utterly lost I looked when she made eye contact. She simply embraced me, and I could feel myself going limp in her arms. I wanted to sob and stay held like this forever. A small urgent part of me told me to pull myself together; not to let Janey know. This feeling grew and I was able to regain some form of composure.

I needed a cover-story to explain the state she found me in and this, I discovered, rolled easily off the tongue. "I'm so sorry to have woken you, I heard a noise outside and thought we might have an intruder. I went to investigate but thankfully there was no-one there. It gave me a fright and I'm sorry to have alarmed you." She guided me inside, away from the frozen scene.

Everything seemed so absolutely normal inside the confines of my house. I began to wonder if I had imagined the whole thing.

"Let's go back to bed, sweetheart," she said, her words again barely registering as I flitted between the two scenes.

I dutifully followed her upstairs and we made our way to bed. She lay curled up beside me, holding me close, her body so warm it should've melted the icy cold feeling which enveloped me, but it didn't.

There was no sleep to be had that night. My beautiful wife lay cocooned in a cosy blanket of sleep, her breathing not fitful. It was the contented breathing of someone in deep sleep. It hit me right at that moment seeing how perfect she was, would I ever sleep like that again?

As I lay awake in the gloom, I pondered the scene again. Did I actually see George, or had I imagined it? Janey saw no one when she met me at the door. However, those two words still rang very loudly in my ears: 'it's time.'

Whether George was there or not was really of no consequence – my demons had finally caught up with me and I knew I had to decide where to go from here.

Monday morning rolled around as it would do any other Monday morning. My world had spun upside down on its axis, yet Monday morning still arrived. Dawn broke but the sun barely penetrated the low cloud in the sky. Without the aid of the sun the frost would permeate every object it encountered. I could almost feel the icy tendrils seeping through my windowpane.

Somehow, I need to muster the strength to get out of bed and go about my day. Janey and Michael can't know anything has changed. I watch as Janey lazily stretches out and gathers herself in the darkness. I know no matter the outcome of events I will always love this woman. The question in my mind is whether she will still love me if she knows all about my past. I cannot ruminate on this for her eyes are opening. Straight away she is concerned, wondering if I managed to get to sleep after the events of the night.

I lie and tell her yes, eventually I had drifted off. Why not, lies have become second nature to me over the years. The deck of cards I have built my life on are based on the very shaky foundations of lies and deceit.

I hear Michael's alarm go off. I reassure myself – I have done a good job in raising Michael. He is a very happy, well-adjusted kid and it occurs to me that he is the very same age as I was on that fateful day when everything changed – 14 years old.

What I wouldn't give to turn the clock back and start things over. Michael has only the normal worries any 14-year-old boy should have to contend with – friends, girlfriends, and getting enough money to keep up with his various hobbies. His friendship circle is as wide as his variety of hobbies. I can't keep up but love to hear all about his life.

He is an open child and it's one of the qualities I love most about him. Clearly, he's snoozed the alarm as the wailing noise has stopped. Another thing I love about him, his laid-back nature and attitude towards life! Nothing is rushed with Michael, 'it all happens in its own good time', he often tells me. Wise words from a mere 14-year-old.

There is no time now to seriously consider anything as Monday morning takes form and I get pulled along – an unwilling participant in the day already mapped out before me. Perhaps I can lose myself in the daily tasks and there will be no time to concern myself with anything else.

Janey is already in full work mode, hastily showering and choosing her outfit. She doesn't stop for breakfast, just gives me a quick embrace and kiss and she's off, taking Michael with her. She is so passionate about her job as an editor at the local paper. Her passion has gained the respect of her peers and the local community who are all avid readers.

We met at University. She had an easy, effortlessly cool nature about her which drew you in. I didn't go looking for love and certainly didn't see it coming my way.

Ours wasn't the instant love that you so often see portrayed in films. Rather, it was one that grew and evolved over the years (as we grew). I was very serious and a large part of this was attributed to what I went through. But she had such a calming influence on me, so much so that I could often forget about events of the past.

On paper we shouldn't have worked. She was a free spirit wanting to change the world through the written word and I, a serious, brooding individual lost in the world of finance. But we worked, we just worked.

We had no ambition to have a huge family. I had followed in my parents' footsteps having Michael at a young age. We knew we wanted a child. We knew when Michael came along (albeit we were very young), what a blessing he would be and how loved he would be. How could we possibly share this amount of love on more than one child? No, our efforts went into doing the best we possibly could in raising Michael and climbing our respective career ladders.

I still lived in Scotland, quite a distance away from where I had been brought up and quite a different landscape from that of my childhood. I had to leave the area I was born and raised in, but somehow I still couldn't leave the country of my heritage.

I love the different changing seasons which come to pass in

Scotland; the way you know you are constantly shifting between one and the next. It can be stark and bleak with driving rain and within the next few minutes, open blue endless sky with the landscape continuously unfolding out before you.

This sense of space allows me to breath and make me think perhaps anything is possible. We live in the Scottish Borders, the most southerly part of Scotland. It is a beautiful area with low-lying hills surrounded by small towns and villages. It is often described as the forgotten Borders with tourists more likely to flock to the Highlands and Islands or the historic capital city of Edinburgh. I think this is why I chose to settle here; I can remain in my beloved Scotland but still retain a sense of anonymity. Add to that, people are easy going and don't pry into your affairs.

This was not the case growing up. Community was everything. I was born and raised on a croft in Dunvegan, a small village on the Isle of Skye. You became intimately involved in each other's affairs and not wholly through choice, partly through necessity. Without everyone looking out for one another, it wouldn't have been possible to thrive. You formed friendships and allegiances which were there to stand the test of time. This was true for my parents (to help with the survival of the croft) and for myself. Communities were small and neighbours could be spaced far apart so you cultivated that relationship with the boy you played with from next door.

Mother did her best, but she had her hands full running the croft and always trying to please the master of the house. Father, I am no longer in contact with and ours was a difficult relationship. He had a presence about him. You knew when he had entered a room. Normally, there was no visible bruising to mother's face (he was too clever for that), but she suffered greatly at his hands. She took the brunt of his sharp tongue, always trying to send us kids outside to tend to this or that whilst she was left to his mercy.

Memories of this time are starting to seep through to my

conscious mind. I am at the edge of a precipice peering down, unsure whether I should start the decent or fix myself to the spot and stand firm. A ringing noise stirs me from my reverie, and I realise I am sat at my desk at work and the caller is a very insistent one. I answer the call and make the switch, my mask firmly back in place, back to my well-rehearsed act of confident, self-assured Thomas.

I manage to keep things in place for the most part throughout the day until I turn the lock in the door and enter the house. It is unusually quiet. Janey and Michael aren't at home. Then something tells me of course, Michael has football practice and Janey will be there showing support. I bend down to collect the mail and make my way through to the kitchen. Just the usual bills, nothing worth even opening so I place them on the counter and notice something has dropped to the floor, something I must've missed under the pile of bills. A postcard. Strange. Do I know of anyone on holiday right now? And who even sends postcards these days?

I take in the scene and, as I do, I can feel my heart beating out of my chest; the hairs on the back of my neck stand on end and my palms are sweating. It's a postcard depicting various beauty spots on the Isle of Skye. We have the Old Man of Storr; the Fairy Pools; Dunvegan Castle & Neist Point Lighthouse. I turn it over and there are only four words: 'Wish you were here.'

Thankfully, I am on my own because there'd be no chance of me being able to conceal the look of fear in my eyes. I lose the ability to stay erect and slump in the nearest chair. I force myself to take deep breaths to slow my heart rate. At first it seems futile but eventually this pays off and I have regained enough composure to try to engage my brain into action. I lift the postcard up again and turn it over. What else can I learn from this? Of course! There is no postmark, this postcard hasn't come from Skye, it's been hand delivered. So last night I hadn't imagined seeing George, he was there, and he has hand-delivered this postcard to me.

I have lost track of time as I sit there staring at my unwanted delivery. It feels as though the initial thoughts I had about whether I wanted to choose to delve into my past and revisit what happened were being snatched away. There was no choice here. George had seen to that. He was forcing me into action. Simply burying my head in the sand was not an option.

I hear the crunch of gravel on the driveway, and it stirs me into action. I hastily shove the postcard into my trouser pocket and ready myself to greet Janey and Michael.

My two favourite people in the world manage to lift my mood somewhat. I get walked through the highlights of Michael's game where he (naturally) excelled, making great passes at opportune moments, and of course scored the penultimate goal in the last five minutes of the game.

"Dad, after the game the coach asked to see me. He thinks I should be trying out for Edinburgh United Junior team!"

"He said, 'it's time', Dad!"

I couldn't let the force of those words impact on the reaction my only son was waiting for. I congratulated him and told him how proud I was whilst those two haunting words rang in my ears – 'it's time ...'

CHAPTER 3

George

I take in my surroundings. This is the first time I have ever visited the Scottish Borders. It is in stark contrast to the landscape of Skye. It certainly has a beauty of its own that's for sure and this beauty is magnified as the pale sun sets over the horizon. Everything Jack Frost has touched starts to sparkle in the half light. I retreat inside into the warmth of my rental house. A coal fire tempts me in; the flames licking up the chimney flu. This at least reminds me of home.

I imagine Thomas will have finished his days' work and will be sat down as I am, mulling over the events of the past twenty-four hours. I recall the look of horror on his face when he saw me stood on his doorstep in the middle of the night. There was really no need to pay him a visit at that ungodly hour, but I simply had to get his attention. I wonder if he has received my delivery. What does he make of it?

He will surely be wondering how I tracked him down after all these years. I am quite sure he thought his old life was dead and buried. I know he hasn't been back to Skye since he left school. But believe me I have kept a close eye on the life and times of Thomas Taylor. It has been a hobby of mine tracking his comings and goings (always from afar). It was unbelievably easy I have to say. If Thomas was trying to stay hidden, he hadn't made a very good job of it.

He started his studies at the University of Edinburgh, graduating with honours gaining a Master's in Finance. (Local sources told me he'd left Skye to go study at Edinburgh University). From there he simply wasn't hard to track down at all. His name often appeared on their website when he'd gained his next accolade.

Social media was also a vast source of information. Thomas himself didn't have a very active profile but you can still tell a lot from someone's friends list. You simply research each of the friends listed and slowly begin to form a picture. He was 'in a relationship' with a Janey McVie. A beautiful girl who had a vibrancy about her and, it seems, a very driven quality. She was an environmental activist and active member of the debating team at Edinburgh University. Beauty and intellect, Thomas, how well you have done for yourself! She was an intriguing girl and yet there was something familiar about her…

Yes, the world wide web is your one-stop-shop for finding out everything you need to know about someone. You only have to type in the person's name then narrow the search criteria to the country you think they live in and the area of their work. 'Taylor' is a fairly common surname, but 'Taylor' combined with 'Scotland', 'Edinburgh University', and 'finance' led me straight to you in no time Thomas. It directed me towards your Facebook profile and, whilst I hadn't seen you for many years, there was no denying who was staring back at me from the computer screen.

My online searches also allowed me to track your career progression over the years. You started off as a trainee financial adviser at Standard Life headquarters in Edinburgh. It didn't take long for you to climb the ranks and make a name for yourself. You were headhunted and went to work for a prestigious financial advisory office in the city centre. The website for this company had a lovely photo of you, Thomas; a section devoted to you headed 'all about me.' Wonderful reading, I must say; hearing about all your achievements and what an outstanding and well-respected financial adviser you had become. You did not stop there, oh no, the sky's the limit with you, Thomas! You made a name for yourself and built up a devoted client bank and settled in the town of Galashiels in the Scottish Borders. There you took the helm as Area Director and lead financial adviser (covering the Borders region) for a large financial advisory service with offices throughout Scotland. And this leads us to present day …

You see, Thomas, you may think you left Skye and you left it all behind but there's a paper trail which led me straight to your front door. I have patiently waited over the years for just the right time to approach you and that time is now. If you were trying to cover your tracks, you did not make a very good job of it. Yes, to the onlooker, you really look as though you have it all – the perfect career; beautiful wife; perfect son; and more money than most people could wish for. This is true. However, there are things you need to face, ghosts from your past. I know things about you, Thomas, perhaps I know you better than you know yourself.

Thomas

As a hush descends in the house, I no longer need to pretend to Janey that I am lying asleep. I sit upright in bed and find my thoughts drifting back to Skye. I wonder what has become of my siblings. In all the years following my departure from Skye they have never tried to make contact. I consider whether this has been a fault of mine or if it's a mutual indifference.

We truly are a broken family. This pains me somewhat when I consider the upbringing Janey had. It was in stark contrast to mine. I wonder what it must have been like to have had parents who dote on you; to grow up without the recurring simmering threat of violence in the air.

I suspect that I, along with mother (although obviously to nowhere near the same degree), bore the brunt of father's moods. I took on board the job of keeping my siblings in check and looked after them whilst mother cooked and cleaned. She was so consumed with chores and jobs on the croft which were never-ending. He would bark orders at me, and I was only too willing to oblige since anytime spent outside of the house was a welcome relief.

There is no contact either with father and I muse over where he is now and what has become of him. Surely he can't be tending to the croft all on his own? Were any of my siblings still there helping out?

I left Skye at age 16. My siblings (Caroline, James, and Juliet) were all younger than me. At a rough estimate, I would suggest they would now be in their early thirties (Juliet, however, may be late twenties). Unlikely they would still be living on the croft and, if they were, I felt heart sorry for them. Left alone with father, what kind of life would that be?

Mother is the only one I am still in contact with. I say still in contact, but only intermittently via telephone. I get regular updates from the nursing home she now calls home. She has early on set dementia and lives in her own little world most of the time. When she has lucid moments, the staff are very good at contacting me and I chat with her briefly. The content of these chats varies drastically depending on how her mood is that day and whether her medication is having a positive effect. Sometimes she has me fooled into thinking she shouldn't be in care, that there's nothing wrong with her. At other times she may have agreed to chat with me and when I speak to her, she can scream at me down the phone, shouting repeatedly, "Go away; go away."

When I first started making these calls with her, I used to bring up father's name or my siblings. Or sometimes I would talk about matters relating to the croft. But I soon realised that this put her mood into a downward spiral, and she reverted further into herself.

Any chat about the past seemed to make her recoil and I pictured a frail little woman on the other end of the phone, so we kept things simple. I would enquire about what she had been up to and what the food was like. Very banal conversation but this was the way it had to be. It was very frustrating as I had no clue what had become of my siblings. Father I was not so concerned about, but I was anxious to know if my brother and sisters were OK.

I recall some of the times we spent on the croft. We stuck together and pulled together when there were jobs to be done, such as cutting the peat or feeding the animals, but when there was some free time it often fell that my sisters would pair up and go off together and I'd be left with James.

All three had very difference personalities. Caroline came across as very quiet and timid. A reserved girl, she shied away from large gatherings and was not confident at speaking out. What people did not realise was that underneath that shy timid exterior, there was a very clever mind at work. She was a master manipulator. How expertly she worked at making you think you had chosen to do something in a certain way, but she was a puppeteer, pulling your strings and making you bend and twist this way and that to the beat of her drum. The truth was you could never be angry at her either because of the timid little girl persona she donned. She was really such an expert in manipulation that you were always left questioning whether she could've possibly had any part to play in the outcome of the situation in the first place.

Juliet was the youngest and, bless her, she just went along and had to do what she was told. She was a beautiful girl and was very open and honest. I felt sad for her growing up as I felt sure she would have been used as a pawn by Caroline. If she was being manipulated, she didn't let it bring her down. Nor did she let father's dark moods penetrate her positivity. She radiated happiness and I suspect this was a source of annoyance to father who seemed to revel in us all emanating his gloominess. Yes, we could all aspire to be more like Juliet.

Then there was James. What can I say about James! The sides of my mouth pinch as I realise a smile is forming on my lips. I have fond memories of James. He was the quintessential naughty schoolboy. He was forever plotting and scheming up new plans, never able to sit still to catch a breath. But you couldn't help but have a soft spot for him at the same time. We all think at one time or another about what we would like to do in a situation, but something holds us back. With James there was no such filter. He acted upon anything which came into his mind. I marvelled at some of the schemes he would dream up. But because he was unable to act on these in father's presence, it was up to me to somehow rein him in when we were outside doing chores or having free time. He was manageable whilst doing tasks as his mind was kept busy but in our free time his creative mind was left to run wild.

I chuckle inwardly to myself when I recall the fascination he had with horses and being a cowboy. It began at an early age. He would pester our parents to buy him a horse. But money was tight, and we were already stretched with the livestock we had. This did not deter James. He wanted a horse and he wanted to look the part, so he set about fashioning a saddle from the cushioned seat left over in an old rusty tractor sitting out back. I didn't see the finished product but what I witnessed is one of the funniest things I think I've ever seen even to this day … there he was in his home-made saddle with father's hat on, riding our tup Bruno full pelt across the field and up the ridge. Give him his due, the boy was holding on, but it looked like a scene that could only end badly! Where are you now, James, and what are you up to? I cannot begin to imagine what a thirty-something-year-old version of James could possibly be like. Had he settled down or was he still the spirited character I remembered?

I must have fallen into a deep sleep shortly after because the next thing I knew, the alarm was ringing in my ears. After gathering myself

I make my way down to breakfast and I am surprised to see Janey still sat there as she is normally out the door long before me.

"I found something curious," she says. I am caught off guard and unsure where this is headed.

"What, love?"

"In your trouser pocket, Thomas … I went to do the washing and picked up the trousers you had dumped next to the bed and a postcard fell out of them. It was a very odd card as it was hand-delivered with only the words 'wish you were here'."

I manage to stand firm and simply say, "Oh that, I meant to put that in the bin. Yes, I thought it was strange too, but it must've been put through the wrong letterbox, nothing to worry about."

I turn my back to her to indicate the conversation is at an end and go about fixing breakfast but when I turn back around and make eye contact, I see an altogether unconvinced Janey staring back at me. She doesn't pursue the subject so for that I'm grateful and give her a quick kiss and make my way to work.

Morning passes in a blur of meetings. I pause for a brief lunch, wolfing down my sandwich, and set about analysing the performance of my client's investment portfolio. My assistant Susie knows not to interrupt me just before a client meeting so I suspect this must be an urgent call when she buzzes through to me.

"Thomas, I know you're busy, but I've got a Mr Smith on line one and he says it's urgent. I tried to put him off, but he was very insistent. Sorry! Is it OK to transfer the call?"

"Yes, no problem," I reason, thinking whoever this is, I'll get rid of them.

"Hello," No reply. "Hello, Mr Smith?" Again, no answer.

Just as I was about to place the receiver down, I hear, "Did you get the postcard?" OK so this was no Mr Smith, George Traynor had also tracked me down at my work! Let's play along and see what he has to say …

"You know I received the postcard, George! Now tell me, what is it that you want. You show up at my house in the middle of the night, deliver a random postcard to me, and now you're phoning me at work. I will not be harassed by you!" Time stands still as I wait for his response. He appears to be in no hurry as I listen to nothing but a faint sound of static on the line. Impatiently I cajole him, "Well?"

He responds, "Thomas, the time has come for you to go back to Skye. You can't run and hide from this any longer. Let's you and I take a wee trip home, son, back down memory lane."

I'm confused, I can't tell if he's being menacing or friendly with that last comment.

"Look, George, I can't just up and leave my business and family just because you show up out of the blue and demand that I go on some random trip with you! Now please just leave me alone. Do not contact me again. Do not show up at my house or my work, just go back to wherever it is you came from and leave me alone!" I am about to slam the phone down when I hear laughing on the other end. What the…?! I can't help myself. "Exactly what part of all this do you find so amusing? If you carry on, George, I'll be forced to contact the Police." With that the laughing ceases.

"Do you really expect me to believe you would go to the Police? This is no matter for the Police, it is personal, Thomas."

With no response, he carries on, "You need to come back, son, there's things you need to know."

I respond, "What things?" but I realise my question will remain unanswered because the faint static has been replaced with a dull tone. George has hung up.

I am late for my 2 o'clock as I take time out to gather myself and find that my usual enthusiasm has waned, the stuffing literally knocked out of me. The meeting went ahead and dragged on for longer than I would have liked. I realise I have no idea what time it is as I stare outside and notice that not only is it now pitch black, but it's also snowing. It starts as a little flurry but gains momentum quickly.

The little flurry had deceived me for it must've came on heavy when I'd been in the meeting. I see only mine and another couple of cars left in the carpark, everyone else must have left for the night. As I set foot outside, I marvel at the snow scene before me. There is an ethereal quality, a beautiful silence. The drive home could be interesting with the snow coming down fast on top of the ice which had never managed to melt away. I don't have time to consider what to do about George as I focus all my attention on simply getting home in one piece.

The night passes uneventfully and for that I'm grateful. It's refreshing to be part of 'normal' conversation; easy-going and light-hearted. I quiz Michael on whether he has a girlfriend and it's just friendly banter back and forth. "Of course I have, dad, who's gonna say no to this face, come on now." Janey as well seems fairly relaxed and if she's at all concerned about our chat earlier this morning, she doesn't show it.

I manage to sleep solidly for the most part throughout the night, resolving to push any thoughts of George to one side for now.

All was going well when I arose and set about getting ready for work. That was until my mobile phone rang. Sunny Days Care Home flashed up on the screen – mother's care home.

"Mr Taylor."

"Hello," I respond.

"Hello this is Beatrice from Home Farm Care. Sorry to bother you and I don't want to alarm you but there's been an incident—"

I don't let her finish, I interject, "What do you mean there's been an incident? What type of incident?"

"She had a visit earlier today from your father and nothing happened so don't worry, she's not hurt or anything, but she has become very hard to handle. It's quite unlike her, she's been lashing out at the staff; kicking and biting and refusing to eat or drink."

"Are you saying this is as result of father's visit?"

"Well, I can't say for sure, but it's been a number of years since he's been here, and he shows up out of the blue and the next thing we know your mother is acting completely out of character … People with dementia can show these tendencies but your mother has never displayed them before. Her illness is one which made her revert more into herself. Anyway, she's refusing to allow any of the staff to come near her and says she'll only speak to you."

"OK, thanks for letting me know. Is she wanting to speak to me just now?"

"No, she's resting up, Mr Taylor, but when she comes around if she is still asking for you would it be possible to give you a call back?"

"Sure, no problem," and we end the call.

What on earth is going on? First, I have George pestering me to go back to Skye, now this! Why has father gone to visit mother in her home if he's not been for years? Why now and what has he said to her to cause her to start lashing out?

I wait on tenterhooks for the phone to ring and eventually it does a couple of hours later. Beatrice passes the phone to my mother and I say a tentative "Hello." A brief pause then, "Hello son." Relief floods my bones, no matter what's happened, at least she is lucid enough now and knows who I am. And, she has calmed down enough to speak to me.

"Are you OK, mother?"

No pause this time. "Bad man; bad man; bad man."

"Who was the bad man, mother?"

"Can't say; not allowed to say."

"What do you mean you're not allowed to say? What has happened, mum? Has someone upset you?" There is no response. I wait patiently but nothing. I don't know if mentioning father would be a wise move or not and I wrestle with my conscious as I dive between concern about mother's welfare and my own curiosity about exactly what happened during the visit.

My curiosity is the victor and I press on, "I know father came to see you earlier today mother what—"

Before I can finish my sentence, she implodes, "No; no; no; bad man ..." The rest I was unable to decipher but I could hear Beatrice in the background calling for back-up. A noise akin to the phone crashing on the ground was next, then the dial tone. I sit there for some time, unable to steady the flow of my breath. My heart feels as though it's beating out of my chest; my throat constricted and my temples throbbing. I am unable to shake the nervous tension which has enveloped me.

I don't hear back from the care home until later that evening. Beatrice had finished her shift so a barely interested Carly phones to tell me mother is OK now. She lashed out at a couple of staff members, but they had the situation under control once they were able to sedate her. I thank her and tell her that I will phone in tomorrow to see how she's getting on.

I realise the events of the past few days are my burden and my burden alone. I cannot share any of this with Janey. This feels very strange because I am used to being able to share everything with my wife and best friend. She doesn't know a great deal about my upbringing. I've talked about my siblings and she knows that mother is now in a care home, but I have never gone into any great detail about how bad things were. Why would I? Ever since I left Skye all I have ever tried to do is move on from it and bury it as deeply as I possibly could. She knows I had a difficult relationship with father but a combination of me not wanting to delve into it and her not pressing me for information has meant we've only ever touched briefly on it.

No, I must figure this out for myself. But how? My thoughts are with mother and I hope the sedation has been effective. Perhaps when she wakes this time, if she's not reminded again of father's visit, she might be able to put it behind her. I truly hope so.

As I lay in bed, sleep only a whisper away, a noise rouses me, and I realise someone has texted me. My brain not fully functioning, I reach out to pick the phone up. It's an unknown number and I feel the veil of sleep diminishing rapidly. Before I open the text, I note the time – 12:30 a.m. This had better be good. Who was trying to make contact at this time of night? I open the message to reveal a text which to an outsider would look perfectly normal, a concerned friend or relative perhaps. It read: 'Is your mother OK, Thomas?'

OK, you have my attention! Who has sent this text? George? But how would he have my number and how would he know about my mother and the incident at the care home? No, that makes no sense. No-one in the Borders could possibly know about mother and what happened today other than father and the staff at the care home. That had to be it, someone at the care home. They had my number and there is no way that father could have my number. Still extremely odd that someone at the care home would make contact at this time of night unless there was an issue with the mobile phone network and the text has only just filtered through.

That's it, no need to panic, it's someone from the care home, it's an innocent text. I resolve to answer in the morning and place the phone down then try to clear my mind for sleep. As I drift back down into that comfortable slummy state, another bleep sounds on my phone. I reach over and look at the screen; open the text and I see, 'Thomas really, is she OK?'

This is clearly not someone from the care home. Whoever this is, they are playing games with me. If I don't answer, even if no further text appears, I know there's no chance of any sleep coming.

I am curious. I am curious and more than slightly alarmed as to your identity. However, there is always another option – to deflect and play it cool in the hope that whoever this is, they lose interest and make no further contact. Let's try this tactic first. I reply, 'Sorry you must have the wrong number.' There. It's sent. I switch the tone to vibrate and turn the sound down so Janey isn't disturbed. I'll wait for ten minutes or so and, if there's no reply, I'll switch the phone off and go to sleep.

Five minutes pass and nothing. Then another five minutes pass and still nothing. OK you leave me no choice. 'Who is this?!' Another buzz, much quicker this time. 'It's your friend here, George. Your assistant Susie was kind enough to pass your phone number onto me earlier today when I told her I had tried to reach you at the office and was unable to get through to you. She was happy to release your number when I told her it was rather urgent and that I had a large sum of money to invest. Very obliging of her I must say!' Fabulous. I can't even be angry with Susie; I've always told her it's OK to hand my personal mobile number out to clients if it's urgent.

So, George knows where I live, he knows where I work, and he has both my work and mobile phone numbers. He is not going anywhere anytime soon by the looks of it. But how on earth could he possibly have known about what happened with mother today? I rack my brains and come up with no plausible answer. He is forcing me to quiz him, and I imagine he is revelling in the power game he is playing.

I type, 'What do you mean by how is mother doing? What do you know about my mother?'

He replies, 'I had a chat with an old acquaintance of hers recently.

I just wanted to know if she was doing OK. I was concerned for her welfare but all in good time, Thomas. I will be in touch tomorrow. I think you and I should meet up and we can discuss arrangements about your forthcoming trip up north.'

My forthcoming trip up north?! I will not be railroaded into taking a trip with some random person from my past who is clearly more than slightly unhinged. (Having said that, I am only too aware that what he is saying is correct, I do have unfinished business up there.) I cannot think of any worthwhile response as he hasn't listened to any of my recent protests, so I turn the phone off and lie down and once again wonder if there's any hope of sleep coming tonight.

CHAPTER 4

Bert

Life had suddenly become more interesting. I must say I was surprised when I answered the phone earlier in the week and heard George on the other end of the line. Well, there's a ghost from the past! It had been quite a number of years since we'd last had any contact, I forget how long but then I forget quite a lot of things these days.

"I need to make you aware of my plans, Bert," he declares. A pause.

"Well spit it out, man!"

"I plan to bring Thomas back to Skye. He needs to know the full story about his past and I thought it was only right you should know. So, if you wanted to reach out to him whilst he's here …"

OK George, I am listening! However, he doesn't stop there.

"I will take him to see Mary too. He hasn't seen her since he was a boy."

Now he has my full attention. I had to intercept this and get to Mary before those two did. There is no way that useless bitch is going to implicate me. She needs told to keep that mouth of hers sealed shut. I am sure that won't be a problem. Lord knows what planet she is living on these days; probably doesn't even know what day of the week it is.

I need to play it cool though, act nonchalant so he doesn't realise he has ruffled my feathers.

"What are you hoping to achieve by bringing him back here?"

"Not so fast, Bert, that's for me to worry about. It is of no concern to you. Let's be honest, when have you ever shown concern for the lad before? So let's not pretend you're suddenly interested now. However, that being said, you have a chance to make amends with him, should you so choose – hence the reason for my call."

He had a point. I never could be bothered with Thomas. He was a useless snivelling boy, not much use around the croft and always in the way when I was trying to give Mary a good seeing to. 'Make amends.' Ha! Not on your life! I ended the call with George just after his 'make amends' suggestion. I didn't let onto him about my plans to go and see Mary. Yes, this could be fun paying her a wee visit, but would she still recognise me in her 'demented' state?

I got up early the following morning filled with conviction. I just hope the old bat recognises me or this will have all been for nothing. I have never been one to concern myself with clothing but with an extra spring in my step, I find myself perusing through my wardrobe considering what would be just the right outfit for today's tete-a-tete.

OK I admit it, I have let things go around here. The croft is dilapidated at best. It is only just ticking over with government grant money but it's an impossible job to sustain it with only me, myself & I. I had no option but to sell off some of the livestock to raise cash. All that I'm left with now are a handful of sheep, a highland cow, and some chickens. Things are grim and if I'm honest selling up is going to be the only option (that is if I can find a buyer).

Never mind, not to worry, let's focus on today. I have already phoned ahead and notified them of my intention to visit. I spoke with Beatrice. What a nosy cow that one is! "Oh, this is quite unexpected, Mr Taylor, it's been quite a number of years since we last saw you. In fact, if my memory serves me correctly was it not when Mary first came to us?" What's it got to do with her? I'm so tempted to give her a piece of my mind, but I rein it in when I realise in doing so she might refuse my visit. "Oh I know but my schedule is so busy, Beatrice. I'm running the croft singlehandedly." "Quite, Mr Taylor, well that can't be easy. Of course you can come and visit Mary. I'm sure she'll be glad of a visitor. The visiting hours are 10–12 a.m. and 2–4 p.m." "I'll be there tomorrow at 10, thanks" and with that I hang up.

Sunny Days Care Home is located in Portree, some 20 miles from Dunvegan. So, I have a half hour or so drive to ponder what I'm going to say to her when I see her … I pull up outside and feel my heart flutter. This is truly an alien feeling as I realise it's a feeling of excitement, something I've not experienced for a very long time. As I recall, it is the same feeling I used to get many moons ago when I took great satisfaction in rattling Mary's fragile cage. Oh, it feels good to be back in the saddle! And the fact that the outcome of this visit is going to result in an upset Thomas, well that is simply the icing on the cake!

I find the staff room/reception close to the entrance and a young blond thing bearing the name Cindy greets me. She doesn't look the full shilling, but I'd definitely give that one a good seeing to! I sign my name in the register and she leads me down the corridor. She is incessantly chatting about Mary's welfare, how she slept last night and what she's had for breakfast – as if I'm remotely interested. "Oh yes, wonderful," I hear myself saying, playing along. I change my mind; this one would have to be gagged if I were to go anywhere near her.

We round a corner and reach our destination. Room 14. Cindy tells me she'll go in first ahead of me to check that Mary is OK to receive a visitor. I hear her tell Mary she has a visitor, but she doesn't mention my name. That's good, there's no way she'd agree to the visit if she knew who was standing behind the door. I feel myself giddy with anticipation. Ooh her face when she sees me! It's almost too much to bear! I remind myself however of why she's in here and the fact she might not recognise me. The lovely Beatrice reminded me of this yesterday too. "Now don't get upset, Mr Taylor, if she doesn't recognise you, she has good days and bad."

I needn't have worried … As I rounded her chair to move to face her, I stood before her and my only regret is not having photographic evidence to capture the look of pure horror which stole its way across her face. No matter, I'll take a mental image and store this away in my mind so I can always recall it and recapture the feelings I have now as I stand before her. It all comes rushing back to me in waves. Oh, what I put this woman through! I knew it was wrong (well a small voice in my head told me that and it was easily silenced) but oh how good it felt!

There doesn't need to be any words spoken yet. We take each other in, lost in our own thoughts. Her, transported back to the times of the croft in her own personal hell and me Lord and master ruling over my domain and this pathetic excuse for a wife. Seeing her sitting there slumped in an oversized chair locked away in a care home because she's losing her marbles somehow made her seem even more pathetic. Why didn't I do this years ago? Well thank you George for making contact, you really have made my year, old chap. This visit wouldn't have taken place had you not phoned me.

She doesn't utter a word, I didn't expect her to, I had her very well trained. To be honest, back in the day she was better trained than our old sheepdog Jess and Jess was higher up in the pecking order. Yes, Mary knew her place and that was at the bottom rung of the ladder. I could sit down in the chair opposite which the delightful Cindy has clearly left out for me, but I choose to stand so I can tower over the wrench, assuming my position of power and authority.

"Mary, look at me, woman," I start, my voice menacing but I keep the tone low, so we don't get disturbed. "How have you been, sweetheart?" I revel in the brief look of confusion as her features start to contort from abject horror to bewilderment. She really is an ugly specimen. In all the years we were together never once did I call her sweetheart, so the word had the desired effect. Perhaps she was considering if I was still a threat to her, as if the years had caused me to mellow out. If that were the case, I was soon going to clear that up.

The thoughts in my head roll off my tongue, "You are an ugly bitch, Mary. No man will ever have you now. Ugly and insane, great combination! Take your eyes off the floor, woman, and look at me when I'm talking to you." She does as she's told. "Bet you can't even wipe your own arse anymore, can you?! These poor bitches in here will soon be feeding you. What's the point of it all, just give up and put yourself and the rest of us out of our misery. No matter, you shouldn't be here too much longer. You've been here what, eight years? The average person with dementia lasts around 10 years so don't worry, sweetheart, you're on your way! I could always give you a helping hand along if you like, nothing is too much trouble." I expect a reaction from the last statement and when I see none I start to wonder if she's slipped away again into her inner world. OK Mary, we'll coax you out, don't you worry.

"So, I've been chatting with George Traynor." Was there a flicker of recognition there? I press on … "A most interesting conversation, Mary. He plans to bring Thomas back to Skye." I leave it at that for the minute, my words starting to have the desired effect I'd hoped for. The mere mention of Thomas' name and she shakes her fugue. Still no words from her but she is paying attention. "Yes, he tells me they're going to take a trip down memory lane. Now, if either of them show up here and they have any questions for you, I need to make sure you keep that mouth of yours firmly shut! Got it?! There is a good chance George could mention something about February 1998. I need to know you are going to be a good girl and keep shtum! Shouldn't be a problem. Looks as though the lights are on but no-one's home." I chuckle inwardly.

The one thing I do know about dementia is there is a good chance she can't remember what she ate for breakfast this morning but memories from even decades ago she will have stored. I bear witness to this as the face goes back to its original contorted state resembling both horror and fury. Oh, Mary, I didn't think you had it in you. She even tries to prise herself from her chair but with her muscles clearly having wasted away from sitting for extended periods, she doesn't make it far and a firm hand from me pressed down onto her shoulder pushes her back down. Things escalate from here. She screams a high-pitched wail, "Help me; help me," and pushes a red panic button located on a box on the side of the table next to her.

Within seconds Cindy appears with a matronly, plump-looking woman by her side. I read the name tag 'Beatrice' – figures! "What's going on here, Mary? Are you OK?" Mary is babbling and is virtually undecipherable and it turns my stomach, the stupid bitch, she is making no sense. I want to tell Beatrice to hook her up to morphine and put her down once and for all. That wouldn't be the done thing, would it? So I interject with deflection, "I don't know what's wrong with her! She was fine one minute and, the next, she went crazy. Have you got her on the right medication? You're clearly not doing your jobs properly!"

Beatrice responds, "Mr Taylor please can you leave now and let us see to Mary." This wasn't a question; it was an instruction and I grudgingly left, which was a shame. It would've been just the ticket to see them restraining her and perhaps giving her a shot of something to calm her down. No matter, I'll just have to imagine that scene in my head. Well George, I think I've done a good job there and make no mistake. I almost skip out of the care home feeling giddier than I have done in years.

CHAPTER 5

April 1998

I awaken as usual to the noise of the animals. I hear the rooster singing his morning song, imagining him striding along proudly showing off his plumage. He's closely followed by the hens. It's lambing time so we have to keep a close eye on the ewes. They are hardy beasts and are used to the tough terrain of the Inner Hebrides and can easily lamb outside, but we have to be aware in case any lambs get stuck in the birthing process, so I keep an ear out for the sound of an ewe giving birth but I hear nothing.

This is my favourite time of the day, early morning when I am alone with no pressure to do anything or be anywhere. I know I could sleep on a bit longer but I've trained myself to wake when the rooster calls so I can have some precious time to myself. I lose myself in my imagination. I wonder what it would be like to be living in a foreign country; to be a different race or religion. Having never left Skye and only ever left the croft to go to school or accompany mother once every few weeks to do food shopping, my imagination was my sanctuary. I fantasize about what it would be like to be rich and live in a fancy house with fancy clothes. Imagine having a butler to chauffeur you around to a posh restaurant or clean up after you because frankly you couldn't be bothered. Or imagine living as a nomad in the desert, what would that be like? The blazing sun on your face and your camel by your side. The weather on Skye could be wild at times and blazing sun was not a frequent commodity so I pause on this thought and imagine the sun warming my whole body.

My happy dreamscape is broken into shards as the jarring voice of father penetrates through my fantasy. "Thomas! Thomas, move it, boy! Shift your lazy carcass." With a heavy heart I jump out of bed and set about going downstairs as quickly as possible. I know not to delay as this only aggravates him. The school has broken for the Easter holidays and this is not good news. Whilst most of my schoolmates are happy to just 'chill out', I know I will have endless work to do on the croft and no escape from father. I don't necessarily love school, but it provides me with a welcome escape for a few hours each day.

Father had adopted his usual position, head of the table sitting waiting to be served. Mother I know is always first up in the household, fetching the eggs from the barn and preparing everything just so, just how father likes it. We're not allowed to speak at the breakfast table so we sit in silence which I find excruciating because I can't bear the noise of him eating. His jaw makes a really odd sound as he chews, and he never eats with his mouth closed so we are all subjected to the pleasure of watching him turning over his food. I see mother anxiously flitting here and there in the kitchen, unable to sit down – she's waiting to see if there's anything wrong with the food she's plated up which undoubtedly there normally is but I pray today everything is to his liking.

I consider what Caroline, James, and Juliet make of the situation and deduce that they are my co-conspirators in the loathing for the disgusting pig-like way father munches his breakfast down and then the ensuing stony silence we find ourselves in. We know better than to utter a single word. Perhaps if I were allowed to eat myself, I could focus on my food and the noises I make when eating but we're not allowed to eat until father is finished and has granted us permission to begin. So, we have no other option than to listen to him slavering and slurping away, that godforsaken jaw of his banging in tandem.

He has the same cooked breakfast each morning consisting of three rashers of bacon (fat removed); two fried eggs (well done); two sausages and beans. It looks promising this morning, he's almost finished, and it appears as though everything is to his liking. He only has one egg to polish off then, all being well, we can eat. He starts off with the yolk, puncturing it with his fork and I watch in horror as a small slither of yellow liquid escapes from the centre. Mother hasn't yet noticed the scene unfolding as she is busy at the sink already clearing away the frying pan and utensils. He doesn't shout or make a scene straight away … he very carefully lays both knife and fork down and sits back in the chair, arms folded in contemplation. This isn't good. I know better than to glance over at him, so I stare down at the table. He is being very calculated about how he's going to deal with her misdemeanour.

Out of the corner of my eye I notice one of his hands reach for the fried egg then drop it on the floor. The noise stops mother in her tracks. With no other sound in the kitchen other than the noise of her washing dishes, when the egg makes contact with the floor the sound is amplified.

"Mary," he says in a quiet menacing fashion. "Get over here." I want to stop this right now before he dishes out whatever punishment he has in store. Every part of my being wants to protect and shield her. I am frozen though, ashamedly frightened for my own skin. My heart is telling me to protect her, and my head renders my body motionless and speech mute. I hear the shuffle of her feet as she makes her way towards us, the shuffle of the condemned. Still no shouting but he simply says, "Get on the floor and eat that excuse for an egg up, no hands."

This is degrading. I am quite sure she'd have preferred a telling off or a quick slap, but this was his forte, dreaming up new ideas to break you down and here is the latest, mother on all fours eating like a dog off the floor and making her do it with an audience. I know he will be savouring the moment; engrossed in the spectacle so I consider whether I could risk a glance over. I cast my eyes towards him and see him totally relaxed, slung back in the chair; raptured with the very edges of the corners of his mouth upturned in a menacing grimace. He was loving this. Do I dare cast my eyes towards mother? I don't want to see this, my precious mother eating like a dog off the floor but a small part of me holds a morbid fascination and I look over. I knew straight away this was a mistake. This scene I know will be etched in my brain forever. Because she wasn't allowed to use her hands and the egg hadn't been chopped up into manageable pieces, she was floundering and failing; bits of it entering her mouth and bits dotted over her face and body. With the yolk not solidified she had yellow stains on her teeth and face.

I willed him to just put her out of her misery and call an end to this but in a further shameful act he took his plate, not uttering a word, then proceeded to smash it within an inch of her face on the floor. This caused mother's body to buck backwards. He was ready for her. He pushed her back down and told her to lick the remains of the yolk clean off the plate then tidy up 'her mess' afterwards. Dutifully she obliged. I'm sure it was only a couple of minutes, but it seemed to be an eternity before it was over.

I was aware of father shifting in his seat, so I quickly reverted my gaze downward to the table. He turned his attention to the rest of us. "Move it; no breakfast for you here this morning. Go and feed the sheep … NOW!" For once I was more than happy to leave the table without a morsel of food. I knew if I were to try to eat anything there's no way I'd be able to hold it down. I could already feel the bile rising in my throat and did my best to swallow it back down.

I wish I could slip back into my fantasy world where none of this torment existed. I just wanted to wrap my arms around mother to tell her everything will be OK, but I know that's not the case. There is no way she'll leave him she'd be too frightened to. She would be forever looking over her shoulder wondering when he was coming for her.

When I was younger, I used to just think this was the way of things and that everyone's household was the same, but now I know better. I've seen the interaction between my classmates and their fathers and it's in stark contrast to my reality. They have a loving relationship. I look on with envy as I see fathers gently ruffling their son's hair and embracing one another as they meet them at the school gates. There is no loaded silence, just easy chat with the fathers displaying a genuine interest and enthusiasm to hear how their beloved son's day went.

This is another fantasy of mine. I often imagine myself as being that boy at the school gates with a loving father; stood there with open arms ready to greet me. He doesn't have father's face; it doesn't matter too much what his face looks like and it can change frequently as I drop into the fantasy, but it's never been father as this would turn my fantasy into a nightmare. At least there are still some parts of me he can't penetrate.

We had experienced a harsh winter and it had been unforgiving on the land. Grass was in short supply, so the ewes needed an extra supplement as they were heavily pregnant, so I haul a couple of buckets of sileage up to them in the nearby field. I deposit the buckets in the feeding tray and watch as they lumber their way over, unable to move at their usual speed whilst carrying their heavy loads. As they make light work of the sileage I turn my attention to my siblings.

James I see is already up to no good. I don't know what he's doing but he's out of sight and that's never a good sign. Juliet is by my side, helpful as always. I'm seriously concerned about what impact father's antics are having on her. She is way too young to be witnessing his behaviour.

I ask her, "Are you OK?"

She beams up at me. "Yes, don't worry, Thomas, I'm fine thanks." Still that beautiful nature of hers. I hope and pray that his actions aren't chipping away at it.

I risk pushing a little further and the words are out before I realise it, "I wish mother would just leave him." A pained look flashes across her face as she considers how to respond but thinks better of it and decides not to answer. I've pushed too far, and I'm annoyed with myself. She's young and is dealing with this in her own way, lord knows I can relate. If that involves pushing it away and not talking about it then I respect that. We are all just trying to find a way to deal with it.

Now the feed is out it's time to check the water bute to ensure there's plenty water there for the ewes. I see Caroline has busied herself with this task. When complete she takes a seat on a large boulder adjacent to the water bute. Her posture tells me everything I need to know even before a single word is uttered. She is slumped forwards, her long hair dangling around her face. There is enough space on the boulder, so I sit down next to her.

As the eldest I always feel a duty to look after my younger brother and sisters. With mother preoccupied the majority of the time with matters around the croft and trying to pacify and please father, the majority of what my siblings have learned around the place has come from me.

I adopt a different tactic this time. Caroline can be fragile so rather than start a conversation I simply put an arm around her. We sit like that for a few minutes in a comfortable silence. Then she breaks the silence.

"She's weak you know."

"Sorry, what did you say?"

"She's weak, Thomas. Mother is weak, she should just stand up to him or pack her bags and get out. Why does she put up with it?"

"Well perhaps she can't see any way out."

Caroline pauses as she considers this and comes back with, "Possibly, but if it were me I'd find a way, I'd get the bastard back for what he'd done."

Her words shock me. Caroline at this point is young too and I'd never heard her use language like this. Even thinking about how she'd plot revenge on father. She was old beyond her years and it scared me. Was this the stamp he'd imprinted on her? Caroline was quite a shy character but clearly the damage has left a simmering fury there.

As I consider how to react, I end up not responding at all for I hear James rampaging in the adjacent field chasing an ewe who'd managed to escape through a hole in the fence. He is way too exuberant – she's heavily pregnant and scaring her could have drastic consequences for the unborn lamb. Rather than shout over and cause more noise I run over to lend a hand. Between us we coax her back into the correct field and she quickly re-joins the flock. It took some doing and we both collapse onto our backs on the grass. Too exhausted to tell him off I just lie prone and then a noise breaks the silence. It's laughter. James starts with a little chuckle then it's a full-on hearty belly laugh. It's infectious and I join in. He takes to his feet and does an impression of the pregnant ewe; legs akimbo cluelessly darting this way and that then it all becomes too much, and he falls down again rolling about the grass in fits of laughter. I am so grateful to this boy. He has provided us with a welcome distraction and lifted our spirits, for now at least.

CHAPTER 6

Thankfully I awaken this morning having managed to get some sleep. It felt as though my body shut down with exhaustion last night, leaving my mind no other option than to eventually follow suite and surrender too. I gaze over and see Janey lying there. She's normally up and about by now but perhaps she's benefitted from a night when her husband hasn't been tossing and turning the whole time. I know she'd want me to rouse her as she's going to be late, but she just looks so peaceful I can't bring myself to do it. At least with some sleep on board I might be able to piece things together. Yes, a clear head is what I need to think about how to deal with everything.

First things first, let's see if there are any more messages. I ease gently out of bed leaving Janey to her slumber and head down to the kitchen. Michael is there just finishing off breakfast. We have a quick chat about what he has planned for the day and then it's "bye dad" and off he goes. I'm left in silence, so I retrieve my phone and turn it on. Nothing. No more contact from George. This is a good thing. It gives me time to think about my next steps. It's 08:30, possibly too early to phone the care home so I fix some breakfast for myself and Janey and take it upstairs.

It could've been me getting back into bed or the smell of the coffee, but a sleeping Janey bursts into life. "Breakfast in bed. Is it the weekend?" I explain unfortunately not. When she realises the time, she takes a quick slurp of coffee and hastily shoves some clothes on. There's clearly no time for a shower so she grabs a slice of toast and with that she's off.

It's now after 9 a.m. and I too should be in the office. Instead, I phone in and tell Susie a little white lie – that I'll be in shortly, that I'm at the doctors. I phone the care home and Beatrice answers after only a couple of rings.

"Morning Beatrice, it's Thomas Taylor here. I was just wondering how mother was doing."

"Well Thomas, she's had a good night and is bright as a button this morning. She had a chat with one of our domestics late last night and was very lucid, able to recall various facts and memories so that was lovely. She has calmed right down. In fact, you'd almost think that yesterday had never happened. Perhaps her illness has erased the memory? Anyway, we have no concerns about her, and I'll tell her you're asking for her." I thank Beatrice and hang up.

This was what I'd hoped for. Her short-term memory isn't good at all and I wondered if she'd recall any of it. That at least provides welcome relief. Before I stow my phone away, I feel it pulse and vibrate in my hand. Another message from George – 'Meet me at 1 p.m. at Bank Street Gardens.' Once again George is in control, dictating the flow of things. I consider replying to his text then think better of it. I will meet him at the designated time and place and hear what he has to say first, then take it from there. He has been persistent to say the least, so I guess I need to hear him out.

I head off to work and the morning passes uneventfully. I curse George for arranging to meet somewhere outside. It's bitterly cold and there's been a fresh flurry of snow. As I approach Bank Street I glance over at the gardens. The snow looks like spun sugar, it's a truly magical scene. Then I catch myself as I remember why I'm here.

As I approach the gardens, I see the solitary figure of George. We exchange pleasantries and George initiates the conversation.

"Afternoon Thomas, thank you for meeting me. I thought you and I could take a walk, it's too cold to stop anywhere." Well, I'm fine with that, at least we agree on something!

My plan to see what he has to say goes right out of the window and I jump straight in; "OK you have my attention. You want me to go back to Skye but why? For what reason? What do you plan to achieve by dragging me back there and what makes you think I'll agree to it?"

"Slow down, Thomas, we'll get to that."

God this man frustrates me. He is always so cool, calm, and collected. I guide us towards the black path, a walk which runs alongside the Gala Water. I see the river is unable to flow freely with large clusters of ice along its length. The path is icy too so we walk tentatively as it doesn't appear to have been gritted.

I know there is no point in saying anything further so I muster as much patience as I can and wait with bated breath on his response. He makes me wait a good ten minutes or so then – "Have you never considered returning to Skye over the years, Thomas?" Is he playing with me?!

"Of course I've never considered returning to Skye! You know fully well why not."

"I have to be honest with you, Thomas, when I say I can't tell you everything right now. There are things you don't know, and I need you to trust me on this when I say you need to go back and see for yourself." This was giving me very little to go on.

"Why can't I just leave the past in the past and continue on with my life? I have a good life here. Why would I want to put that in jeopardy by going on a wild goose chase up north?"

"Why indeed? Well, I'm sorry, but that's where we have to leave it but like I say there are things you don't know. I'm heading back in a couple of days and I'll stay in touch. You need to address this,

Thomas. You think you've moved on with your life, but you haven't, you're living a lie. Without addressing what happened in your past, you can never fully move forwards. Goodbye for now, Thomas, and we shall speak soon."

With that, he about turned and left me standing there. I had no new information, yet his words struck a chord with me. I'd always known deep down that there was unfinished business in Skye. I thought the best remedy was to flee and never return but in dark moments I have flashbacks to my childhood and of course that fateful day in February 1998.

I consider the consequences of returning. Would I get closure, or would it break me? If I remain in the Borders, I would never know, but if I head to Skye who and what will I be confronting? The thought sends a shiver up my spine.

I return to work and find myself checking my diary to see what my schedule is looking like over the coming weeks. With no prior thought, here I am checking my schedule to see how I could possibly free up some time. There are no 'free days.' The very efficient Susie has meetings booked out for the next six weeks or so. This was not going to be easy and what do I even tell Janey and Michael? Then there was George's lack of information – he didn't give me any indication as to how long I should plan the trip for.

I buzz Susie through to discuss the matter. "I don't like to ask but how feasible would it be for you to re-schedule some of my meetings? I'm feeling run down and the doctor has recommended that I take a couple of weeks off work." She doesn't do a very good job of hiding the pained expression on her face.

"Well it won't be easy but of course it can be done."

"That's great then. I'll come in next week as those meetings are too soon to reschedule then I'll take the following two weeks off."

"No problem, Thomas," and off she goes, clearly relishing the prospect of the numerous phone calls she had to make. I figured two weeks would be more than enough time and if it took less then I could always return to work earlier.

This was a huge decision I'd made in what felt like a heartbeat. I only hope I have made the right decision. And what to tell Janey and Michael? I have to come up with a convincing story. I can't tell Janey I'm going back to delve into my past, she'd only worry and undoubtedly want to come with me and there's no way I can have that. Then it hits me, I have a plan.

I wait until after dinner and I present my wife and son with my cover story. "So, it looks as though I'm going to have to go up north soon on business. Our Inverness branch are looking to recruit a new financial adviser and they've asked me to be involved. There were keen for me to help as I've had a lot of experience in recruiting in the past. There are two candidates currently in the running for the post and they both work on the Isle of Skye, so I'll be based there." I pause to hear my family's reaction.

The first question is from Janey. "And what do you feel about that, Thomas? Are you OK with spending time on Skye?" her voice loaded with concern.

"Oh yes, I'm purely there on business, I won't be seeing any family or anything."

The next question is from Michael; "When are you going, dad?"

"The week after next, son."

"That's really soon, dad, I hope it doesn't clash with my football try-outs." Oh, I'd forgotten all about that with everything that had been going on. Michael continues; "It's OK, dad, don't worry. If it does clash, mum will be there to see me. You go on your trip."

I'm so proud of him, he has a big heart. He gets up and leaves the table, leaving Janey and I to our thoughts. I gaze over at her and see her brow is furrowed, clearly she has serious doubts about my announcement. Eventually she says, "I'm not sure this is a good idea, Thomas. I'm worried about you going back there. I know you've never went into any great detail with me, but I know you didn't have a happy childhood. Is there anyone else they could ask to go in your place?"

"Don't worry, Janey. I wouldn't have agreed to this if I didn't think I could do it. Yes, I didn't have the best childhood but I'm not alone in that. Anyway, I am not there to catch up with anyone, I'm simply there on business."

She considers this. "OK, if you're sure. Would it help if we came through with you even for part of the trip?"

"No, not at all, I'll be fine. You need to be here; I know how crazy busy your work is right now and Michael can't afford to miss out on his schooling or this football try-out. Don't worry, it'll all be fine." I get up and go to her side and we embrace.

The following morning, I wake early and consider whereabouts on Skye I should find accommodation. George has given me no clue, but I reason that Portree would be a good idea. It's the main town on Skye and would provide a good base for my trip. Being almost in the centre of the island everything is accessible from there and there are plenty of amenities. For a brief moment I wonder about staying at Dunvegan then think better of it, I don't want to be a mere stone's throw away from the croft. Also, mother's care home is situated in Portree so it seems like the best option all round.

I search for some time then settle on a quayside apartment which sounds perfect. 'Industrial chic meets Victorian charm at this luxury harbour-front apartment overlooking Portree's picturesque harbour', so the advert boasts. It looks cosy and has a large wood burner so that'll be perfect and the view out to sea looks lovely. At this time of year, the weather can be wild so it'd be quite something staring off to sea should a storm hit, watching the waves crashing into the harbour.

I reflect on how quickly things have moved along. There is a distinctly tight knot in my stomach but interestingly mixed in with that there is also a tingling nervous anticipation. I marvel at the impact George's presence has had. He knows only too well my reluctance at venturing anywhere near the Isle of Skye and yet here I am only a matter of a few days after his visit having arranged the time off work, broke the news to my family, and sorted out accommodation. I wonder how much of this I have control over and how much I am getting pulled along. Well, there's no going back now, I knew that when I told Janey and Michael about my plans. Does George think I will remain in the Borders or venture to Skye? I am tempted to contact him then think better of it. He has been in control the whole way along, why not wait until I am ready!

George

I realise I have enjoyed my stay (albeit brief) in the Scottish Borders. It has a landscape made up of undulating hills and arable farmland. With such green lush fields, it's perfect for farming. Skye doesn't provide such fertile ground with farmers and their livestock alike having to adapt to the often harsh and unforgiving climate.

However, I know that I could never leave Skye. This is where my heart belongs. I am planning to retire in the not-too-distant future, and I can already feel the mountains beckoning me. I will avoid those well-trodden places where all the tourists congregate, choosing instead to go off the beaten track into the wild and remote corners of the island. These are the moments I truly come alive when I am immersed in the rugged terrain using my senses to navigate my way around. It is a truly magical island where mountains meet the sea; the Cullin mountain range providing an awe-inspiring backdrop. The colours are remarkable, and no two days are ever the same. The

Cullins tower over the land and, when they're not covered in snow, they're inky black; dark and foreboding.

Then you have the dramatic coastlines. To the north-west of the island, it resembles a Jurassic coast with the huge cliffs and boulders at ground level all jutting out at different angles. You see a good example of this at Neist Point Lighthouse. The wildlife too is in abundance and, if you are lucky, you can spot seals, whales, dolphins, and red deer. It is wild and dramatic and beautiful, and I struggle to find the words to best describe it as it truly has to be seen to be believed.

I pause as I think about how my chat went with Thomas today. He looked somewhat bewildered when I left him. I'm not surprised, it's a lot for him to take in. He's bound to be wondering what to do for the best. However, he needs to take my advice and take a leap of faith and head back to Skye. I can't go into any great detail with him about everything at this stage. He just needs to trust me as he once did many moons ago.

I know how Thomas ticks and he is not easily won over. Turning up at his house in the middle of the night was pretty dramatic but I had to get his attention. The other tactics as well were genuinely a little over the top, but I was feeling positive that my plan had worked. I truly believe he has listened to me and pray that he is in the process of planning a return visit.

My only regret (and it is a regret which niggles away at me) was that I involved his mother in all of this. Mentioning her in that text to Thomas was a mistake and it has weighed heavy on my mind, the call I had with Bert. The man is unhinged. I told Bert about my plans to take Thomas to see Mary when (and if) he comes to Skye. After ending the call, different scenarios started playing out in my mind. What if he went to pay her a visit? (This only occurred to me after I had spoken with him, so I was anxious to hear how she was, hence the text messages to Thomas). I accept that I went about it the wrong way. Thomas (probably rightly so) was very defensive when I asked after her. It was also ridiculously late to send a message. He is bound to be un-nerved. It had seemed like a good idea at the time but, with hindsight, I am not so sure. Anyway, I can only hope enough has been done to lure him to Skye. We shall see …

I pack the last few belongings into my case and set off out the door. My heart soars as I jump into the car and set the satellite navigation for the Isle of Skye.

CHAPTER 7

June 1998

The days are long as Spring bows its way out and surrenders to Summer. The sun rises around 4.30 a.m. so my friend the rooster is sounding his morning song very early now. That is fine with me, I love this precious time on my own before the rest of the house wakes up.

I draw my curtains and gaze up at the sky. There is still quite a lot of cloud cover but if today is anything like yesterday it'll only be a matter of time before that burns away. Since I was a small boy, I'd been fascinated with clouds. My imagination runs wild as I picture different scenes and objects. Although I'm now 13 and I've been told you lose your imagination as you grow up, I can't say that has been the case with me. As I look up at the clouds, I have played out a whole scene before me. It's quite fanciful! I see a huge elephant dancing and leaping around; a crown adorning his head and his master atop his back getting swung along. The clouds change in shape and form and the elephant drifts awa, giving rise to a child's face, a very expressive face, and I consider whether this child resembles anyone I know.

We only have a few days left of school before Summer break. Is it too much to hope that I might get at least a few days to take off on my own? How I would relish that prospect of free time to myself!

There are endless possibilities, but I know exactly what I'd do. I would take off on my bike. The freedom I feel as I pedal faster and faster is intoxicating. It's as though I'm taking off into the unknown and I'm very much at peace with no one to bother me and only adventures to be had. I allow myself to dream, why not!

I rise early as always on father's call and the morning passes uneventfully. (I appear to have completed my chores around the croft to father's liking since I hear no word of complaint, so this is looking promising.) I get the bus to school and settle behind my desk ready for the school day to begin. It felt as though everything was going well so I am surprised when the teacher asks me to stay behind at the end of the class.

I notice the normally composed Miss Davies looks somewhat flustered. This has me confused. She takes some time before she says anything, and I sense she is struggling to formulate the words.

"Thomas, this is a little bit sensitive." OK where is this going? "Is everything OK with you?" This has completely thrown me off guard. What could she possibly know about my personal life and how I am feeling? I start to panic and hope she doesn't know about my situation at home, then I reason with myself, but how could she?

I use a predictable default response, "Yes, I'm fine", hoping that it's case closed and I can disappear out the door. No such luck; a somewhat flustered Miss Davies now looks downright downtrodden, and the colour has risen in her cheeks.

She carries on, "It's just that a few of us have noticed that you're not quite yourself. I have to ask, is everything OK at home?"

Oh, now we get to the crux of it. And how do you know what it's like for me at home Miss Davies? Do you have any idea? And am I likely to tell you? Not a chance. I shudder involuntarily at the thought of father finding out about this chat if I were to give her any kind of an insight. To face his wrath is a fate worse than death so I go with,

"Yes, everything's fine, can I go now?" Please let me go, this is excruciating.

She persists, "Well I have noticed changes in your behaviour and your grades are starting to slip. We can leave it at that for now but if things don't change, I'll have no other option than to speak to your parents."

What does she mean by she has noticed changes in my behaviour? I don't dwell on it. With a green card to go, I'm out of there quick as a flash. There are only a few days to go before the end of term, so I'm not overly concerned about her speaking to my parents either so off I go.

I think no more of the matter and put it to the back of my mind. However, later in the day father is shouting on me to "Come here now, Thomas." I feel the all too familiar hairs on the back of my neck start to prickle and stand on end; my system already in a high state of alert with both pulse and heartbeat quickened. I reason with myself – calm down, you've done nothing wrong, there's no need to panic.

Juliet is in the room with me and, as always, she has comforting words of reassurance; "Don't worry, Thomas, it'll be nothing, he's probably just wanting help with a job or something." Her beautiful big doe eyes staring up at me do offer some solace.

"You're probably right, I'll go and see what he wants."

"Come on, lazy arse, get here now, son!" I pick up the pace and stand to attention in the front room, assuming my submissive position of eyes downcast to the floor. "Well, what have you got to say for yourself?" I'm confused! What is he talking about? To the best of my knowledge, I've not made any mistakes with my chores around the croft, and he can't possibly know about my chat today with Miss Davies, so I'm baffled but extremely anxious none the less.

"Sorry father, I'm not sure I know what you are talking about."

"Father, father?! You know full well you should address me as Sir."

"Sorry … Sir."

"Let's get that lazy bitch in here as she's part of this. Mary, Mary… move it! Get in here NOW!!"

I don't know where mother was in the croft as I couldn't hear her but in no time at all she's flanked by my side. I swear she's never far away, ready for her summons at the drop of a hat – she knows better than to keep him waiting. "Right Mary, you take it from here, tell that good-for-nothing son of ours what he's in trouble for this time. I swear he gets it from you. There's not so as much as two brain cells in that thick skull of his to rub together to figure out why he's stood before me right now." There is a momentary pause whilst mother gathers herself. She is clearly not used to taking the lead and he can't stand it. "Well spit it out, woman, we've not got all day." The tension in the room is palpable. When he says the words 'spit it out' some spit actually projects from his mouth and lands on the top of my nose. I feel my stomach heave at the thought of his spittle on my body, but I know better than to even shift in my position, so I stand strong and steadfast.

Eventually mother responds and in a small timid voice we hear the words "there was a note." I can't see his face as I'm still staring at the floor, but I sense that he is less than satisfied with her input.

"Fuck sake, Mary, you can't even do the simplest of things! 'There was a note'," he mimics in her quiet voice. "No more of it," he bellows, "it takes a man to get things done around here. Well son, here's what went down. You did a shite job when you hung your coat and bag up because a wee note fell out of your bag and drifted its merry way to the floor. This pathetic excuse for a woman here went to pick it up and no doubt would've destroyed it had I not been watching. You see, I am never far away. I've got eyes on the pair of you and don't forget it! So, Thomas, let's start again, what have you got to say for yourself?"

A note, a note?! What note? I am completely baffled! Has someone at school put a note in my bag?! This is not good. I don't have a clue what he's talking about. I can only respond with, "Sorry Sir, I don't know anything about it." He pauses and I feel the veins in my neck throbbing and beads of sweat starting to form on my forehead. He takes a couple of steps towards me and I can smell his stale breath on my face, a disgusting cocktail of whiskey and cigars, vile! "Look me in the face, Thomas." I was hoping this could be avoided and I can sense the contorted features before my eyes gaze upon his face. I raise my head to meet his eyes and he is mad. His face has turned a dark shade of red with visible purple thread-like veins darted over his cheeks and his eyes are staring to bulge in their sockets.

"Correct, Thomas, you won't know anything about this. Why? Because the note is addressed to Mr and Mrs Taylor." Oh God, this could only be from the school! What has she done?! She told me she wouldn't say anything to my parents for now! He carries on, "Well, don't you want to know what it says?" With that he slams the note at my chest, winding me and knocking me backwards, my arms flailing. I hear mother gasp inwardly. "Read it then, stupid."

My throat is dry, and it takes me a few seconds to gather myself before I can feasibly formulate the words. "Dear Mr and Mrs Taylor, I just wanted to notify you that I've had a chat with Thomas today. I told him that I wouldn't be involving you at this stage but after due consideration I feel that it's only fair that you're kept involved so we're all aware of the situation. With your co-operation and input, hopefully things can improve. Thomas has always been a capable student but over these past few months his grades have been slipping and it's giving us cause for concern. Also, he has become very withdrawn, choosing to spend more and more time by himself. I hope the chat I had with him helped and perhaps you could possibly provide some input? I look forward to hearing from you. Yours sincerely, Miss Davies."

"Well then, what have you got to say for yourself? Speak up boy!"

I don't know what to say, I don't want to aggravate the situation any further, so I simply say, "Sorry Sir."

"'Sorry Sir; sorry Sir'," he mimics. "Well, it's too bloody late for sorry. That meddling teacher of yours is poking her nose in where it's not wanted and either one of you or both of you need punished for it. I mean, on the face of it, it would make sense that you, Thomas, should receive the punishment because after all it involves you. But, if we stop and think about it, Mary, you're the useless bitch who gave birth to this pathetic excuse for a human being and you raised him, so hmmm … this really is tricky! What am I to do? Let me think."

A loaded silence fills the room and every part of me wants to turn and flee but another part tells me it'll be far worse if I don't surrender to his mercy, so my feet stand firm. "Ah ha, I have it," he says. "Mary, have you prepared dinner yet?"

A little voice pipes up, "Yes."

"Wonderful," he says. "In that case, follow me, you two." We shuffle behind him, both too terrified to even attempt eye contact with one another. He leads us to the kitchen then has mother plate his food up. "First things first," he says, "you two sit down; arms around the backs of the chairs." We oblige, fearful of what is coming next. "Why the long faces?" he says, clearly delighting in seeing our suffering. "Let me just get something. He is back in a flourish with four lengths of rope. He proceeds to bind each of us to our chairs by our hands at the back and around our ankles. The rope is so tight it is chaffing at my ankles and wrists and it feels as though the blood supply is being cut off.

"There we go, you're all strapped in nicely the pair of you and here you shall remain until tomorrow morning. If you mess yourselves, you needn't think I'm coming to clean the stinking mess up! You can sit in your own piss and shit for all I care!" With that he sat down to his dinner and set about wolfing it down. The noises emanating from him whilst he ate were truly abhorrent. When he'd finished it, he flung his plate in the general direction of the sink, let out a very loud belch, and then he was off out the door, leaving mother and I strapped to our chairs, two lost souls.

We sat like that for Lord only knows how long, lost in our own thoughts, trying to comprehend the grim situation we now found ourselves in. Perhaps it was a combination of shock and fear, but we were rendered mute for quite some time. Eventually I gathered myself and asked mother if she was OK. "Yes, love, don't worry about me, I'll be fine. It could've been worse." I find myself nodding in agreement with her but that's really to quell her unease. 'It could've been worse' is not exactly my sentiments right now sat here bound to a stiff chair for an indiscriminate period of time with (as father kindly informed us) no toilet breaks. Clearly no food or drink to be had either but, even though I'm starving, it's probably not a bad thing in the light of the toilet situation.

I realise my senses are heightened with nothing to do other than listen out for noises or take in objects around the room. I can hear the chatter of my siblings from the adjacent room, and it is getting louder and more animated. Then the noise shifts in direction and grows in volume as they make their way towards the kitchen, obviously looking for food.

Leading the pack is James and he is his usual exuberant self. He fails to hide the look of shock when he sees us and shouts, "Mum; Thomas; no, what has he done?!" I shake my head violently and tell him to hush quickly. In a quieter voice he carries on, "No I can release you both. Come on you two, help me!" I stop him in his tracks.

"No James, please just leave us. If you release us, he'll go mad, and we'll be in way more trouble. Please just go back to your rooms, all of you."

Juliet is just staring, wide eyed, not sure what to say and she simply comes over and plants a kiss on my cheek and mother's cheek. "Thank you, Juliet, that was lovely. I bet you're all hungry? There's some bread and butter over there if you want to fix yourselves some."

James is still unfazed. "I'm not bothered about fixing myself food, I want to get you both out of here! How long is he leaving you here for?"

"Overnight," I respond. "Don't worry, it's not so bad and I'll look after mother."

"That's not on," he says and with lightning speed he is around the back of my chair trying to loosen off the bindings. I'm panicked now but try to keep my voice low so as not to alert him. "Get off, James, now I mean it! You're only going to make things worse for us." I feel his hands loosening their grip and at the same time I exhale a sigh of relief.

I address all three of them; "We both really appreciate you trying to help us but if you really want to help us the best thing you can do is grab yourselves a quick bite to eat and get out of here as soon as possible. If he catches any of you in here, you might find yourselves in the same position as mother and I."

Mother seconds this, "Yes just go, all three of you, be gone now!"

James and Juliet seem to be pacified with this, but I sense there's something to come from Caroline.

"Are you in pain?" she asks, and I can't tell whether this question is borne out of concern or a morbid fascination, you were never too sure with Caroline. I assume the former.

"No, we're OK, thanks, Caroline, we're not in pain, just a little bit uncomfortable." There is more to come.

"Did you know that you can lose fingers and toes if the blood supply is cut off for long enough?" This was worrying. I am starting

55

to think the things she's seen in the croft are having a really bad impact on her. This needs nipped in the bud.

"I'm sure we're not going to lose any fingers and toes, Caroline, so don't worry." With that last sentence I hear a sharp intake of breath from mother. I have to call time on this because it's clearly distressing her even more. "Just be quick the three of you, please, that's all I ask in case he comes back and you get into trouble or get us into further trouble." It looked as though finally my words had penetrated as they set about making a quick snack for themselves before reluctantly leaving us to it.

I had no idea what time it was as there was no clock in the kitchen and being June there wouldn't be a sunset until after 10 o'clock. I stare across at mother. She had what could only be described as a weary acceptance scrawled across her face. I wasn't old but I was old enough to realise that she was a broken woman. This was mental torment what he was putting us through, and I couldn't help feeling guilty. Mother was being punished for something I'd done. I broke the silence; "I'm so sorry, mother, for all this, it's all my fault. If it weren't for that note, you wouldn't have got into trouble."

She beams across at me, "That's OK, son, but what note? What are you talking about?" What are you talking about? What am I talking about?? What was she talking about?! How could she not remember about the note?

"The note, mother, from my teacher. That's why we're both tied up!"

"Sorry, son, but I don't have a clue what you're talking about."

This place is literally driving me insane! Why couldn't she remember what happened earlier this evening that led to us being tied up to the chairs? I'm too young to understand the workings of the mind and ponder whether she's becoming forgetful (although I think she's too young for this) or is she suffering somehow with trauma over what he's put her through over the years? Perhaps she is adapting and evolving to her circumstances and has found a way to blot it all out? I decided there is no point in forcing the issue as I don't want her to have to relive the experience all over again. Anyway, I have a more burning issue to attend to. What I feared would happen has come to fruition – I have a full bladder and I can't hold out much longer.

I distract myself by looking out of the window and notice that sundown is approaching. The sky is vibrant, one of those summer skies where you get flashes of red, pink, and blue etched across the horizon and you know it's going to be a hot day the following day. This provides only a momentary distraction as my bladder snaps my mind back to the fore. Instead of just a niggling sensation, it has developed into something far more insistent. It feels as though every square inch of my groin and stomach are fit to burst. I cannot go in front of mother, I just can't. I wonder if she is enduring a similar torture and I glace over, surprised to see her head lolling gently back and forth resembling a nodding dog as the first signs of sleep begin to envelop her.

I can hold it no longer and just let go. I feel the hot liquid gushing down my leg, the tell-tail stain spreading its way across my jeans. I watch in fascination as I see the liquid pouring forth out of my jeans, some choosing to saturate my socks and stay put in my trainers; the rest pouring out across the wooden floor, spreading out in all directions. I'm sure this is what father was hoping for and only gives him ammunition to further berate me. I take a deep breath and let out a heavy sigh. The pungent smell of ammonia hits my nostrils from the puddle at my feet and makes me gag.

One thing I can be thankful for is the bindings around my wrists and ankles have loosened off somewhat. I can only assume mother's bindings weren't as tight as mine as she's managed to drift off, bless her. I have no idea how long I stayed conscious for but eventually I managed to find some rest.

It was very much a fitful night's sleep. I woke several times throughout the night and even in the gloom I noticed a similar puddle to mine under mother's chair. When I heard the rooster call, I was more grateful than ever before. Surely my impending release was coming.

Life on the croft started early so I was confident that father would be through shortly to untie us but there was no sign of him. Mother woke after me and she was as confused as I was as to his whereabouts. He had to be here soon, I have school this morning and the bus to catch! My siblings had already paid us a visit earlier this morning.

Eventually we hear the loud footsteps along the hallway. His towering presence fills the length and breadth of the doorway when he reaches the kitchen. He bends over, gagging and retching. When he stands upright again, he addresses us. "You pair are a couple of stinking dogs. I knew you'd piss in your pants." There is no response from either of us, better to just let him get it all off his chest. "I imagine you'll be wanting set free like two little birds?" He then recites the nursery rhyme 'Two Little Dicky Birds' in a sing-song voice as he roughly sets about loosening the ropes (the sound of that nursery rhyme being sung by him is truly sickening).

However, the feeling of having my limbs back into their normal place of alignment is incredible. I am still very sore, yes but oh, what a relief! "Not so fast, boy! Don't either of you move a muscle. You're not going anywhere until this lot has been cleaned and polished up. I'm off to feed the hens. When I get back this had better be sparkling."

We set about making the best job we possibly could of cleaning the place up. In no time at all however he was back in the room inspecting my work. "OK, now off to school, you better run or

you're gonna miss the bus. No time for breakfast or to get changed."
What?! He's expecting me to go to school in my urine saturated
clothes?! I try to reason with him, "But—"

"Don't you dare try to answer me back. Out that door now or so
help me God I'll strap you back in."

I walk out the front door gripped in a state of panic. What should
I do? If I get on the bus everyone will smell me and my life won't be
worth living any longer at high school. It's bad enough at the
moment with only another couple of the outcasts choosing to
associate with me. If I go into school in this state, I'll be targeted and
bullied mercilessly. And what about Miss Davies? What is she going
to say or any of my other teachers? They are bound to start asking
more questions. Will they contact the social work department? I
shudder at the thought. What punishment would father dish out next
if this went any further?

My brain feels as though it's going to explode with all the thoughts
churning over and over and I have to reach a conclusion soon as the
bus will be here any minute. I notice my heart is pumping at an
alarming rate and my throat is constricted. I am struggling to draw a
breath and I barely notice Caroline is at my side.

"Looks like you're having a panic attack," she says. "Are you
struggling to breath?" Unable to speak I simply nod. "I read about
this, all you have to do is take deep breaths and extend the exhale." I
take her advice and after a few rounds of deep breathing I feel the
edges of the panic beginning to subside.

"Thank you," I manage.

"What are you going to do?" she asks.

"I don't know but there's no way I can go to school like this! I
need to think of something, the bus is going to be here soon."

A voice pipes up from behind me, "You're not going to school
with those clothes on, I've got a plan." James, you've got to love him,

James to the rescue! "Make your way down the glen to the outskirts of town. There's an old payphone there. Use it to phone the school pretending to be father to say you're sick and unable to make it in."

It was a plan but how feasible? "I can't do that; I don't know how to speak like father!"

"Oh yes, you do," he says. "You're always mimicking his voice. 'Thomas, come here now, Thomas do this, do that.'"

"I guess so but even if I get away with it what am I going to do all day?"

"What are you going to do all day?! You're going to taste freedom that's what you're going to do. You're going to lose yourself for the day and love every minute of it!"

Well, this puts a new spin on things. Something positive coming out of this nightmare situation. Where would I go with my newfound freedom? I catch myself. I have to get through the first stage and pray this call to the school works. No time to waste, the bus is rounding the corner so off I dash.

It takes me a good half an hour or so to get to the phone box and I step inside. I can't help but laugh inwardly as I imagine the look on father's face if he could see me right now! The steam would be coming out of his ears! En route to the phone box I passed a couple of people going about their business but I felt sure they knew there was something amiss, such is the way of it when you know you're doing something you shouldn't be doing.

I pick up the receiver with my left hand and hold it to my ear. With my other hand I reach for some loose change. Everything was going well, and my right hand was tracking its way towards the coin slot but then I lost my nerve and quickly replaced the receiver. OK, deep breaths (taking Caroline's advice) and I also remembered the chat I'd had with James. 'I can do this!' I say to myself. Before lifting the receiver again in my head, I create a mental image of a recent conversation I'd had with father, playing it out as a movie scene taking note of the pitch and tone of his voice and any nuances. I didn't want to overthink this either but decided it was probably best to have a practice run first. I have a quick look around outside to ensure there is no one there (as this would surely look odd, me having a conversation to myself!), then I begin; "May I speak with Mr Hedley please? ... Ahh, Mr Hedley, this is Bert Taylor here. It was just to let you know that unfortunately Thomas won't make it into school today, he's feeling unwell." I laugh involuntarily as I realise I'm quite good at this. Yes, full marks, Thomas, managing to lower the pitch and tone of my voice to emanate father's deep gravelly tone.

I'm ready. Without hesitation this time I once again lift the receiver and this time the money makes its way into the slot and I punch the numbers in. I take a few deep breaths as I wait to be connected and even if I do say so myself it all goes swimmingly well. Mr Hedley (our headteacher) is 'very sorry to hear Thomas is feeling unwell' and wishes him a speedy recovery. Bingo! Job done; I now have free time to myself but what to do? Of course – spend the day at Dunvegan Castle.

I hadn't been to Dunvegan Castle since I was just a small boy, and it held a place in my heart. It was the stuff of myth and legend. There was no need to go into the castle itself (and I reminded myself I was still smelling ghastly and should avoid crowds!) but just to be in the grounds of the castle taking everything in would be enough. I could lose myself and pretend to be someone else for the day and that's exactly what I did. The time flew by as I savoured the sights and sounds en route to the castle, the sense of freedom intoxicating.

Then I eventually came upon it, the castle rising sheer from the perpendicular edges of the rock, its massive battlements 'holding fast' against a spectacular backdrop of sky, mountains, and sea. It is awe-inspiring and takes my breath away. Father is unable to penetrate this magical scene before me and this newfound freedom as I say a silent prayer for time to stand still so I can stay locked in this happy state for as long as possible.

I make the most of the day, taking in the surroundings and walking the perimeter of the estate. Happily, I also had enough money to buy a snack from the snack van, so the hunger pangs were satisfied. It was a day I never wanted to end but end it did. I made my way back to the croft, carefully timing the trip to coincide with the time the bus would make it there so as not to arouse suspicion.

I felt giddy with excitement. It felt as though I had one up on father. He thought he had completely broken me but here I was having had the most perfect day I could remember. The feeling lasts for the majority of the duration home but as I round the last corner and look upwards towards our croft, I feel an impending sense of doom, every step now torturous. With heavy feet and a heavy heart, I take the final few steps up the path and open the door.

CHAPTER 8

Thomas

The past week or so has flown in and I realise that my trip to Skye is only a matter of hours away. All that remains is to pack a bag, get some shut eye, and, first thing in the morning, set off. It hits me with full force the enormity of the decision which I had taken so lightly. Have I made the right choice? There's still time to change my mind. There are so many questions. I realise I could drive myself crazy as I know they will remain unanswered until I journey up there to see where this is all leading.

In the past few days, thoughts have been returning more and more vividly of the time spent on the croft and my siblings; memories I thought I'd quashed. Realistically, what was I hoping to achieve with all this? Would it be good therapy for me, or would it simply be a case of picking at old wounds? Picking at them and letting myself bleed out? I feel the panic rising as I picture myself being drawn into a downward spiral. I'd spent all these years clawing my way back up and was this about to be torn wide apart in a matter of a few days when I confronted the demons from my past?

I hastily pack a case; my mind not fully focused on the job in hand. I pack with warmth and comfort in mind. This is the tail end of winter after all in Skye and it can be a very unforgiving climate. A couple of work shirts and ties are placed strategically on the top so as not to arouse suspicion should Janey sneak a peek.

With that completed, I make my way downstairs to spend the rest of the evening with my family. Michael is his usual easy going self, the conversation in full flow. We get all the details on the latest love of his life – a girl called Ellie who is apparently 'very popular' and 'do you know she's been asked out by three of my mates and turned them all down but said yes to me!' I'm in awe of the confident young man I see before me. He has the world at his feet, and he doesn't even realise it. Had I had the upbringing he's had and the confidence he exudes, then I can only imagine about what I might've become.

Janey, I note, is not so easy going. She is participating in the conversation, but I can sense she's somewhat guarded. Michael will be blissfully unaware but as her husband I know her better than anyone and pick up on the slight edge to the tone of her voice and the extra line along her brow giving it a furrowed appearance. She's worried; she's concerned about me going to Skye, but she won't say anything about her concerns in front of Michael. I suspect she might talk to me later …

My suspicions prove correct. Michael leaves the room after an hour or so and I move in closer to her side. She smells amazing and I take a mental picture of her face in the half light and try to capture it all so I can recall this moment if I come upon hard times when I'm away.

"Thomas, are you absolutely sure this is for the best? I am worried about you. I know you're going there on business but what if you run into anyone from your past?"

"We've been through all this, it's fine, don't worry, nothing's going to happen, and I'll check in regularly with you."

"Well, if you go and see your mother, tell her I'm asking for her. I know she probably won't know what you're talking about but all the same."

"Yes, of course I will."

"You're not going back to the croft, are you? I know you don't like to talk about your upbringing so I don't fully appreciate what it was like for you, but I know it wasn't easy and I would worry about you going there, especially on your own."

"Janey, honestly, I'm going on business so don't panic. Yes, I'm hoping I might get some time out and I'll be able to do some sightseeing, but I have no plans whatsoever to delve into the past." We leave it at that, neither one of us wanting to push it any further. We were both keen to end our last night together on a happy note.

Janey

Something just doesn't feel quite right, and I can't put my finger on it. This was quite unlike Thomas to just up and leave for a couple of weeks on business and at such short notice. And Skye of all places! I don't like it and I smell a rat.

Why could his company not draft in someone from their Inverness branch, wouldn't that make much more sense? After all, the successful candidate is to eventually work from the Inverness branch. It didn't add up. What did Thomas say? Something about all the experience he's had in the past with recruitment so that's why they've asked him to get involved? Yes, don't get me wrong, Thomas has climbed the ranks within the firm and done exceptionally well (to have reached Directorship at his age was practically unheard of) but he's not the longest serving member of staff, not by a long shot.

He's also been acting pretty strangely these past few days and it's quite unsettling. We are used to him being a permanent fixture downstairs, but my usually affable husband has become altogether more secretive, spending a lot more time on his own.

There is also the matter of his phone ringing late at night, the bleep of messages going back and forth. He thought I was sleeping but I was only too aware of what was going on. Has he got himself involved in something and he's going to sort it out or (God forbid) is he having an affair?

This was my Achilles heel. If Thomas was found to be cheating on me, I really do wonder if I could possibly stand by him. I have been sorely tempted to pick up his phone on many occasions, the suspicious wife on the trail. I can't decide what's stopping me, whether it's the fact that I do trust him, and I'm not prepared to go there, or is it that I'm frightened of what I might find?

I also think back to a couple of weeks ago when he'd got up in the middle of the night claiming that he'd thought there was someone at the door. When I had approached him and laid a hand on his shoulder, he'd barely registered this. It took him a long time to gather himself and when he turned around his face was a spectacle, he looked as though he'd seen a ghost. He did a good job of trying to gloss over why he was there; that he'd heard a noise but 'not to worry he was mistaken,' but there was no mistaking the look of horror I saw in his face.

Perhaps most worrying of all was the postcard. A random postcard depicting famous tourist hotspots on the Isle of Skye; no stamp or postmark, just the words 'wish you were here.' He came up with a lame excuse about how it must have been posted through our letterbox by mistake. I wasn't buying this. As a journalist and now editor of a paper I have a naturally inquisitive nature and a good nose for telling when I'm being spun a story, and this felt very much like I was being lied to. I think he knew I wasn't taken in with it as he looked rather uncomfortable and flustered when I spoke to him about it and couldn't get out of the door quick enough!

Yes, there was no denying something was up. A very strange postcard of Skye's beauty spots is discovered crumpled in my husband's trouser pocket and the next thing we know he's off to where – Skye! Pretty coincidental! Also, why did he hold onto the postcard if it was as he said, delivered to us in error?

And today when he was preoccupied, I had a quick look through his case. I know I shouldn't have but I couldn't help myself. Everything looked plausible to start off with, there were shirts and ties at the top of the case but on rummaging further through the case I could find no trousers or work shoes. There is no way Thomas would attend work or go to a meeting without his work trousers and shoes on. The whole situation had me baffled.

It would be great to think he was simply going on a business trip, but my mind was beginning to conjure up all sorts of weird and wonderful conclusions. Do I dare confront him though? He has given me no cause to doubt his fidelity all these years. How could I simply accuse him of potentially cheating on me? Or if it wasn't that then what was he up to and how would I find out? Thomas certainly has skeletons in his closet, that I know for sure. He has only ever given me snippets about his childhood, and it leads me to wonder, was there more to this than meets the eye?

CHAPTER 9

I set off nice and early – 8 a.m. – having said my farewells to Janey and Michael. It's a six-hour journey so will take the best part of a day to get there, factoring in a lunch break etc. My nerves are jangling, and I honestly can't decide whether this is through a nervous excitement, or as a result of a poorly made decision on my part to make this trip in the first place. No going back now though, and I reason with myself that this time on my own as I make the journey will do me good. There's no one there to disrupt me; just me, the car, and the open road, and I like the sound of that. I set the satellite navigation, select a random playlist of songs, and hit the accelerator pedal.

Not long after setting off, I start imagining what the next couple of weeks are going to have in store. I haven't let George know that I'm on my way yet or even that I'd made plans to go up north. I figured I'd get there, get settled in, and maybe a bit of sightseeing first before I make that call. With that in mind there's no way he can have made any prior arrangements for me to go anywhere/meet anyone as he doesn't even know about my imminent arrival.

I wonder whether I might get reunited with my siblings if any of them are in the area? It would be a relief if they were, not only to catch up but to discuss mother's welfare and to hear what they have to say about the visit father paid her in the care home. Since I am no longer in contact with them it feels as though I bear the brunt of worry when it comes to her care and I relish the idea of lightening that load somewhat.

Would George be planning on taking me to the croft to see father? I shudder at the thought. I left home at a young age and I have never been back. What would our meeting (if it were to take place) be like? I imagine he still has a fixed image in his mind of what I look like and what my demeanour is like. He will be expecting that same terrified boy to be stood before him. Would he even recognise me? I imagine I'll still recognise him; his wicked contorted face sometimes still darkens my dreams.

I have come a long way over these years and would like to think I could meet him face to face; man to man and not cower in his presence, but would that be the case? If I were to stand before him now, could I stop myself from falling apart?

I daydream about standing before him; imagining that I stand a foot taller than him; peering down on him as he used to do with me. He is weak now in my dream; leaning for balance on a cane and he is unable to give me eye contact. I don't speak to him, I simply smack him square in the face with my fist and send him reeling backwards. Without the cane to steady him he falls to the floor and I shake my head at him indicating that no, it is not OK for him to get up off the floor until I grant him permission. He bows his head in a submissive gesture. This feels so good; the roles have reversed, and I have the power over him. I imagine mother isn't in the care home, she's there to witness the scene. She's aware of the shift of power, he's loosened his grip over us, and I've taken charge. She relaxes as she understands he can no longer hurt her whilst I'm there to protect her.

Dare I let my mind drift further into concocting weird and wonderful ways to punish him as he has done to me or do I rein it in, unwilling to let my mind tap into that dark place? There is a sense once you go there it may become a descent. Did I really want to descend to the deep dark places he resided in?

There's no time to ponder this further as I'm momentarily aware of movement in front of the car; there's a loud band and the windowpane cracks and splinters; the spiders web of broken glass extending to either end of the window. Instincts kick in and I bring the car to an emergency stop; the back having jutted off to the right with the force of the impact. My mind has yet to catch up and comprehend what has just happened. A searing pain has clawed its way from the base of my skull and rooted itself across the top of my head, sending shockwaves of pain along my nerve endings. My chest feels so tight, and I struggle to catch a breath but realise the cause of this as I glance down – the airbag is pressed firmly against my chest, so the impact must've activated it.

I have to breathe; this is the first thing I have to attend to, so I manage to adjust the seat into a reclined position to remove the weight off my chest and I take a huge breath into my lungs and release.

Focus. I hear a remote part of my brain urging for clarity; to shake the fugue and allow me to collect myself. I feel the veil of fog starting to lift and with it the pain sets in. OK, don't panic, where am I hurt? My head has clearly taken a knock as it is pounding but think positively, I'm still conscious. Is everything else OK? I take a mental scan of my body and locate the source of my pain, my lower back. I take some deep breaths, not wanting to move in any direction quickly and without any due thought. I surmise that at least nothing appears to be broken. My heart is racing as I brace myself for what's out there. What did I hit? An animal, another vehicle or a person? Oh God, I wince at the last thought. It all happened so quickly I had no time to process the images or form them into any kind of order.

The window is barely open a crack as I muster the courage to wind it down further. Before I do however, a figure is standing at my window. I'm so startled, I hadn't even thought about there being anyone there but of course, there were a couple of cars behind me. "You alright, mate? You've taken a bit of a knock," he says. "Yes," I feebly manage to say. Again – focus!

If he's been behind me, he might've seen what happened. "Can you tell me what happened?"

"Sure can. Wind your window right down, mate, and take a look." Oh God, my fingers are operating the lever for the window involuntarily, but my head is screaming 'don't look!' The motion continues until the glass is fully down. I gently twist my head to the right, ignoring the stabbing knives exploding in my brain. There, laid out flat on the road is a stag, a beautiful creature. *Was* a beautiful creature I should say. His antlers, his crowning glory. I count them and note sadly that he was a Royal Stag. His vacant eyes gaze heavenward and his beautiful coat is no longer gleaming; tarnished a ruddy red colour with the gathering pool of blood he is now lain in.

A strange noise escapes from me and my body visibly sags into the seat. I realise it was a full body exhale; all the tension I had been holding onto releasing in that glorious exhale. I'd hit a deer; a magnificent deer none the less but it was a deer and not a person, for that I will be eternally grateful.

I look up at the stranger. "Would you mind helping me out of the car? I want to see if I'm able to stand up."

"Is that a good idea? What if you've done something to your back, if I move you I could make it worse!"

"It's fine, let's try and, if there's a problem, we can call for help."

"If you're sure …" I make some micro adjustments to edge closer to the outside of my seat to assist him in manoeuvring me. I pray he doesn't see the pain etched on my face which I try to mask as I make these adjustments, I feel sure he'll refuse to touch me if he does.

He leans in and fixes an arm in front of me, and one secured around my back under both arms. I wrap my arms around his neck best I can. "OK, I've got you, let's go for it." I try to apply as much pressure as possible into my thighs to aid him and I step one, then both feet out of the car. I'm now almost erect but my full body weight is leaning on him. I apologise and he motions me back towards the side of the car and instructs me to lean against it. I've done it! Hurts like hell but I'm alive and in one piece and I haven't killed anyone.

I take a few minutes to rest after the exertion of being heaved out of the car then I ask him to aid me in taking a couple of steps towards the backseats (there's no point in trying to squeeze back behind the front wheel). Tentatively I take my first step and it goes better than I expected. I note that my spine feels compressed and I picture an accordion being squeezed tightly; imagining the folds of the accordion are the vertebra of my spine. It is somewhat forgiving however as it unfurls slightly and allows me to take another couple of steps. We make it to the backseats, and he guides me in, and I am grateful to be sat down again.

My initial thoughts of this situation being better than it potentially could have been started to wane when it crosses my mind that this could be a really bad omen. Hitting and killing a Royal Stag and injuring myself in the process. That's a big red flag right there saying TURN BACK NOW! Do not go another minute further on this journey! Well, there is some truth in that for sure as this car won't be going anywhere. I don't know what the damage is like elsewhere, but the windscreen is shattered.

The stranger's name I ascertain is Oliver and Oliver kindly gives the car the once-over for me. All the damage is towards the front end of the car. This was a huge beast I killed, and he has certainly left his mark. Both lights are out, the bumper is off, and there's a huge indentation to the front of the vehicle so we can only imagine the damage under the bonnet. Oliver suspects the stag hit the front of the car then bounced off the window, shattering it in the process.

I guess we should notify the Police to get it off the road safely but then I catch myself. Where am I? Where did I get to? I recall I had been so caught up in the vengeful fantasy about persecuting father that I'd lost all sense of time and place and realise I must've been driving on autopilot. With no chance of referring to the sat-nav now for directions, I ask Oliver where we are.

He informs me we are just on the outskirts of the village of Inverarnan which is located by the river Falloch at the south end of Glen Falloch (near the head of Loch Lomond). He points it out to me on his phone and I get my bearings. It looks as though I've been on the road for a couple of hours or so and a quick check at the time on his phone confirms this. It's around 10.30 a.m. He offers me a lift into the village, but I thank him and tell him to carry on with his journey. I am anxious about leaving the car and decide the best plan is to phone the Police and take it from there.

They arrive in no time but then I imagine there's not a lot of crime here! They secure the scene and then drive me into the village. It's a picturesque little spot and visited almost daily I'm informed as it forms part of the West Highland Way. A short distance away, apparently, are the Falls of Falloch. I feign interest. I have more pressing matters to deal with like what do I do now? I am in the middle of nowhere feeling sorry for myself and with no transport to speak of I don't know what the next step should be!

The female officer has been quite persistent in asking me to seek medical attention, but I keep refusing. With nothing broken there's really no point. I just ask her to point me in the nearest direction of somewhere I can buy some painkillers from. She drives me to the local inn which dates back to the 17th century and the bartender proudly declares that it is well known as being a haunted location. This is the last thing I really wanted to hear after the day I've had but I smile at him whilst he regales us with some stories and folklore. She orders some coffee and cake for me then tells me she'll be back in a minute.

True to her word she appears back a few minutes later with a varied assortment of painkillers. We get chatting about what happens next, and she says first things first, they will arrange to tow the car to the nearest garage and that I should notify my insurance company. Then she asks if I know of someone to call to come and collect me. I tell her of course and to just leave me to it. She looks hesitant, clearly a caring soul, not wanting to abandon me in this vulnerable state. However, again I am very insistent and grateful for her help, but I am even more grateful when I'm left on my own to collect my thoughts.

Thankfully, the painkillers are starting to work their magic and the coffee and cake have done wonders in uplifting my mood. OK, who do I phone? Normally there would be no question – it'd be Janey. But is that wise? She would be there in a heartbeat and I'd be ushered home to rest and recuperate. I realise it's more a question of whether I want to continue with this trip or abandon it altogether. What my heart and my head are telling me are two different things.

Without further thought, I select my chosen contact and hit 'call.' He answers after just two rings.

"Thomas, how are you?"

"I've been better!"

"What's happened, are you OK?"

"I'm en route to Skye but I've been involved in a car accident. I'm fine but I'm stuck here. Both the car and I are pretty battered and bruised. So, I'm thinking to forget all this and make arrangements to go home."

Is that strictly true? I'd phoned George. Now why phone him if I wanted to go home? Surely, I would just have phoned Janey and asked her to take me home. Was this inadvertently a plea for help because I wanted to continue the journey? George replies, "Tell me exactly where you are. I'm coming to get you."

I decided not to phone Janey at all. She'd only worry needlessly and insist on me coming home so instead I waited it out at the Inn. Four long painful hours pass, then my chaperone arrives. His opening line – "Well, Thomas, you are a sight for sore eyes, let's get you into the car." I swallow another few painkillers down, the thought of the long journey ahead cramped up in a car with my injuries not filling me with much glee. He's managed to park just outside so with his help and the assistance of the bartender they flank either side of me and, somehow, we make it to the car then they bundle me into the passenger seat.

It occurs to me that I hadn't even planned to let George know I was making the journey to Skye and yet here I was sat by his side with him having come to my rescue. I don't know whether to be grateful for his kindness in making this journey or angry at him for not talking sense into me and telling me to go home.

This was going to be a long awkward drive. What would we talk about and would I have the ability to even hold a conversation? All my energy was currently focused on breathing through the spasms of pain exploding in my head. He seemed to sense this, and we started the journey off in a mutually agreeable silence.

The effect of the painkillers sets in and I no longer have to concern myself about anything as I fall into a deep sleep. But it doesn't last long. When I eventually start to waken, I'm doing battle with my head and body. My mind is screaming for more sleep, but my body won't allow it. The pain in my lower back tracks its way up my spine and into my skull, meeting the tender painful areas already present there. I have no option but to open my eyes and sit up.

I look out of the window and instantly recognise where we are – Bridge of Orchy. People often refer to Stirling as being the gateway to the Highlands but, for me, the Bridge of Orchy represents the gateway. It is from this point onwards that the spectacular landscape unfolds. The transition from low-lying hills and populated areas makes way to vast wide-open spaces; snow-capped peaks all around and the odd croft and farm dotted here and there. The feeling is one of unbounded possibility. Having been away so long from this landscape I am surprised to note there's a wistful feeling developing. I realise that I had to leave because of everything that happened but the wild untamed beauty of the area still holds a place in my heart.

"Thomas." Where did that voice come from? It wasn't George, that's for sure. It was a female voice, a tender voice. I sense its source, it's coming from behind me, but I struggle to turn my neck around with the pain only allowing a very restricted movement. I am forced to try to mentally place the voice and realise it's familiar. It has the same lilt as mine and it hits me with full force.

"Juliet?" I venture.

"Yes Thomas, I'm here!"

"Oh Juliet, it's been so long! How are you?"

"I'm great, Thomas, but never mind about me! How are you? You don't look so good. I see you've been in an accident."

"I'm fine, honestly, just a few bumps and bruises, nothing which won't heal up. How did you know about my accident and the fact I was headed for Skye?" I don't know why I'm asking this question. I already know the answer, the information could've only come from one source.

"It was George of course, he told us a couple of weeks ago that he had contacted you and I was so looking forward to seeing you again. When he told me you'd been involved in an accident, I came straight away and I'm pleased I did, it looks as though you're going to need my help."

I started to feel emotions clearly pent up inside me, bubbling and rising to the surface. Juliet's presence was the catalyst. I'd always had a soft spot for her and as she said, here she was when I needed her, and it felt wonderful; like having a warm cosy blanket wrapped around my whole body cradling me. The tears formed and started to roll down my cheeks and the sobbing came of its own accord; my head no longer in control of the situation; my body surrendering to the tidal wave of emotion bursting forth. It actually felt great to let it all out. It felt liberating as though a weight had been lifted off my shoulders. I hadn't given any thought or concern as to how it would look, a grown man bubbling away uncontrollably like that. I mean, that wasn't the done thing, was it, a man should keep his emotions in check, right?!

If George had any opinion about it, he wasn't letting it be known. His eyes were fixed firmly on the road ahead. Juliet, however, was really concerned. "Oh Thomas, oh dear, is it your wounds? Can I help with anything?" It was enough to jolt me out of it and no new fresh tears came. I couldn't have Juliet getting all upset, what was I thinking?

"I'm sorry, Juliet, I don't know where that came from! I'm OK, I just need a few minutes to gather myself."

"No problem, Thomas, take all the time you need."

Yes, Juliet was the catalyst for this burst of emotion but, if I was honest, it was the whole build up to this point – George coming back into my life, facing up to the reality of my past, and opening that box I'd held so firmly shut. The car accident also attributed to it but just hearing Juliet's voice had the effect of unravelling me.

We drove on in silence and I realise with gratitude that the distraction of Juliet being here has also taken my mind momentarily off my aches and pains. The scenery as it unfolds takes my breath away. I see we are approaching Glencoe. This is not somewhere you want your car to breakdown mid-winter as there is a very good chance you'd have no phone signal and no way of calling for help. I've been lucky enough to have travelled all over the world, but I can honestly say there's nowhere I can think of which has such a raw natural beauty.

Each corner you turn around opens to a new panoramic vista of snow-clad peaks. And every new view you come upon is undeniably more impressive than the last. All the other cars on the road appear to agree with me as people have slowed to a snail's pace; the drivers unable to keep their cars on the road at a speed greater than 30 miles per hour whilst taking in the views. Many have stopped off in one of the layby's and are taking photos or peering through binoculars. I suspect only a very few experienced mountaineers would even contemplate climbing any of those peaks today – the ice is compacted, and the snow is still thick and dense, enveloping most of the mountains. Only a small grassy area at the foot of each mountain remains intact where a few hardy, black-faced sheep graze here and there.

It appears that George and Juliet are equally as awe-struck as I am for neither of them utters a word as we pass through the glen. George is the first one to break the silence and informs us when we are leaving Glencoe that we should reach Skye in about two and a half hours, just in time for dinner. He insists that I eat with him and, given the shape I am in, I'm in no fit state to argue so I agree.

I feel my phone vibrate in my pocket and go to retrieve it – two missed calls and three messages, all from Janey. Of course, what was I thinking? She'd be worried sick wondering why I hadn't phoned or texted to let her know I'd arrived safely – she would have expected me to be there some time ago I realise. I call her straight away and tell her I'm so sorry, but my phone dropped signal and not to worry, I'd arrived safe and sound. A little white lie but made with the best of intentions. I keep the conversation brief, not wanting to say anything too personal with an audience in the car.

The weather I see is starting to close in. The sky is already darkening, and it has gone eerily quiet outside. I realise this is the prelude for a snowstorm. The flakes start lightly; beautiful, delicate little geometric crystal shapes landing on the windscreen. Then in no time they give way to huge flakes; the kind which happily lie and cover any surface which they come into contact with. We are all too aware if this continues for a long time it will make completing the journey difficult. Driving in this can't be easy and George slows down somewhat.

Again, George breaks the silence. "So Thomas, I've been thinking... Given the current shape you're in, it would make sense if you came to stay with me." I am relieved for the shroud of darkness so he can't see the look on my face. I wait for Juliet to interject and say don't be silly, that I should stay with her. She does no such thing. In fact, she says that she thinks this is a great idea. This leaves me with very little room for manoeuvre. It looks like there are only two options; to stick to my original plan and stay in my rented accommodation or move in with George. I can't deny it's a nice gesture. He has offered me a place to stay and came to collect me (both things he didn't have to do) so it would just be rude to shoot him down in flames. "I'll have a think about it, George."

Thankfully, the snowstorm is short-lived, and we're back up to speed and on track in no time. The rest of the journey passes uneventfully and under the cover of darkness we eventually reach Kyle of Lochalsh; the bridge over to the Isle of Skye. We cross this and head in the direction of George's house near Portree and I am grateful he has offered to feed me – I'm ravenous!

His house is located on the outskirts of Portree and even in the darkness I can see how impressive it is. I imagine the views are spectacular across the bay because he has uninterrupted views. As we enter the house, I am not surprised to see he has made full advantage of the view. Off the main living area there are bifold doors which seem to span the width of the living room and open plan kitchen area. I approach them and see they open out onto a huge expanse of decking.

George excuses himself and asks me to make myself comfortable whilst he prepares supper. I say a mental thank you to that female officer for providing me with these painkillers. It hurt like hell but, without them, even stumbling over the length of the living room would've been an insurmountable task. However, taking little baby steps and lots of breaks, I managed unaided. I then take his advice and relax onto the sofa. I close my eyes and think about what a day it's been. I never envisioned any of this when I set out this morning! A car crash, Juliet's appearance, and then spending the evening with George having supper!

Whilst George isn't in earshot, I take the opportunity to chat with Juliet. "Were you just saying that in the car for George's benefit so you didn't hurt his feelings?"

"Not at all. Don't look a gift horse in the mouth. He is offering to put you up and look around, Thomas, you're not going to be badly off here! You are not in a position to look after yourself right now and have you thought about how you'd get out and about? You don't currently have access to a car and, even if you did, you're in no fit state to drive one right now. It makes sense." I couldn't argue with that and no, I hadn't even given it any thought, the fact I'm unlikely to be able to drive anywhere. She wasn't offering up any other possibilities, so I didn't push it.

"Thing is, Juliet, how do I know if I'll even get on with him?"

"You don't but, let's face it, you're not going to know unless you give it a shot."

Supper was ready much quicker than anticipated, a dish of langoustines with lemon and pepper butter and crusty bread on the side. Clearly freshly caught, they were delectable. I had forgotten about the amazing selection of fresh fish on Skye. We eat in a contented silence, savouring our meal and devouring every last piece of the shellfish and bread. It gave me a chance to think about George's proposal.

"George, if the offer still stands for a place to stay I'd like to take you up on it." A smile spreads across his face.

"Wonderful, you've made the right choice. When we're finished up here, I'll show you to the guest room and you can relax, I'm sure you're in need of it after the day you've had."

I certainly was and I was also grateful for the fact I'd have some time out on my own. I had no energy left for making polite chit chat and had a feeling the minute my head hit the pillow I was going to go out like a light which is exactly what happened. It was a drug-induced sleep with all the painkillers I'd been on and, as a result, I didn't rouse until after 10 a.m.

I noticed the pain in my head had eased somewhat (a result of the rest?) but as I tried to prop myself up into a sitting position in bed, I realised every bone and joint in my body was stiff as a board. My plans for doing a little sightseeing seemed unlikely unless I were to be driven somewhere and I didn't want to see mother until I was feeling more agile. Thoughts then drifted towards George, perhaps I had no input in any itinerary? He brought me here to confront my past, not to visit Skye's tourist spots. This is a wakeup call as I'm reminded of why I'm here. I need a clear head for what's ahead of me ...

CHAPTER 10

Janey

My concern yesterday that something was wrong had now escalated and all sorts of horrifying thoughts and scenarios were playing out in my head. He knew I would be anxious to hear from him, to let me know he'd arrived safe and sound, yet nothing. I'd tried repeatedly to contact him via phone and text with no success and when he eventually did make contact later that night, he said something about his phone having no signal, but I felt certain the Thomas I knew would've found a way to get in touch and let me know he was OK long before he did. I'd also tried to reach him this morning first thing but again his phone just went to voicemail. You have left me no choice, Thomas!

I look the number up online. A polite well-rehearsed voice chimes, "Good morning, Gibson & Mason, how may I direct your call?"

"Morning, I'm not sure who I need to speak to, but my husband works as a financial adviser from your Scottish Borders branch and he's travelling to your branch to carry out some recruitment over the next couple of weeks. I've been trying to contact him repeatedly over the past day or so, but his phone seems to keep losing connection. Perhaps you could pass a message on and get him to call me?"

"Of course, what is his name?"

"Thomas Taylor."

"I'll be sure to pass that message on," and with that she ends the call.

I hear nothing from Thomas for the remainder of the morning but an unknown caller ID flashes on the phone around mid-day and, when I answer the call, I recognise the polite female receptionist's voice from earlier this morning.

"Mrs Taylor?"

"Speaking."

"It was just to let you know that I've checked with some colleagues and we're not expecting a visit from Mr Taylor. In fact, we're not currently in a position to carry out any recruitment either so I think there's been a misunderstanding." I politely thank her for looking into this and I lose grip on my phone and it tumbles to the ground.

What is going on? Where is my husband and was he even in Skye? If he is in Skye, who is he with?! I made my excuses at work about a bad migraine coming on and headed home. I had to do some digging but where to start? Of course … the P.C.

I log on and immediately check the search history. This is slightly reassuring. There are lists of websites listing accommodation for rent on Skye. At least he's not lied to me about where he is going but there was something going on here. In all the years we'd been together I couldn't think of a time he'd ever lied to me like this. If he's not there on work, then what?

I select five of the most recent links to properties he'd been looking at and start dialling round. "Hello, yes, I am trying to locate my husband Thomas Taylor. He was due to check in with you yesterday but there's an urgent family matter I need to discuss with him, and I can't get through to his phone." No luck with the first three calls but on the fourth call I strike gold. "Yes, Mr Taylor has booked to stay with us but I'm afraid he's yet to check in. If you do manage to contact him perhaps you could ask him to call us and let us know if he'll be needing the room. If I don't hear from him by this afternoon, I'm afraid I'll have to re-advertise the accommodation." I pause briefly.

"There'll be no need for that. I'll take the booking, thanks. If there is any surcharge for amending the details, please let me know."

I hang up and the enormity of what I've just done hits home. I'm going to abandon work and Michael to go on a wild goose chase up north to try to find out what the hell is going on!

Potentially I could keep trying his mobile and if I managed to get through to him, we could have a chat about why he's not been answering his phone. I could even go so far as saying I'd spoken with his work and they have confirmed they're not expecting him. But even if I did this, could I trust his response? He has lied to me repeatedly over these past few weeks. There have been the texts going back and forth late at night; that postcard; the fact he said he's going there on business and most worryingly where he was staying. OK he didn't give me the details of the accommodation he was staying at, but I'd just discovered he'd booked and paid for accommodation and had never arrived there.

I could think of only two scenarios. Either he is having an affair and he's shacked up somewhere on Skye (that's if he's definitely in Skye) with his mistress or (God forbid), he's been involved in an accident and that's why he was unable to check into the accommodation and return my calls this morning. I don't want to run away with this and force myself to calm down. I need to rule out that he has had an accident and decide to try calling him again.

He answers on the third ring. Relief floods my system. Thankfully, he's not been involved in an accident. He tells me he's fine, doing well in fact, and taking in some sightseeing before starting work tomorrow. The earlier feeling of relief is oh so quickly replaced with an intense anger. I can't believe this is the same man I married all those years ago. He is so happily spinning lie after lie to me. Through gritted teeth I somehow manage to maintain some decorum and tell him that sounds wonderful and that I hope he gets on well in his search for a new financial adviser. Yeah right! As I hang up, I can feel a huge knot which has formed in my stomach twisting and tightening and, with it, a painful throbbing in my temples and tightening in my chest. This only leaves the other possibility, that he is having an affair, I can think of no other logical explanation.

Another worrying prospect is that I travel all the way up there and there is no Thomas to be found! If he hasn't checked into his accommodation was he even in Skye? I reason that I don't have anything else to go on and his latest search history did show that he was looking at accommodation there (albeit he hadn't checked in) so it's the best I have to go on for now.

I need to make arrangements for Michael whilst I'm away and phone my best friend Amy. Her son Lucas is also good friends with Michael, so I think he'd be happiest staying with them. She is a saviour. I've given her next to no notice and she's got no problem whatsoever in taking him in. I tell her it'll only be for a few days, that something urgent has come up. And, like a true friend she senses that I don't want to go into it and doesn't push me for any more information. Let's just hope Michael is on board with this arrangement too.

Work already think I'm unwell so there's no problem there, I just need to keep the pretence going and phone in daily to notify them of my absence. My mind wanders ... if he is having an affair, what then? Could I remain married to him or would this be the end of us? If we split up what would this do to Michael? He is at a crucial time at school with exams coming up and the thought of disrupting his little world with this bombshell (if it is true) makes me feel physically sick.

It then occurs to me perhaps there is a third explanation. I'd ruled it out long ago because he was so matter of fact about going there on business. I had had no reason to doubt him because, up to that point, to my knowledge he had never lied to me before. I recall a conversation I'd had with him when we discussed what he was going to do when he arrived. I had asked for reassurance that he wasn't going to delve into his past and he said there was no way he was going down that road, that he'd stay away from the croft and all the ghosts from long ago. He said the only person he'd contact would be his mother. Perhaps this was a lie?

Thomas had done an excellent job over the years of putting a brave face on and burying things, but I know him better than even he realises, and I can see the cracks and chinks in his armour. There have been many occasions over the years when I've seen the little lost boy look come over his face; when he's completely left the room lost in his own world. He always snaps back to reality, a false smile scrawled across his face for my benefit, with him thinking he has successfully covered any momentary lapse in his otherwise happy demeanour. I've also heard him cry to himself (and, on occasion, talk to himself), always when he thinks I'm out of earshot. He does such a masterful job of trying to cover this up when I approach him after such an incident that I don't have the heart to push him and then the moment passes.

If this was the explanation and he was finally going to confront his demons, then he'd need my support. Either way I reason I've made the right choice in going there but decide for now to keep my visit a secret from him until I have more information. Thomas is not the only one with secrets, perhaps he might find out more about his wife than he bargains for when we re-acquaint in Skye ....

CHAPTER 11

October 1998

The long days of Summer have been replaced with shorter daylight hours. But with it, Autumn has brought the most spectacular sunsets I think I've ever seen; a result perhaps of the intermingling of the two seasons before Summer lets go of her grasp completely in surrender to Autumn.

You are never quite sure what weather October will bring on Skye. We have had Autumns where the rain is relentless, flowing down the mountains and hillsides and saturating everything it comes into contact with. This is particularly difficult on the croft. The soil is predominantly peat based and when it's saturated there is backbreaking work to do to ensure the ditches and drains are clear for the 'run-off.' Mercifully, October thus far has been mostly dry, which is unusual as we normally expect to see a fair bit of rainfall. Instead, we have the start of cool crisp days and these mesmerising sunsets and for that I'm grateful.

I had completely forgotten what day it was until I sat down at the breakfast table. There was a card sitting there for me and as a special treat mother had made pancakes which I devoured in no time. I open the card and it simply says, 'Happy 14th Birthday Son, love Mum.' There is no pile of gifts waiting to be opened but she whispers in my ear and tells me that she has bought a bar of my favourite chocolate and put it in my schoolbag. When you don't have much in this world your expectations are low and little gestures like this mean a lot, I know I'll savour every mouthful.

Our happy moment is short-lived as I hear the thud of his heavy footfall approaching. I'm not quick enough to remove the card from the table and with a flourish he snatches it away. "Lots of love, mum?! Aah, right enough, son, you only have one parent, it only took one of us to bring you into this world, didn't it, Mary?! Did you simply forget about this, Mary, you simpleton, or are you trying to belittle me on purpose?" He doesn't give her a chance to answer as he ploughs on "No, you two are as thick as thieves, always conspiring together, I never quite know what the pair of you are up to and I don't trust either of you. You have your own 'thing' going on, don't you, and you seem to have forgotten about little old me! Well, I will not be cast aside. Perhaps it's time to make my presence truly known!"

It occurs to me that his fiery temper and episodes of emotional abuse (especially towards mother) were escalating. Before it was every so often he seemed to need to let off steam and you prayed you weren't in the firing line. Now it felt as though there was no escape. He was so volatile, prone to an outburst at any time, often with no provoking required. I had noticed he was drinking more too, whisky being his tipple of choice so perhaps there was a link between the two?

Anyway, by now I knew the drill. Do not give him eye contact and under no circumstances, ever answer him back unless he specifically asks you to do so. We were at stage two now; the interlude after the initial outburst where he collects himself in a relative silence, pondering our destiny. This I realise is always the worst stage, where we are left to sit and conjure up what weird and not so wonderful fate he has in store for us. I wonder whether I'll be involved in this punishment today. He is angry at mother for not including his name on the card and it's my birthday so perhaps he'll let me off? Then I chide myself for wanting mother to face his wrath alone.

I wish there were some way we could stand up to him but each time I let my mind drift towards ways we could 'get our own back' I am reminded of what life would be like then, it would be completely unbearable. Would he then resort to physical violence too? If he did, mother would be number one target and I couldn't have that. I've seen it in his eyes and the colour of his face; that anger he has is barely under control. He looks as though it'd take nothing for him to reach that tipping point. I couldn't bear the thought of him using mother as a punchbag. Her life wouldn't be worth living.

I feel a burden of responsibility as far as mother and my siblings go. I do all I can to protect them all. As time goes on, my siblings are becoming more aware of the situation and their anger and frustration is growing too. Caroline especially is losing patience and I'm concerned that she will push things too far. Only the other day she confided in me that she has dreams about dishing out punishments to father; more severe and fanciful than what we have ever had to endure. She also talks about what would happen were we to pick up the phone and notify the authorities. She has convinced herself that were the Police to be informed, all our worries would be a thing of the past as they would sort everything out. I've tried to explain it's not as simple as that. I feel sure father would turn on the charm if needed and what would the chances be of mother speaking out against him? Not in your wildest dreams, he has her exactly where he wants her. No, it would be quickly dismissed then we'd really be in for it!

James is also growing in confidence and, with it, his sense of restraint is dwindling. Along with Caroline, he needs checked and kept in line because he too is simmering away, growing increasingly intolerant of father's behaviour. It seems as though the fear they both once had has been gradually replaced with anger and a sense of injustice at why we have to put up with this! He is also frustrated with mother. He thinks she should 'grow a back-bone' and stand up for us all and do something about getting us out of there. I explain it's not as simple as that; she's unable to do this but I suspect this is falling on deaf ears as his anger, frustration, and intolerance grow.

The only one who doesn't have a lot to say on the subject is Juliet. She is like a little sponge taking it all in and I often worry about her the most. What is going on in that little head of hers? There is simply no shielding her from what is going on.

The responsibility I bear when it comes to them all feels like a heavy burden on my shoulders. It feels as though I have no one to vent my feelings to. I can't speak to mother about anything as I don't want her to deal with any more than she's currently going through. Her mental health doesn't look too good just now. I'm no expert but she's becoming increasingly forgetful. I'm getting up extra early in the mornings to lend a hand with feeding the animals and laying out the breakfast things because there's been a couple of occasions recently when she's forgotten to do the morning feeds and God forbid if she gets anything wrong with his breakfast so I'm there to make sure that doesn't happen.

I can't say anything to school friends or teaching staff either for the same reasons. Our lives would not be worth living if any accusations were pointed in his direction. I sometimes wonder, however, if our lives are worth living as things currently stand. The thought that things could worsen is too much to bear and I know I'll never utter a word. I dream about leaving at 16 as soon as I am able to but then I'm torn. This would mean leaving mother to face his wrath alone, without my support.

I snap back to reality as I'm aware he's shifted in his seat. The tension in the air is palpable. The kitchen window is ajar, and I can hear the familiar noises around the grounds of animals calling to each other, snuffling and happily grazing. It always astounds me how utterly normal everything around me is. The world just carries on; everyone and every beast living their own little life and then there's me, stuck in this recurring nightmare. Sometimes reality is indistinguishable, and I question whether this is actually happening or if I'm in some sort of quasi dreamlike, nightmarish state.

We move towards stage three now, the dishing out of the punishment. He breaks the silence; "Well I suppose you'll be expecting special treatment today, son, on your special day and who am I to deny you that! Mary, look in the cupboard, woman, have you got any of my chocolate muffins left?" This had me baffled. Where was he going with this? A chocolate muffin is something I can honestly say I have never tasted in the confines of the croft (they are his special treats, and we would never be allowed to touch one). I've only ever tried one a handful of times at school.

Mother dutifully obliges and retrieves one and places it down on the table. "Excellent. Don't ever let it be said that I'm not good to you, son. By the looks of it that's my last one so you're in luck. It wouldn't be right though if your mother and I didn't join you in celebration now, would it? I'll have a Scotch. Mary, move it, I'm thirsty, woman, come on now." She doesn't delay and fetches a whisky over ice for him from the dining room drinks cabinet. This is all way too civilised and I'm nervous. What has he got planned for us? I daren't look up; my eyes still obediently downcast towards the table and the muffin looking expectantly up at me.

There is a pause whilst he takes a large swig from the glass and the noise when the glass makes contact with the table again echoes around the room. "Fill her up, Mary. Would you have me die of thirst, woman? Your idea of a measure and mine are clearly worlds apart. Fill her up good this time, we're celebrating the lad's birthday, are we not?" She shuffles back through and does as he asks, then returns to her seat alongside mine. I imagine she's a bundle of nerves wondering what he's got in store for her.

"Well, let's take a look around the table shall we. Birthday boy has a chocolate muffin, lucky old him, and I have a rather large glass of Scotch here thanks to you, Mary, but there's something missing, isn't there? Mary, you have nothing in front of you and that we need to remedy! We can't have you sitting watching us tuck in with nothing for yourself now, can we? Come on, lad, follow me because I have an idea." Follow him? Follow him where? All the food and drinks were inside, but he'd already strode out heading towards the front door. I kept up as best I could. He appeared to be on a mission striding out towards the field adjacent to the croft where our Highland Cows were grazing. Oh no, he can't be …

He stopped walking and motioned me to come over. He handed me a bag and instructed me to collect some of the steaming muck one of the cows had clearly only recently defaecated. I have a strong stomach and working on the croft has hardened me to all sorts of sights and smells, but I can feel the bile rising up rapidly as I realise his intention for the stinking deposit. I lose control and the contents of my stomach are there on show for all to see and the bag he handed me lies at the bottom of the pile of my vomit.

He looks as though he's going to really lose it with me. He is absolutely fuming. The cool, calculated persona now replaced with blind fury and he's barely able to contain it. "Get back in there now, you useless piece of shit, and get me another bag … NOW!" Resistance is futile so I move as quickly as I can and fetch one of Jess's poo bags from mother's coat pocket in the porch. If there had been anything left in my stomach it wouldn't have remained there because the stench of the fresh manure intermingling with my vomit was indescribable. He seems completely unperturbed with the stench, standing only inches away from it, his eyes and attention solely focused on me.

"Hurry up, you lazy brute," he roars at me. My feet deceive me as they make their way towards him as no part of me wants to be there. "Get on with it then, get a decent dollop." A decent dollop? Caroline's words ring in my ears, 'it's time to show him a piece of his own medicine', and I am sorely tempted to get more than just a 'decent dollop' to throw right at that smug face of his! How wonderful would that be? Watching him stood there with a mixture of my vomit and cow dung plastered all over him! As always, however, the voice of reason takes over and I know taking matters into my own hands is only going to make things worse for mother and I. So, with a heavy heart and limbs, I bend over, doing my best to block off my nose, breathing instead through my mouth. I attempt to take a small portion but he's watching me with hawk eyes. "I don't think so, smart arse; you can easily double that! No more time wasting; fill her up and back inside with you now, boy, before I change my mind. Do you want to forfeit your muffin and join your mother?" He takes one look at my face which says it all. "No, I didn't think so, now get moving!"

I glance up at the kitchen and see movement. Bless her, mother has clearly been watching the scene unfold, she knows her fate. As we make our way back into the kitchen, however, she's sitting there in the same seat as though she'd never moved. The only difference in the scene is that Jess is now lying at her feet. She doesn't lay there long; the stench has clearly piqued her interest and she's up on her haunches sniffing the air. "We've got you a wee treat, Mary girl! A little mud pie for you so you can join in with the birthday celebrations." His voice has lost the wild anger and has been replaced with a boyish giddy excitement, he is loving every minute of this. "Out of the way, Thomas; let me do the honours, I want to plate it up for her."

I sit down next to mother and whilst he busies himself plating up the disgusting offering, I reach my hand out under the table and find her hand and give it a reassuring squeeze. She reciprocates and squeezes my hand back. I just want to guide her out of here; to run away somewhere far away from this stinking hell hole but she releases her grip, and I am forced to also move my hand back. With his back to us I sneak a look over – he is in his element. He has used one of mother's scone cutters and has created a perfectly formed little dung pie placing it smack, bang in the centre of her plate. Jess is in on the action; both her paws are up on the counter next to him, eager to see what he's up to, the smell too much for her to resist. He pushes her off. "Fuck off, Jess, you stupid mutt. OK 'et voila', Mary; especially for you, a little Mississippi mud pie – 'Bon Appetit'!"

He places it in front of her and the tiniest little voice pipes up, "No." It was so faint I was unsure whether I'd imagined it or not but clearly I hadn't for he'd heard it too.

"No?! No?! You are to deny me, woman?" With that he pulls her chair away from the table and stands in front of her, towering over her, standing between her and the plate. "Mary so help me God if you don't clear that plate up and lick it clean you just wait for it; you do not want to take me on!" His voice is now booming, the words reverberating around the small room. "Do I make myself clear?" he says, the words coming out in staccato fashion, a pause between each emphasising that he is not messing about. With a flourish he bends over; his face right on hers; his hands steadying himself by holding onto the top of her chair. "Well?"

In the same little meek voice, "Yes."

"Yes what, bitch?"

"Yes, Sir."

"Aah good," he says, the bluster now gone and he's back to being Mr cool, calm, and collected. "Well don't let me stop you then, tuck right in." He moves out of the way and pushes her chair back in towards the table. Then he makes his way back around to the head of the table and gaily takes a large swig of the amber liquid.

There's silence and no movement from either mother or myself, neither of us ready to 'tuck right in.' He's ever ready with instructions though. "Right, you two, how will we do this? Bite for bite or dive right in?" If he's wanting a response, he gets none as we remain silent. He's oblivious to this and ploughs on. "Oh how remiss of me! We haven't sung Happy Birthday to Thomas!"

This really is beyond weird. To the onlooker I imagine it'd look like a happy scene; mother and father singing Happy Birthday lovingly to their son, ready to tuck into a 'cake' to celebrate, but the reality was a far cry. He goes for it, belting the song out; the whisky clearly starting to take effect along with the heady anticipation he is experiencing over his latest punishment. Mother's contribution is barely audible and I feel my heart breaking for her as she knows her fate at the end of the song.

When it's over he signals for us to begin and I find I have no appetite; feeling yet again sick to my stomach so I can only imagine the horrors mother is enduring. I'm aware of movement to my left and realise she's picked up her fork. I am momentarily frozen, unable to move a muscle; gripped by this sickening scene. He doesn't miss a beat. "What are you waiting for, son, eat up!" Reluctantly I too raise my fork. The combination of smells in the room from the chocolate and cow dung is a vile cocktail. There is a momentary pause and silence before the next sound – mother's fork being placed back down on the table and she barely whispers, "I'm sorry, Sir, I can't do it."

I expect to hear him roar and confront her, but he goes eerily silent as he contemplates his next move.

"I'll give you one more chance, eat up, Mary – now!"

I'm thrown as mother turns her gaze towards him, looking him in the face and replies, "I'm sorry Bert, I can't do it." He will lose it now; we are not allowed to give him eye contact. What was she thinking?

He blows his top. He sends his glass flying across the table, the contents pouring everywhere, and it smashes into little pieces as it makes contact with the edge of the sink. Jess lets out a whimper and I said a silent prayer that it was over the noise and not a little shard getting into her paw or her face. He is over at her chair in a flash. "OK you insolent bitch, I'll teach you a lesson." He grabs the back of her head and pushes it downwards with force onto the steaming muck. "Eat it up now, bitch!" I want to lunge at him for what he has put her through. He transitions again from fury to giddy excitement, "That's it, little piggy! Oink oink! Eat up, that's a good girl." He momentarily turns his attention away from her and looks towards me. "Well what are you waiting for, boy? Your mother is tucking right in so get that muffin into you."

I can hear all sorts of strained muffled noises coming from mother as she battles to catch a breath. I panic – is he going to let her come up for air? "Please," I hear myself say. "Please Sir, let her breathe." It takes him some time to register I've spoken; his focus solely back on torturing mother and when he does, he's clearly happy to continue to let her suffer.

"Aww isn't that lovely, Mary, the lad is full of concern for you; haven't you done a good job of raising him." The panic I felt earlier has now escalated beyond anything I have ever experienced before as I see she's now thumping the palms of her hands on the table. Fortunately, the noise of this shakes his reverie and he loosens his grip on the back of her head. Like a drown victim bursting through the surface of the water to get air, her head whips up at break-neck speed and a huge, panicked gasp ensues as she gets that blessed oxygen into her lungs.

I realise I am off my seat and need to re-position myself in my chair before he notices but I'm unable to as my legs are rooted to the spot like two solid oak trees. My body is rendered motionless as I take in the horrific scene before me. Mother is still eagerly gasping for air; this is her priority. Her survival instinct having kicked in. Dealing with the mess and the degradation of what he's done to her obviously secondary at this point. I, however, am simply left with this vision of my beautiful mother looking like something from a horror movie, bits of cow dung plastered all over her face and hair; the unrelenting stench doing nothing to quell the unease in my stomach. I needn't worry about being unable to take my place back at the table for mother has grabbed his attention again. Obviously now that her lungs have recovered somewhat, the rest of her bodily functions have taken over and with an unimaginable force she expels everything in her stomach, the projectile vomit bursting forth with such ferocity, some of it makes contact with the wall opposite us. How is he going to react to this? That's both of us now been sick, this is not going to go down well.

With all this going on, I hadn't been aware of James and Caroline's presence in the room. James like myself is aghast at the spectacle, seeing mother like that covered in a mixture of excrement and vomit. He is ashen and momentarily unable to utter a word (I know how he feels). Then, "No, no, no!"

"Shhhh," I attempt to silence him, but Caroline is straight in there.

"You've taken it too far, you brute, enough!"

"OK Caroline, I know, sweetheart, but hush, please!" I sit back down at the table, now praying for an end in sight.

"What's that? What's going on and what is all the mumbling about?"

I speak on behalf of us all, not wanting my siblings to jeopardise things any further. "Nothing Sir, sorry Sir." It seems enough to pacify him as he turns back towards mother.

"You really are a stinking bitch, Mary, look at the state of you! No-one in their right mind would want you, what was I thinking? Not even good for one thing if I'm honest but let's spare your blushes and not get into that with prying ears listening in. Fuck it, I've had enough, I don't want to spend another minute in your company, you pathetic excuse for a woman. Just don't even think about cleaning yourself up until this place is spotless!"

Whilst he reads her the riot act, Caroline whispers in my ear, "If you don't do something about him soon, I'm going to take matters into my own hands. I can't put up with this any longer. He needs locked up and the key thrown away."

Under my breath I whisper back, "He's still our father." Who am I trying to kid? I know his behaviour is outrageous and I often fantasise about leaving but there's still a part of me which is pulled towards staying here. I've reasoned over the recent years that this is borne out of a need to protect mother but what if I was falling victim to Stockholm Syndrome?

"Father, father?!" Caroline presses on. "He's not worthy of the title."

I am shifting back and forth in my seat now, petrified that he is tuned into the conversation, but he is too busy finishing off ranting at mother. James, who is on the other side of me, chips in too, "She's right you know, no one should have to live like this." I decide the best way to deal with the two of them is to simply not interact. This works only for a short moment as there is no pacifying Caroline.

"Thomas, I love you, you know that, but I'm starting to think it's not only mother who needs to grow a backbone!" Mercifully, they're both now quiet; Caroline having got this off her chest. I didn't think it was possible to feel worse than I had before but with her parting comment I've sunk to a new low and I can feel a simmering rage in my stomach directed not towards Caroline but towards him. You have done this, I think to myself, you've tortured us and now you're turning my siblings against me!

At that moment I start to wonder what I could be capable of. The mental anguish is too much to bear, and I feel as though I'm coming undone, ready to explode. Thankfully he beats a retreat and storms back through to the dining room and fixes another large Scotch then slams the door shut, leaving us to it. I can now properly engage with mother but I'm not sure what to do or say. I venture a meek "Mother" and I get off my seat, arms outstretched to give her a hug, but she backs off, too ashamed with the state she is in and says simply, "It's OK, son, you go to your room, sweetheart, I'll see to this. Sorry about everything on your birthday too of all days." Sorry about everything! She is apologising for him! I can feel that hot fury bubbling away again. I am fit to burst!

"He shouldn't be allowed to do this to you, mother." I realise Caroline's words are having an impact on me as I normally avoid the subject, fearful of making things worse for her. I look at her and her eyes are full of sadness. Sad for the wretched life she's living and sad for the impact he's having on the rest of us. She doesn't know how to fix this. Of course she doesn't, otherwise she'd have found a way out long ago so she simply reverts to the usual tactic of cleaning up the mess and brushing the incident under the carpet as though it had never happened. Her eyes are pleading with me to leave her to it, and I relent, then motion to James and Caroline to join me.

Caroline has to have a final say though, she can't help herself, "One of these days he'll take it to the next level and you're not going to walk out of here." I turn around to see my mother before leaving the room and for once she hasn't just 'jumped to it' busying herself cleaning the place. She is slouched in one of the chairs, looking as though all fight and hope and resolve have left her body entirely. A solitary tear traces its way down her cheek, navigating its journey past stinking excrement and vomit.

CHAPTER 12

Janey

With work still thinking I am unwell, I waste no time in making final preparations to set off. It was difficult saying goodbye to Michael. Not because he was upset, far from it. He was over the moon to get to spend a few days with Lucas and Amy's cooking is legendary, so I know he is more than well taken care of. It was more that I didn't like lying to him about why I'm heading up there. I made up an excuse about work being so hectic lately and needing some time out. "Whilst your father is working through the day I'll relax or do a little sightseeing then catch up with him later, it'll be just what I need." Bless him, he didn't ask once to join me, sensing from the thread of conversation that I was looking forward to some 'time out.'

We hugged briefly on Amy's doorstep then he was off in search of Lucas, leaving Amy and I alone. I thank her again for taking Michael in and she waves it off as though it was no big deal then steps towards me and squeezes me in an unusually tight embrace. Amy always has been very intuitive, and I sense she knows there's more to this trip than meets the eye. Being held like that fires up some of my pent-up emotion and I'm so close to telling her everything, imagining some of the relief I'd feel at sharing the weight of this heavy burden I'm carrying about just now. But thankfully, she loosens her grip and takes a step backwards before I have a chance to blurt out anything I would later regret. She looks me directly in the eyes and says, "Don't hesitate to call anytime, Janey, if there's anything at all. I'm here and don't worry about Michael, he'll be well taken care of." I thank her again and head towards the car.

I set out on the long journey northwards. My stomach is churning, and a dull throbbing sensation is ever present at my temples with all the thoughts turning over and over in my mind. There are too many loose ends to tie up and the only way to address this is face to face. I know this truth, but I vision standing before him and hearing something awful then see myself going to pieces. To quell the unease, I turn the radio on and try to immerse myself. But my brain has other ideas. It is a clever fellow and persistent in its quest to keep pulling me back in towards the churning anxious thoughts. I decide to wait until I reach Portree and get settled into the apartment before contacting him. If I phoned him now and told him about my plans, I am certain he would do everything he could to get me to turn around.

It is inky black when I arrive at my destination. When I pull up at the apartment and exit the car, I gaze heavenward and see a blanket of stars. With very little light pollution on Skye the stars are on display in all their glory. It is breath-taking and I realise I have been star gazing for quite some time as my neck aches when it snaps back into position.

Well Thomas, you certainly have chosen well! I'm looking over the harbour and the lights from all the properties surrounding the harbour are twinkling and give the whole place a mystical, ethereal quality. The sound of the waves lapping up is hypnotic. It is captivating at night, but I imagine through the day it will be equally captivating or even more so as the colours explode.

Wearily I haul my luggage out of the car and drag it in the direction of the apartment. Once inside I am pleasantly surprised, and it lifts my mood. It is very quaint. Someone with a keen eye has been involved in dressing the place, picking out some beautiful bespoke pieces. I particularly like the brass telescope set in front of the picture window which I see holds the same view out over the harbour I had just bore witness to. There is also a wood burner and large stockpile of wooden blocks sitting adjacent to it so before I do anything, I set about getting the fire going.

In no time at all I have a roaring fire and the sight and smell of it seem to evoke a sense of calm in me. I start wandering around the apartment, finishing up in the kitchen where to my surprise there is a welcome basket. Happily, I realise I won't have to leave my cosy fire because the owner has provided some pasta and accompanying sauce. Perhaps not my favoured cuisine but it certainly beats trailing around outside looking for food after the long day I've had so I quickly rustle this up.

With feet up resting and a full belly I feel somewhat contented and decide to phone Thomas. I realise just the thought of phoning him has caused my whole body to tense up then I chastise myself for feeling like this. This is the man I fell in love with and went on to marry. He has to be given a chance to explain everything. He answers after only a couple of rings and it takes me by surprise (I was half expecting the call to go straight to voicemail).

We start by going through all the pleasantries. Then I enquire about what he's been up to today and I get fed a pack of lies about how he's visited one of the potential candidates for the position; him going into great detail about the imaginary fellows credentials and it simply becomes too much to bear. I'm straight out with it, "You're lying to me." I give him the opportunity to change his story and tell the truth instead.

"I don't know what you mean, Janey."

He's not going to give me any other version of events, so I press on; "I know you're lying to me because I've spoken with your work when I was unable to contact you and they told me there was no recruitment drive so I'll ask you again, what were you up to today, Thomas, and where are you now?"

There's silence on the other end of the line. He is clearly gathering himself and fine tuning his cover story. I don't interrupt, too interested in what he's got to say for himself. Eventually, "I'm sorry, Janey. It's quite hard to explain and I don't like lying to you, but I said what I said thinking it was the best way to deal with the situation to avoid you getting involved or upset. I'm sorry if you've been worried but please don't be. I am in Skye on a personal matter, but it is honestly nothing for you to worry about. Just give Michael a big hug from me."

"That won't be possible, Thomas."

"What do you mean?"

"Well Michael is in Galashiels and I'm in Skye sitting in the apartment you rented for yourself wondering where you could possibly be!" He buys time for himself again, not addressing his whereabouts straight away.

"Who is Michael staying with? He's not been left on his own?"

"Of course he's not been left on his own! He's at Amy's. So I'll ask again, where are you?"

"I'm just staying with a friend."

"Would this friend happen to be male or female, Thomas?" My voice falters with that last statement as my mind conjures up a vision of him sitting cozied up with another woman.

He wastes to time in replying to this, "Male of course. I know I've lied to you, honey, but I have never been involved with anyone else – EVER!"

He sounds so convincing when he says this and emphasises what he's saying with such determination that straight away any concerns I had about his fidelity just dissolve instantly. Of course my husband isn't cheating on me. My Thomas: I feel my heart open. However, this was closely followed by a feeling of concern. What was he up to then? It had to be something to do with his past.

"OK thank goodness for that," I venture. "Thomas, please just be honest with me, what's going on? Where are you and why have you come to Skye?" He asks me to fetch a pen and paper and he relays an address to me of where he's staying. He asks me to drive out there in the morning so we can chat further. I object and say I'll come out tonight, but he insists I rest up after such a long journey. He seems unperturbed that I am here, and this also gives me some reassurance. Perhaps he will be happy to see me?

The tension I felt when I initially lifted the receiver has dissipated somewhat and I realise I'm able to breathe more freely as though for the past twenty-four hours I'd been holding onto my breath. But I wasn't unconcerned. There were still lots of questions to be answered. What was he up to and who was he staying with? I reason that (hopefully) all will be revealed tomorrow and with that knowledge on board I take myself off to bed and drift off.

Thomas

Another turn of events! I cannot believe Janey is in Skye and it makes me anxious. How do I explain to her about why I am here and what do I say about George? It sounded as though she was worried I was with another woman, but perhaps that would be an easier tale for her to digest. How do I explain why I'm really here? I can't very well send her packing; she's ventured all the way up here. Do I turn to George for assistance or come up with something myself (but the last thing I want to do is lie to her again!)?

Where is George anyway? I haven't seen him at all today. He simply left a note saying, 'Gone out; be back later, rest up.' To be honest I needed today to rest. The car accident has taken its toll and my bones are weary and stiff. The rest has helped the pain in my back, neck, and head all ease up but I feel a dull throbbing starting up in my head again, more likely than not as a result of my call with Janey. I have the night to sleep on it so hopefully I can come up with something credible when I see her tomorrow.

Janey

I wake up feeling refreshed, with a renewed vigour, ready to face whatever I am up against today. The fact I know he is not cheating on me has just opened up something in me. Our relationship can get through this whatever it is. I feel confident of that.

Using the directions Thomas gave me, I make the short journey to where he is staying. I am intrigued. This is beautiful. It looks like a fairly new-build property but it's evident that lots of careful thought has went into its design as it manages to maintain its new look whilst simultaneously merging perfectly into the landscape. There is a long private driveway which sounds my arrival as the gravel crunches underneath my tyres. On approach I notice a section of decking to the left-hand side of the property and there sits a solitary figure. Instead of making my way to the front door to ring the bell I decide instead to get a closer look at the decking. Even from a distance I can see that it's Thomas, so I shout over to get his attention and he responds, "Come on in, the front door is open, come out and join me." He is clearly enjoying the view too much to see me in.

Once inside, there is further reassurance that he is not staying with another woman. The house is beautifully decorated but has a masculine feel to it with black sofa, black and white prints on the walls, and everything is minimalistic. What strikes you straight away, however, is not the décor; it is the view – utterly breath-taking. The bifold doors are expansive and draw the outside inwards. I head towards them and make my way onto the decking. I am unable to acknowledge Thomas' presence until I have absorbed this view. I take it all in; the sight and smell of the bay directly in front of me with waves gently lapping up. Then, in stark contrast, the jagged mountainous area on the other side of the bay. "Wow," I hear myself say.

"It certainly is," a voice to my left pipes up. This snaps me back to reality.

"Thomas!" I join him, sitting in a rocking chair by his side.

"You made it," he says and leans over to pour me a coffee. He does a good job of trying to mask it, but I saw him wince as he leaned over.

"Thomas, are you OK? You look as though you're in pain?"

"I'm fine, Janey, honestly, it's nothing, probably the way I was lying in bed or something." I let it go.

"This is some place, Thomas. I am intrigued to find out who you are staying with and what is going on."

We sit for some time in a comfortable silence enjoying the coffee and taking in the spectacular view. Without pressing him, Thomas leads the conversation. "So, apologies again, Janey, for lying to you. I did that with the best of intentions. I had to come up here on my own and didn't want you worrying so it seemed like the best idea at the time.

Why am I here? It's complicated and since our phone call last night I've wrestled over and over in my mind as to what to tell you. In the end I concluded that the wrong thing to do would be to lie to you anymore so here goes … Someone from my past came back into my life recently. I don't know if you can remember the night you found me in the freezing cold at the front door in the middle of the night?" I nod in acknowledgement. "Well, there was someone there who I hadn't seen in years. In fact, he is the owner of this house. He wanted me to come back to Skye because I have unfinished business here. He was also responsible for the postcard."

I can't help myself, "This is all very cloak and dagger, Thomas. What do you mean by 'unfinished business'?"

"To tell you the truth, Janey, I'm not entirely sure myself. It's hard to explain but something happened here years ago, and I've never came to terms with it, and he knows this. When he asked me to come back, I didn't want to, but I knew I had to. I plan to stay here at his house to get to the bottom of the situation."

My head was spinning. I had suspected this could all be related to his past but what on earth had happened? What was it all about? It had to be something significant for him to just up and leave and come back up here and all these years later too. I test the waters. "Can you tell me about it? Can you tell me what happened?" I watch him visibly shrink in his seat as though he was retreating into an invisible shell.

"I'm not sure, I haven't been able to talk about it, ever."

Before we get a chance to say anything further, we are interrupted by the sound of footsteps approaching. Thomas' mystery housemate is about to be revealed and I feel a nervous anticipation. He doesn't stop in the living room; heading instead straight out onto the decking to join us. It is instant recognition. Yes, he has aged but there is no denying who is stood before me – George Traynor. I also see the flicker of recognition across his eyes as he takes me in. Neither of us acknowledge this as we politely shake hands when Thomas introduces us.

CHAPTER 13

January 14th 1998

It has been a particularly harsh and unforgiving winter. No longer have I been able to find solace carrying out duties around the croft because the biting cold and snowstorms have made the simplest of tasks arduous. The animals too also seem to emanate this weariness as they hunt for shelter and hungrily devour any food available.

Life within the confines of the croft has taken a turn for the worse which I didn't think was possible. Father's drinking has escalated and with it his behaviour has become more and more erratic. I am living in fight or flight mode, my whole being on high alert ready to do battle and to expect the unexpected. The alcohol is affecting his sleep too because he is keeping the strangest hours now. On a few occasions he has writhed me out of my bed in the middle of the night to help with one thing or another, seemingly oblivious to what time it was.

Mother too is worrying me; her bouts of forgetfulness seem to be increasing and neither mother nor father have acknowledged this. Only the other day she had packed my school lunch and laid it out – on Saturday! I didn't have the heart to say anything, so I ate the lunch and brought the empty container back through. She didn't seem to acknowledge the fact I hadn't left the croft that day to go to school so I couldn't work out whether she thought I was at school that day or at home.

The alcohol is doing nothing to dampen father's fury. If anything it's adding fuel to the fire. He is a walking, talking, ticking time bomb, ready to explode at the drop of a hat and woe betide you if you happen to be at the wrong place at the wrong time.

Christmas had been a particularly hard period and I am relieved it's all over. There was no giving and receiving of gifts, no decorations adorned the croft, and no feast was to be had. It didn't stop me waking on Christmas morning with the vein hope that perhaps this year things would be different. I tortured myself with the vision of what my school friends' Christmas Day would look like. The only blessing was that father drank even more than usual (perhaps his way of celebrating?) and drank himself into a stupor where he slept most of the day. My siblings wanted to take advantage of this situation and take off somewhere, but I was unsure. What if he woke up and we weren't there? However, in the past couple of months this has been happening more and more frequently. He gets a few jobs done around the croft then parks himself in the dining room: bottle of Scotch at the ready. It has happened enough times now for us to get a feel for how long he'll be 'out cold.' So, today, we take a huge decision and leap of faith as we decide to venture when we see he's shut himself away in the dining room.

Caroline has been the driving force behind our destination of choice. I can barely recall being there but she's adamant we went years ago on a rare afternoon out. With the only times we leave the croft being to either go to school or accompany mother to the supermarket, this (like my jaunt to Dunvegan Castle) was a treat. It was also extremely risky. We (or should I say Caroline) had decided to go to Neist Point Lighthouse. It was the most westerly point on the island and takes around half an hour to get there by car. We were going by bus, so slightly longer.

We decided to allow two hours all in for the bus trips and a further couple of hours to explore. We will have to say our silent prayers to the gods that he is out long enough to allow us to leave and return un-noticed. We didn't have to worry about mother, bless her, that was easily remedied. On return if she said anything about our disappearance, we were going to use her forgetfulness to our advantage. Not something I am proud of but feasible none the less. There was no chance she would risk waking him to alert him of our disappearance, so we simply had to cross everything and pray he was out for long enough.

We had been plotting this for some time now; waiting on an opportune moment and intermittently checking his supplies of Scotch to ensure there was enough there. When he plants himself in the dining room he doesn't leave until he's emptied the contents of a full bottle. James checked only a couple of days ago and there were three full bottles there, so we decided now was as good a time as any. Juliet was 'coming along for the ride.' She had no opinion either way on whether we should stay or go but was happy to come along with us. With father safely ensconced in the dining room, I rustled some food together and packed it in my rucksack and we were off. Mother didn't see me packing the rucksack, so she was easily appeased when I made the excuse that we were off to check on the cows.

I was only too aware that throughout the day I would have that little voice in my head reminding me not to stay out too long; to get back before he's aware of our disappearance. But I tried my best to quash this. We were out for the day and had to enjoy it. It wasn't too difficult because just leaving the grounds of the croft and heading towards the bus stop, I could feel a weight being lifted off my shoulders (a feeling I often experienced on the same walk to the bus stop for the school run). It was a break away; a break from him and we had to enjoy it.

The bus was fairly empty, and we took it all in; the scenery as the bus trundled along and the excited chatter about the afternoon ahead. None of us mentioned anything about father. I saw Caroline and

James' moods noticeably lift as a result of getting away for the day. Caroline in particular was giddy with excitement, eager for us to see Neist Point and at the same time hoping we wouldn't be disappointed since it was her idea to go there.

As we get off the bus the cold hits us. It's a biting cold which penetrates through your skin to your bones, and I'm relieved we ate on the bus because I shiver at the thought of removing my gloves to eat. Neist Point, like many of the other tourist attractions on Skye, is normally overrun with tourists but at this time of year there are only a small handful and the odd dog-walker. Only the hardy would venture out in these temperatures! The cold however does nothing to dampen our spirits and we take off along the path with wild abandon at breakneck speed, slowing up only when we hit a particularly icy patch. The aim was to get to the lighthouse and the end of the cliffside as soon as possible to make the most of our time there.

We make it to the lighthouse in no time and sadly the grounds are all locked up, so we are unable to explore but this doesn't stop our imaginations running wild. James happily regales us with ghost stories and it's very apt. In the cold dusky winter afternoon, the last of the light beginning to disappear over the headland, and with hardly anyone else in sight, the whole place has an eerie quality. Until recently, the Lighthouse cottages were let out to tourists and James asks us to look at the window of one of the cottages where the face of a little girl can be seen. We look over and of course there's nothing there but he's an excellent storyteller and we imagine seeing her peering out anyway. It's enough for us to pick up the pace; not wanting us to stay a minute longer; fearful she might just come to life.

We head all the way to the tip of Neist Point and pause to take it all in. The view is panoramic and jaw-droppingly spectacular. You look out over Moonen Bay to Waterstein Head and out over the Minch to the Western Isles. The point is often regarded as the best place on Skye to see whales, dolphins, porpoises, and basking sharks.

It is normally teeming with various species of sea birds but not at this time of year. Like the rest of Neist Point, it is eerily quiet at the tip because all the nesting birds will have migrated when the cold weather hit. The only noise to be heard is the wind as it whistles and cuts past us, causing the waves below to crash up against the cliff edge. It is a warning sign, and we take a step back.

James suggests we get a closer look at the waves below, so we take to the ground and lie flat peering out over the edge. It is captivating. This is mother nature in all her glory. The wind picks up and causes a swell in the waters below. As a result, the ensuing waves crash with such a force when they make impact, we can no longer hear ourselves speak. We are left to our own thoughts and a horrific image comes to me.

Father is stood at this very spot holding mother by the neck in front of him in a vice-like grip. He gives her an almighty shove and her fragile body tumbles to the depths, making contact with fragments of rock on the way down, bouncing limply from each like a broken rag doll. The waves suck her under, but I see her glassy lifeless eyes staring up at me before she's gone.

"Thomas, THOMAS; get up – QUICK!" Juliet's shrill voice penetrates the noise of the wind and waves. It takes several moments for me to process what all the commotion is about. The wind speed and force has picked up again and it's now very dangerous. We can't stay a minute longer. I push myself up and realise to my horror mother nature has other ideas, she pushes me back down again. There is a large boulder to my left, so I motion to everyone to grab a hold. We crawl over, hunker down, grab on tightly, and hope for the best.

Thankfully, it doesn't take too long for things to die down and we don't hang about, running towards safety away from the cliff-face. "Whoa; what a ride!" James is clearly enjoying himself; not one to shy away from danger; this was right up his street. "Is everyone OK?" a concerned Juliet pipes up. Caroline is noticeably quiet, and I probe her.

She breaks down instantly; "I'm so sorry. I know how much it meant for us to get away for the day and I nearly got us all killed in the process. It was a stupid idea to come out here at this time of year."

"Hey, don't be so hard on yourself," I reply. "You weren't to know it was going to get so wild; you're not responsible for the weather."

"I guess, but we shouldn't have been so close to the edge! We were lucky to get out of there in one piece."

"Well, we've lived to tell the tale and I can see why you brought us here, it's beautiful." She calms down somewhat. With the lull in conversation, my mind drifts to the scene at the cliff face and I am angry with myself for conjuring this up. We were supposed to be enjoying time away from him! However, with his image now fixed in my mind, I check the time then spring into action. We only have half an hour to make it back to the bus stop.

The mood on the way home is far less jovial. There is very little conversation as we wind our weary way back home. Everyone is frightened to say it, but it is clear we're all thinking the same thing. Has he twigged we snuck out? There is no more light left as we make our way up the dirt track towards the croft and it only intensifies the feeling of foreboding. The gloom has spread out not only over the horizon but also gripped and blackened our hearts as we continue to plough on even though every bit of common sense is telling us to flee.

Like the scene at Neist Point, it was eerily quiet when we entered the croft. Promising? Surely if he had been alerted to our disappearance there would've been a confrontation at the door? Tentatively, we make our way through the porch and towards the kitchen. The kitchen is quiet too and shrouded in darkness. I wanted to make my way quickly to my room, but James was having none of it. "Let's just check he's in there." I was just about to protest but he dragged me over to the dining room door. It wasn't fully shut so we were able to give it the gentlest tap and it gave way, allowing us to peek around it.

It was dusky in there too but thanks to the candlelight I was able to make out his substantial frame; collapsed into the chair before the hearth. The slurred speech revealed he was very intoxicated, "*Well, whaaat do we have heeere then?*" What to say? We don't know how much he knows! Has he left his perch today and realised we were missing? Or has he never ventured anywhere and just drunk himself into oblivion? I think positive and pray it's the latter ...

"Nothing Sir; I just wondered if you needed anything. I was in the kitchen making some food and wondered if you wanted anything." It is too gloomy in there; I can't tell how he has taken my response.

Eventually ... "Just piss off would you! You're trying to sober me up, so you are! Plying me with food to try to stem the effect of the booze. I didn't sink all this just to waste it stuffing my face!" With that, he brandishes his bottle of Scotch up, tipping it over for effect so we can see he's downed the entire bottle. There is no mention of us being away anywhere, so I murmur a "Sorry to have disturbed you, Sir," and take off to my room. With no mother in sight either, no exuberant James is going to stop me this time.

It feels like a small victory. We have escaped unnoticed for the day and we got away with it. This gets me thinking ... Caroline has been pushing and prodding me to come up with a plan to get one over on him; to get back at him for some of his punishments. On two occasions I have managed to escape here unnoticed. What if there were a way for me to play him at his own game with me in the driving seat this time? He's not as sharp these days with all the alcohol he's consuming. In my room I begin to plot ...

Over the next few days, I came up with various different ideas then instantly lose my nerve when I convince myself that something will go wrong and the plan will fail. Caroline knows I am up to something. She is so intuitive, so it doesn't take long before I confide in her. She has a cunning mind so this we could use to our advantage. It is a blessing she is helping me because it is distracting her from her latest hobby – manipulating Juliet. It is quite disturbing to watch and Juliet, being the trusting character she is, falls into Caroline's trap each time like a moth to the flame. It is never anything too outlandish but just little things she makes Juliet do.

For example, she tests mother's memory lapses vicariously through Juliet and it is quite cruel. She will ask Juliet to switch things around in the kitchen under the guise that she's helping mother out to get things in order. In reality, she's making life difficult for mother who is blaming herself and her forgetfulness in putting things in the wrong place. Caroline simply sits back watching it unfold with a satisfied grin on her face. It's hard to see mother suffer when she is going through a torturous enough time right now, but Caroline is losing her patience with mother; becoming increasingly resentful at her inability to stand up to father or stick up for us. So, when she plots and schemes at manipulating Juliet into tricking mother it's a double whammy to her; she gets great satisfaction from it.

There is no question in both of our eyes; neither of us wants to involve Juliet. I am quite sure Caroline would jump at the chance to use her as a scapegoat, but I've made it quite clear to her that this is not going to happen. Caroline's reluctance is borne not out of concern for Juliet's welfare, more out of her uncertainty in Juliet's ability to execute the plan with precision and we couldn't slip up; we were both in full agreement on that. However, we both decide it makes sense to bring James in on it. The only thing we have to watch with James is that his ideas are not too gung-ho, he can get easily carried away!

As we plot and scheme our way through the next few days, Caroline can't help herself. She is itching to put the wheels in motion and get one over on him, so she's been playing tricks on him to pacify herself. Earlier this afternoon we got our kill. Father had been drinking from late morning so, by mid-afternoon, he was none too clever on his feet. She could see he was relying on the chairs of the kitchen table to stay upright and steady himself as he negotiated his way around the table. Right at the very moment he was about to grasp for the chair adjacent to her, she kicked it away from him. Not enough to arouse suspicion, just enough for him to miss the very edge of it. He grasped nothing but fresh air and it was a sight to behold. The realisation only dawned on his face in the instant before he hit the floor and it was a sweet moment! He fell like a mighty oak and I refrained from yelling 'timber!' (only just!). At first there was nothing; then as his brain began to assimilate, a sequence of obscenities were yelled at no one in particular. It was oddly fascinating watching him trying to heave his useless carcass upright. Much like when a beetle lands on its hard shell and is temporarily incapacitated, he floundered helplessly until he eventually rolled onto his side and pushed himself upwards from there. I whipped my head around to see mother's reaction and there it was – a huge smile spread across her face. However, the minute he regained some form of composure and was back on his feet, the smile had disappeared, and that timid helpless lost look formed in its place. Way to go, Caroline! Another little victory: he is licking his wounds and it gave mother a little boost, albeit short lived.

With spirits high in the aftermath of this, we take to my room and have an animated discussion about our next move. I come up with a few ideas, but they are immediately quashed by James and Caroline. "We can come up with something far better than that," James politely informs me. They're both keen for him to get hurt and I have mixed emotions on this. What he's put us through these past few years is beyond redemption, but he's never been physically violent towards us. I don't know how I feel about initiating violence. It's one thing to push a chair out from under him but to put him seriously in harm's way, that's another matter entirely. I wrestle with my emotions. I know how good it would feel to give him a taste of his own medicine, but I need to pause and seriously think about how far I'm prepared to go with this.

Meanwhile, Caroline fantasises about what life would be like with him out of the picture. "Imagine, just imagine how peaceful it'd be here if he had an unfortunate accident and had to convalesce in hospital for a week or two. We'd have the run of this place here too; mother wouldn't bat an eye."

"What exactly do you have in mind, Caroline?" I interject, curious and anxious at the same time to hear what she has to say. "I have a few ideas, Thomas … patience. I'm just trying to figure out what would work."

I try James. "Any ideas, James?"

James has been pretty quiet up until this point. "Well I do have something which might work." There's a brief interlude then he ploughs on. "What if the girth on Sadie's saddle wasn't tightened properly?"

Sadie is our nine-year-old Cob. Father rides out on her at the same time every week, checking the boundary of the croft perimeter to ensure there are no repairs needing done on the fencing or any of the dykes. It's my job to tack her up ready for him. Why didn't I think of that? If the girth is too loose and he picks up speed on Sadie, then the saddle will slip, making it very difficult for him to hold on. Inevitably he will blame me for not tightening the girth enough but it's not something which is easily proven.

"Yes, let's go with that! Caroline, are you on board?"

"I guess so but if this doesn't work, we go with one of my ideas – OK?"

"OK yes, no problem."

We had to wait a couple of days to put our plan into action. He always rode out on a Wednesday morning so before heading to school as is always the case, I made my way to the stable block to brush Sadie down and tack her up. She is a beautiful mare with black and white markings and a great temperament. Because she is only nine years old, she is still high spirited and can take off at great speed with only a little coaxing required. You wouldn't think it as I approach her. She is so placid and snorts in acknowledgement when she sees me. "Hey girl, how are you this morning?" I say whilst stroking her muzzle. She responds by nuzzling her head into me, rubbing it up and down. "Let's get you ready."

This has always been one of my favourite jobs to do around the croft. There is something really calming and nurturing about spending one on one time with her. This morning this is an extra special relief because she's helped massively in quelling any anxious feelings I have about the task ahead.

Brushing over, I reach for her tack which is currently balancing on her stall door. As always, she willingly lets me insert the bit into her mouth and fix her bridle in place. Next, I reach over for her saddle and heave it up and over onto her back. The girth is in my grasp and I feed it through to the other side where it will be secured (well, loosely secured!). A sly grin appears on my face, I can't help it. It does feel good thinking we are finally doing something which is going to hurt him. It's certainly not life threatening but, if he comes off at speed, he could have a nasty fall.

I fasten the girth at the other side a good three notches looser than normal and have a look and a feel of it underneath. Perfect, nothing out of the ordinary visible to the naked eye but it is certainly loose enough to slip when Sadie breaks into a canter. Finally, I pull the stirrups down and as I do so, I can hear his footsteps approaching.

He is walking with purpose and strides into the stable, opening her stall door with a flourish. He doesn't even acknowledge my presence; he simply pulls Sadie around by the reins and marches her into the yard where he will mount her. He is not a great horseman and has never mastered the ability to mount her from ground level, so he uses a mounting block to get to the right height to heave himself up onto her back. This also works to our advantage – far less chance of being found out. Had he been able to mount her from ground level when he put all of his weight on the left-hand stirrup to pull his body upwards, there's a good chance the saddle would've slipped then and game over. But, because he's using the mounting block, there's far less pressure going into that left stirrup.

It still doesn't stop me from feeling anxious. I hold my breath and time stands still as I watch him get into place. So far, so good! He is sitting abreast Sadie and I can relax somewhat. Then I dutifully make my way around to the front of them to fulfil my final task, checking his stirrups are even. Again, there is no communication between us and I'm OK with that. I give him the thumbs up to indicate all looks good and he's off.

With a good hour or so left before the school bus arrives, I will forget about showering and get a ring-side seat watching this unfold! There are quite a few chunks of his ride I am going to miss because the boundary is fairly vast, but I know a good vantage point on the edge of the field where the Highland cows graze. I should be able to see quite a lot from there, so I head over. Being the highest point in our grounds, it has the best uninterrupted views.

I waste no time in making my way there and select just the right spot. At this point, he isn't too far away, and Sadie is just getting warmed up. He has coaxed her on from a solid walk into a fairly brisk trot and she is looking frisky so there'll be no problem in her picking up speed. All it will take will be a little nudge into her belly and she will respond. I wait with bated breath and my co-conspirators have joined me. There was no way these pair were going to miss out on the action!

"Ooh, this is exciting!" Caroline can't contain her emotions. "Come on, give her a kick on, get her moving; what are you waiting for?"

"Damn it!" James chirps in and I see the reason for his frustration. Rider and horse have disappeared out of sight over the brow of a small hill. We have an excruciatingly painful wait to catch sight of them again. It felt like ten minutes but, in reality, it was probably only a couple of minutes. Then, we were lavishly rewarded. They burst into sight, Sadie now in a rapid canter, covering ground easily and looking quite at ease with it all.

Then, disappointingly he reins her in. Something has caught his eye. He guides her over to a section of the fence and takes a closer look. We are all impatient and James speaks for us all when he says, "What are you doing? Get on with it man! Get her moving, you daft bugger; it's no use stopping still. Aaahhh!" But stopping still is exactly what he did and undoubtedly the break in flow will have calmed the feisty Sadie down.

Obviously, there is a section of the fence needing repaired so he's now being more methodical in his approach; frightened to miss anything which of course unfortunately means the pace has slowed right down. We sit and wait, there's nothing else for it! We keep expecting him to kick her on and get going again but it doesn't happen. In fact, it looks as though he is heading back this way.

He is heading back this way! "You have to be kidding me! What a waste of time and effort!" He is clearly heading back to get materials to repair the fence. We can wait no longer, otherwise we'll miss the bus. Cautiously, we make our way back to the croft via the stable block. I misjudged how far away he was (thinking there was plenty distance between us) but I hear it as clear as a bell; "Stop right there! Do not move a muscle." I tell Caroline and James to head back, it's me he wants to speak to.

Oh God, this plan has seriously backfired. As requested, I stand still, and he approaches. Sadie once again gives me an affectionate nuzzle. It is temporary relief. "Explain yourself, boy!" That is all he says and I'm not sure how to respond. "Cat got your tongue? Well, let me enlighten you then! You have proven yourself once more to be a useless waste of space. Even after all these years you still manage to mess up when it comes to tacking Sadie up. The girth was way too loose, I could feel it the minute we picked up the pace going over the brow of the hill! I had to slow up and tighten it before we set off again. If I hadn't done that and she'd taken off, I'd have had a nasty accident!"

"Sorry Sir. Caroline was helping me this morning. Perhaps I was distracted with her being there. Sorry, it won't happen again."

"Don't be stupid, boy! Don't go blaming Caroline for *YOUR* actions! Use your God-damn brain next time you imbecile!" With that he dismounts and leads her back to her stall.

I take stock. Not the desired result; our plan had backfired. However, at least he didn't suspect foul play. Why did I bring Caroline into the picture though? Trying to deflect all the blame away from myself? I immediately feel ashamed. And it was back to the drawing board. This time we needed something fool proof. Then I remember my promise to Caroline – we would use her plan if this one failed. What did she have up her sleeve? I felt trepidation and excitement in equal measure.

CHAPTER 14

I am curious to find out what George has in store for me today. He has said very little about what he has planned, and I am left guessing. Reluctant to let my mind run away with itself, I resolve to letting it play out and to try to go with the flow.

Juliet is by my side and has been very supportive. We sit at the breakfast table waiting on both George and Janey appearing. I asked Janey to come and join us for breakfast last night. How could I not? Whether or not I'm doing the right thing remains to be seen. She is in Skye and I see no other way around it other than to involve her. I just have to hope for the best. I have to pray that our marriage can survive this, and she stands by me no matter what ugliness is uncovered from my past.

"Juliet, this is all a bit of a mess. I don't know if I'm strong enough to deal with all of this."

"Listen, Thomas, you listen to me. You are strong enough; you always have been. You were always there for me when I needed to lean on you and now, I am there for you." She always knows just what to say and her kind words reassure me somewhat. "What is it that worries you the most?"

"That I won't be able to deal with re-visiting my past and that Janey is going to look at me differently and maybe decide she doesn't like what she sees and take off."

"OK, I think you are jumping the gun, Thomas. I haven't known Janey long but you two have been together a long time and she's here too as I am at your side so trust in that." Of course she's right but it doesn't stop me feeling anxious none the less. Physically I am feeling much better, now able to walk about with very little pain so that's something. I really didn't want to distress Janey any more with a tale about me being involved in a car accident.

My host makes his appearance. He appears to be in a jovial mood. "And how are we on this fine morning?" There was no denying it was a fine morning. The mist and freezing fog had just cleared up over the bay to reveal one of those beautiful cool crisp winter mornings. However, I could not share his enthusiasm for the day ahead. "Let's get ourselves a hearty breakfast to set us up. Have you eaten, Thomas?"

"No, I was waiting on you and Janey arriving, but I can help you prepare if you like?"

"No need, you sit still, you are my guest, and you are still recuperating."

I try to put his mind at ease; "Yes but I'm already feeling much better thanks."

"That's as may be, but you took quite a knock and it's best to keep your strength up for the day ahead."

"About that, George—" My intention was to quiz him on where we were going but I was interrupted by the doorbell.

"Thomas, please can you get that if you don't mind. No doubt that's Janey. I'll just get the breakfast started, thanks."

I make my way towards the front door and am pleasantly surprised at how I am able to walk with minimal effort or pain. Everything was healing up nicely already. I open the door and find Janey standing there looking radiant. Every so often I look at her and catch myself. What a lucky guy I am, she is truly beautiful. She senses something is up, and I have been caught staring.

"Are you OK, Thomas?"

"Of course I am, I was just taking you in."

"I can see that! I hope you like what you see."

"Naturally! You are a fine-looking woman, Janey Taylor. Come here." I embrace her, and we kiss on the doorstep. I feel layers of anxiety which had been building up start to melt away.

"Can I come in?"

"Of course; of course, sorry! Clearly I was preoccupied."

We head back to the kitchen and Janey strategically places herself at the table looking directly out over the bay. "Wow George, that view is quite something. I don't think I'd ever tire of it."

"Thank you, Janey, and no, I never do."

"Thank you very much for having me over, that was kind of you."

"Not at all, you are Thomas's wife, you are welcome here anytime. In fact, if you like, why don't you stay here? It makes no sense you going back and forth all the time to that apartment." That was a surprise and we both turn to her to gauge her reaction.

"I couldn't possibly impose. It was very kind of you to ask but I wouldn't like to put you out and the apartment I am staying in is lovely so it's no problem. It has beautiful views too; not as spectacular as these views but lovely none the less."

"It's no imposition whatsoever and it'd make life easier for you both. Have a think about it at least."

"OK thanks."

"That was very generous of him," Juliet whispers in my ear.

"I know, it really was." As I respond to Juliet, I notice Janey shifting uncomfortably in her seat and a strange look has come over her. "Is everything OK, sweetheart?"

"Yes, of course," comes a fairly abrupt and clipped retort. What has got into her? Maybe she doesn't like getting put on the spot, but, like Juliet said, it was nice of him to offer.

We are all distracted with the smell of food. George is serving up a delicious, cooked breakfast and my mouth is salivating. There is very little chat as we all tuck in. Then, Juliet once again whispers quietly into my ear, "I sense tension."

"Nonsense," I reply, meaning to gently whisper this back but it came out a lot louder than I'd intended and rather than look at me, George and Janey share a look. It's a knowing look and I find it disturbing. Maybe I am being paranoid? They don't even know each other. Why would they be 'sharing a look?' Clearly my mind is playing tricks on me which is not surprising given the stress I have been under.

It has to be said though, it does feel wonderful to have the support of both Janey and Juliet. I have worried endlessly about bringing Janey into this; frightened about the prospect that her feelings towards me might change when confronted with the demons of my past. But now there is another part of me countering this voice … remember those vows 'for better or for worse.' You can only run away from your past for so long. Inevitably it always has a way of catching up with you and at least when I face it, it won't be alone (hopefully). Juliet, I have no concerns about. She knows all about my past, she was there. Perhaps it's having her here now which is giving me the strength to stand strong and to include Janey.

It has also been playing on my mind to go and see mother. I will need to have a chat with Juliet about her. That, however, will have to wait as we are all apprehensively waiting on George announcing our plans for the day. He has taken the longest time to finish his breakfast, clearly in no rush at all and I find myself champing at the bit. Is he toying with us? He realises my eyes have been boring a hole into his skull as he looks up and gives me a smile which looks more like a smirk. Am I being sensitive or is he playing games with me? No, I really am being oversensitive I decide. It is just the uncertainty of what lies ahead in the next few days.

He finishes up and addresses me. "Well Thomas, I bet you are anxious to know where we are going today? Am I right?"

I can't help myself. "Of course I'm anxious but it's why I'm here in the first place, so let's get on with it!"

"Very eager, Thomas, very eager, well done, lad." No, I am not being oversensitive, that last phrase was definitely condescending. How many years have passed since I was last addressed as 'lad'? I show restraint and refrain from rising to it so he has no option but to press on. "All in good time, Thomas. Now, let's clear up here then we can head out to the car and all as they say shall be revealed."

"I will be right with you, George; I just need a quick word with Janey first."

"No problem, take your time. I'll sort this lot out and we can leave when we are all good and ready." There is something else which has been weighing heavily on my mind, something I need to speak to Janey about.

We head to the guestroom I have been staying in so there is complete privacy. I motion to Janey to sit beside me on the bed, and she tentatively takes a seat. "Thomas, what is this about? You have got me worried."

I take both of her hands in mine and lock eyes with her. "There is no easy way to say this. I haven't been able to talk about it before with you, or anyone else for that matter." I watch my wife mentally brace herself. "It feels like the right time to tell you about it now. Being here in Skye, it's forcing me to face things I have quashed for many years."

I take a few deep breaths then press on. "I know I haven't been very transparent and open about everything that happened years ago, and I hope you can understand why – it was just too painful to talk about." She gives me a reassuring nod. "You know relations broke down with my father as there was an incident years ago which culminated in me ending up in hospital then ultimately being placed in foster care?" Again, that reassuring nod comes but slower this time, an indication that she agrees with what I've said but is wary about what is coming next. "Well, it wasn't just me he hurt that day. He killed my sister Caroline."

There, I've done it. It's out there and it feels like a weight has been lifted off my shoulders. The only other person in the world I have discussed that with is George. Many times I had considered speaking to Janey about it but either I was unable to form the words or I was worried about the consequences of opening the proverbial Pandora's Box.

I look at Janey to gauge her reaction as she hasn't said anything. She appears to be in shock. I am so close to probing her to find out what she thinks but she beats me to it. "Thomas, I can't believe it! You have lived with that knowledge all your life, keeping it all bottled up? You should have spoken to me; I would've tried to help you! You poor thing! That must've been so traumatic for you." She is off her seat now and cradling me in her arms. The pain which, as she so correctly pointed out, had been bottled up over the years rises to the surface and I weep like a child in her arms.

It was the right time to tell her. I haven't got a clue what George has planned for me, but it was only right Janey wasn't left in the dark. She had to know about what really happened that day. Since she is accompanying me on the journey, I know I have to be upfront and honest with her.

Eventually the sobbing starts to subside, but Janey maintains a tight embrace and it feels so good just being held. I raise my head and whisper a thank you. "Don't thank me, Thomas. I am your wife, and

I am here for you no matter what. We are going to get through this, believe me, and do you know how I know that? Because we are going to do it together."

I manage a fleeting smile. She wipes the remnants of any tears from my cheeks and stands up, holding out her hands to help me to my feet. I dutifully oblige. "Ready?" she asks.

"Let's go," I hear myself say. The voice was meant to portray conviction but behind it the reality was that I was shaking like a leaf. I notice Janey didn't ask any questions about how father killed Caroline. Perhaps she was wary of pressing me for more information, knowing full well what it took for me to tell her about it in the first place. My rational mind takes over ... no point in over-analysing it, the main thing is she now knows what happened that day. No more secrets. As she said, we're going to get through this – together.

We leave the guestroom and join George. Why can't I shake the feeling that we are like two spring lambs getting led to the slaughter ...?

CHAPTER 15

February 12th 1998

It was no ordinary day. We had patiently waited and planned for this day. As promised, we were going ahead with Caroline's plan since mine had failed in spectacular fashion. However, her plan was also extremely risky so I prayed that we could pull it off.

We didn't have a lot of space in the barn for the livestock, so the majority of our stock were out in all weathers. The Highland cows had the advantage over the other animals because they were able to use their horns to dig through the snow to get to the grass underneath. Still, it was laborious for them and, without a helping hand, most of the other animals wouldn't make it through the long winter. This is where the snowblower comes in.

It was a lifeline. It was able to quickly clear the lane up to the croft and a pathway to the fields and onto the feed bunks. In years gone by, during heavy snowfall, we were literally cut off from civilisation for days or sometimes weeks at a time with the lane being completely backed up and blocked with snow. (The winters up here can be long, harsh, and unforgiving). This made it very difficult for us to get any supplies in or any deliveries of animal feed etc. But, no more!

It was an expensive purchase last year. I can remember listening to the debacle between my parents as to whether it was a good investment or not. It had paid off. The animals all remained in a good shape throughout the winter months, and we only had a couple of casualties who didn't make it through to the spring.

At the start of this winter, father set about teaching me how to use it. "You're old enough now so I might as well make use of you," so he politely informed me. I did not relish spending time with him whilst he went over the instructions, but it wasn't too hard to operate and actually quite good fun. There was also a real sense of satisfaction at the end when you had cleared a large area. The downside was if there were frequent dumpings of heavy snow you were right back to it.

Father had indicated mid-week that he wanted me out on the snowblower at the weekend (since we were already covered in a thick blanket), so this is when we seized the opportunity to put our plan into action.

There are two things you have to be really wary of when it comes to snowblowers. Firstly, injuries to the hands are very common when unclogging snow from the discharge chute. This often can involve amputations as the blades easily slice through fingers. This can happen even after the engine is switched off as the blade can still move. Secondly, you must be wary of rocks and sticks being caught up in the blower and shooting out from the chute in a direction which could injure someone when projected.

Caroline was in her element. We had talked at great length about how we were going to execute our plan.

"OK," she says, voice animated with excitement, "let's run through it one more time." Early Saturday morning we had a final chat, with Caroline taking the lead. "Are you quite happy you know what you are doing, Thomas? We want to make sure we clear the pathways effectively but some strategically placed rocks and large sticks as you near the end of the clear up job will have the desired effect. The chute will be clogged up with the snow and debris and we will have to shout on father to help unblock it."

"Got it," I say, interrupting her mid-flow.

"OK good. Now, you repeat back to me the full plan, start to finish."

I resist the urge to roll my eyes as we've already been through it so many times, so I give her the edited highlights.

"Like you say, I clear the majority away then hoover up some large rocks and sticks at the end of the lane which will cause the chute to become blocked. I then call on father to unclog it and as he reaches his hand inside the chute, I fire the blower back up. He either gets a finger or two sliced off or he gets a nasty smack in the face when the debris ejects. Afterwards, I say it was a complete accident, my hand slipped."

"Very good! Do you feel OK about going through with it?" That was a good question. Do I? If you had asked me that question when he was dishing out one of his punishments, I'd have had no hesitation. But to intentionally cause injury to him when at the time I am not being threatened myself, I don't know where I sit with that. Not wanting to show any sign of wavering whatsoever, I remain strong and steadfast.

"It's not a problem, I'll be able to see it through."

"Excellent, then let's do this!"

James has said very little throughout our recent discussions, so I am not wholly convinced he is completely on board. Perhaps his nose is out of joint because we haven't used any of his suggestions. Although, at the same time, he hasn't gone against the plan. We stuck with the decision of not involving Juliet which we all agreed was for the best.

Normally I would have a large hearty breakfast before heading out on the snowblower but this morning I settled for a single slice of toast, unsure I'd be able to keep anything else down. I had butterflies in my stomach and my heart rate had sped up dramatically. I could literally feel the pounding of my heartbeat in my chest and hear it reverberating in my ears. All of my senses were heightened. My biggest concern was what was going to happen when I came up with the excuse that my hand had slipped. That was the oldest line in the book, and I felt sure he would see right through it. What then for me? Yes, he will undoubtedly sustain an injury of some form but what will he do to me? It's highly unlikely he's going to buy that excuse. I knew it wasn't ideal but there was a more determined voice within me telling me to press on, that it'll be OK.

I had hoped to eat my toast and slip out un-noticed but no such luck. "Erm, where do you think you are disappearing away to?"

"To make a start clearing the pathways, Sir."

"Just hold your horses. You ain't going nowhere until I've given the blower a once-over so pipe down." That's me told then! He has one nasty scowl on his face, and it occurs to me at that moment how hard it must be going through life as perpetually angry as he is, it must really weigh you down. I don't want to stay here in his presence one more minute than is absolutely necessary.

"Is it OK if I get myself sorted to go out and I can meet you there, Sir?"

"Fine with me. Fuck off out of here just now, give me five minutes peace will you." At least we agree on something.

I wrap up for the weather. Layers of clothing, waterproof trousers, hat, gloves, and scarf. Suitably warm and trussed up, I make my way outside. A winter wonderland awaits me. It is not the picture postcard winter wonderland you see depicted in romantic movies. It is wild and untamed.

There is a high wind and it's picking the top layer of snow upwards and dispersing it all around so you're not quite sure whether the wind has caused the snow to appear in the atmosphere or whether it is actually snowing. I'm going to be exposed to the elements today. Thankfully the snowblower is a ride-on but without a cab to sit in, I am going to be frozen and windswept in equal measure.

The temptation is there to start her up and get on with the job (before I lose my nerve!) but I must be patient. If I do anything without him giving me authorisation, it will not go down well. I survey the area I am about to tackle. It looks untouched; virgin white snow as far as the eye can see. However, I know the secret it holds.

At the far end of the lane only yesterday morning, we strategically deposited some rocks and sticks, ready for the blower to gobble up today. We were forecast a heavy dumping of snow yesterday afternoon and all through the night. Mother nature hadn't let us down. Our offerings were covered in a thick blanket of snow.

Like the proverbial bad penny, he turns up. "Good luck to you today, lad, you're gonna need it!" If you didn't know him, you'd have thought that was a genuine message of concern, but it was of course loaded with sarcasm. We both knew there was no way he'd attempt to clear the snow today. It was too wild for him, but he was more than happy for me to brave it. I'm quite sure he'll be tucked up in the croft, nice and cosy, his favourite amber nectar warming him from the inside out.

"Right stupid; out of the way, give me some space will you. I need to get her fired up." I am only too happy to get out of his way. He does various safety checks to ensure everything is as it should be. It is quite amusing to watch as he talks his way through it all. I refrain from smiling. God forbid he looks up and sees a smile, he would know straight away he was being mocked! After his checks have been completed, he sits astride the snowblower and starts the motor up then proceeds to jump off immediately. Without so much as a glance in my direction, he stomps off, shouting as he goes; "Don't you bloody dilly-dally! Get this lot cleared quick-smart or so help me, you'll see what's coming to you!"

Thank you sincerely! That was just the motivation I needed to see this through. What was I thinking even wavering slightly on this? If there was ever someone who deserved their comeuppance, it was him. The weather was not going to beat me, I had renewed vigour and was going to battle the elements and get this done. And no *'sir'* I wouldn't dilly-dally. You see how quickly I can get through this field with the sweet thought of knocking you down a peg or two at the end of it!

I jump aboard and set about clearing the field. I picture my siblings and mother in my head as I mentally say, 'I am doing this for you, for all of us!' but I snap back to reality when the wind picks up. This was no easy task and was taking all my focus and concentration to plough on. I am convinced now that a snowstorm has set in, there is far too much snow in the atmosphere now to simply put it down to being the wind whipping it up. I cannot stop, I have to see this through.

With grit and determination, I keep going and am rewarded as halfway through, the storm starts to ease off. Visibility has increased and instead of seeing snow and very little else, I can now see the pathway ahead and my goal – the far corner where I know what is lying in wait. On and on I go cutting through the snow; the uniformity of it starting to have almost a meditative quality to it which I enjoy as it has the effect of calming me right down.

A noise breaks the silence and stirs me from my reverie. It was the unmistakable sound of a large stone being swallowed up. It didn't appear to have done any damage as the snowblower continued on. Then again, another clatter and bang as another large stone is devoured. And again, and again she goes, swallowing up the debris and coughing and spluttering and choking with the effort until finally she could take no more. With a last gasp, she simply gave up and came to a standstill; unwilling to hoover up another inch of the white powder. I left the engine idling. I sit in smug contemplation – phase one of the plan is complete.

Now for phase two. I dig deep within myself and summon the courage to call out to him. "Father! Father! I need your help!" I wait patiently but nothing. I try again another couple of times, but again, nothing. I realise he is tucked up indoors. Of course, why would he be out in this? There is nothing else for it, I'm going to have to go inside to retrieve him. This (strangely) breaks my nerve a little. It makes no sense because one way or another I know I'll get him to come out, but I think it's because it wasn't part of the plan which we'd discussed and rehearsed at great length. Also, I need to ensure he doesn't go out alone to fix it or once again, game over! I shake the nerves off (as they will not serve me well) and walk as nonchalantly as possible in the direction of the croft.

He surprises me. I expect him to be nestled into his comfy chair in the dining room, glass of Scotch in hand. However, I find him in the kitchen sipping what smells like a cup of tea. This also has the effect of un-nerving me. As I'd been making my way towards the croft, I'd told myself he'd be starting to feel the effects of the alcohol which would numb his senses but unfortunately it looks as though he is very much clear-headed.

"Been watching you out the window. What's all the bloody commotion about?"

Stay strong! "I was trying to call for you. The snowblower is completely blocked. I got the majority of the lane cleared but the last little bit is still covered because of the blockage. It just stopped working the minute it became blocked, sorry."

"Fucking useless so you are. Getting a boy to do a man's job, should've known you weren't up to it. Well, you needn't think you're getting out of it that easy. I'll get it cleared and *you* will finish it off." As he says 'you,' he pokes me quite painfully in the chest. I take an involuntary step backwards. Then, he slurps up the remainder of his tea and beckons for me to follow him.

I maintain a steady distance behind him, watching him as he strides purposefully in the direction of the snowblower. If only you knew! I thought we were getting a reprieve, but it was clearly short-lived as the earlier snowstorm which had left had now returned in earnest. The wind had also re-joined us and even the act of walking was proving difficult. I had a wobble – what if he turned around, choosing instead to let the storm pass and to clear the blockage later? However, he was showing no signs of slowing down. I am quite sure he had other plans for this afternoon, and they certainly wouldn't involve clearing out a snowblower.

He is trying to communicate with me, but I can barely hear anything with the storm now in full force. We reach our destination, and he indicates to me that I should climb aboard. I do as I am instructed. Again, I hear snippets of words, but it is all indecipherable. I feel sure he is cursing, judging by the look on his face. He approaches me and leans right in, realising I can't hear a word. I feel like recoiling, barely suffering the stench of his breath so close to me. He barks his orders; "Make sure she's off and your foot is nowhere near the clutch. The spark plug should be disconnected but fuck it, I'm not pissing about with that in these conditions!"

OK, here goes nothing. Time to put this plan into action. The engine was still idling but the noise of it was suffocated with the roar of the wind. There was a very slight shaking motion to the snowblower since it was still idling but would he notice? The plan had been to turn the engine off then put it back on as he set about clearing the blockage but was that necessary if he didn't realise it was still on? Keep your cool, I tell myself. Just wait a minute or two and see if he notices. The storm I had been cursing not so long ago for making my job difficult was now working to my advantage. He didn't seem to notice that I hadn't turned it off. All the reassurance I needed came in the form of a sequence of hand gestures. We couldn't hear one other whatsoever, so he did a motion in the air with his right-hand mirroring turning the engine off. This was closely followed by both hands outstretched in a gesture which depicted 'well, have you done it?' Here goes nothing. I reciprocated by giving him the thumbs up and he copies, providing me with a thumbs up. He was ready to go in.

It did occur to me that he might have equipped himself with a broom or shovel to assist him but no, he was going in with both hands! He had put his trust in me to turn the engine off. What a fool! At that moment it felt as though time had stood still. His fate and mine were in the hands of the gods, inexplicably intertwined. I watch intently as he removes some of the blockage from the top of the chute, his hands nowhere near the impeller unit. Encouraged by the ease of which he managed to remove the top layer of compacted snow and debris, he goes straight in again without delay. This time I watch memorised as he heaves a large boulder out of the chute. Those blades attached to the impeller unit were going to fire into action imminently ...

He digs deep a third time and there is no containing the shriek. It pierces and cuts through the storm. I watch the scene unfold as though I'm seeing it through the eyes of someone else, feeling somewhat detached from reality. I have never heard father scream before, and it is a sight to behold. He is a writhing, screaming, snivelling wreck; his face devoid of any colour, clearly in shock. Then I see the blood. The perfect ruby red droplets land on the brilliant white snow and the contrast is striking. It is my sole focus in that moment, and I am completely unaware that he is desperately trying to communicate with me.

Thankfully, he makes steps towards me and it is enough to jolt me into the present moment. I act quickly, cutting the engine off dead. He is completely unaware of my actions; too consumed with tending to his bleeding hand. I cannot ascertain the extent of the injury he sustained since the snow is coming down thick and fast and is being blown in every direction, making visibility extremely difficult. I mentally prepare myself as best I can for what I am about to witness. Caroline's words are ringing in my ears – 'He has it coming to him.' I think of Juliet and mother, both so helpless and easily manipulated by him and it helps me strengthen my resolve.

He is right up by my side now and he brandishes the bleeding digit in my face. Sadly, he has only sustained an injury to one of his fingers – the thumb of his right hand – so not as gruesome as I had anticipated. It was difficult to tell in the storm, but it looked as though the majority of his thumb was still intact; just the very top was missing, sliced clean off. He is very distressed; in pain and desperate to have it out with me but it would be impossible to hold a conversation in the midst of this storm, so we revert to hand signals again. He (thankfully) removes the bleeding thumb and motions me to follow him back to the croft.

I maintain the obligatory six feet distance behind him and again I feel that detachment set in as I am captivated with watching the droplets of crimson blood make contact with the snow. He will leave his mark; an offending trail of blood; staining the perfect crisp white virgin snow.

As we near the croft, I cannot help but cast my mind to my siblings. Will they be happy with the outcome? (Well Juliet knows nothing about our plan so I imagine she will be shocked.) And I am unsure what James will think as he said very little when we were plotting it all out. Have I succeeded or have I failed? I set out to cause him injury and I have succeeded on that count but at first glance it didn't appear to be as bad as I had thought it might be. He was lucky not to have lost the whole thumb or to have damaged any other fingers. He also escaped unscathed from any debris flying out of the chute which could've easily happened when he unclogged it (since the engine was still running). I felt fairly satisfied I'd seen the plan though with the desired outcome, but would everyone share my point of view? Caroline in particular was baying for his blood, desperate to see him suffer. Understandable, since he had pushed her to the limit, and she was looking for retribution.

He is cradling his hand tenderly like a new-born baby, every so often glancing down at it, clearly still in shock about it all. The normally swift walk back to the croft takes us considerably longer than it should do thanks to the forces of nature. We were being blown this way and that and enduring driving snow in our face. I am fearful of how he is going to react when we make it indoors. We reach the croft, and he uses his good hand to fling the door wide. He does it with such gusto that it flies back towards me and I have no choice but to step backwards. The door rattles loudly as the hinges moan and groan when they are activated, such was the force applied. This is not looking good; he is clearly fuming.

The only presence in the kitchen is mother and I can see the slam of the door already has her scared witless. Like a frightened rabbit caught in the headlights, she jumps to attention, all wide eyed and fearful about what is to come. I catch sight of her reaction as he enters the room, and she looks genuinely shocked.

"Bert, what happened? Goodness, are you alright?" She rushes to find the first aid box, witnessing the blood beginning to pool at his feet.

"Do I look alright, you daft bitch?! This one here is out to get me and make no mistake!" He points towards me. What to say, what to say? This is going southwards, rapidly. "He had me put both hands down the chute of that godforsaken snowblower to unblock it with the engine still running and look; just look at the result would you!" He thrusts his bloody, torn, and tattered thumb right into her face and she snaps her head back but somehow manages to regain some composure.

"Don't worry, Bert, we'll get it bandaged up and stem the flow."

She busies herself with getting dressings and tape from the first aid box and meanwhile he turns his attention towards me.

"Well come on then, we are all ears! What the fuck happened out there?! Give me one good reason not to string you up right now!" Again, I have that detached feeling come over me as though if I leave my body, even for a moment, I can pretend this is not happening. I can be there witnessing myself from outside of myself. It is at that point I can clearly hear the voices of my siblings. They have my back; they are the voices of encouragement, of love and support and they help me to formulate a response.

"I am so sorry. It was an accident. I don't know how it happened, honestly! The engine was turned off long before you went in to unblock the chute. The only thing I can think of is that there was still torque left in the system after I cut the engine which caused the impeller to keep spinning." A stony silence fills the room as he takes in my response. The only noise to be heard comes from mother as she expertly tends to his wounds. I am feeling brave and confident with my response and give myself a virtual pat on the back. Not half bad considering I'd just came up with it on the spot! The original plan had been for me to cut the engine off completely then turn it back on, using the excuse that my hand had slipped, but since that's not what happened the rest I was making up as I was going along.

"Aah, smart guy huh? Mary, we have one smart ass here, do we not? What do you know about 'torque in the system' and 'impeller blades'?" he says, mimicking my voice. "Bullshit Thomas! That engine was never turned off, you knew exactly what you were doing! You meant for this to happen. In fact, I imagine you were hoping I lost far more than just the tip of my thumb! Look at me boy! LOOK AT ME!" he says menacingly and with such ferocity, I have no option. I stare him straight in the face and we take each other in, weighing each other up and our opposing versions of events.

I am more than aware that whatever I say next could have a

ground-breaking effect. This is pressure like I have never felt before. And we are in unchartered waters here as he is on the receiving end for the first time. OK, here goes nothing.

"I cut the engine off, I swear to you. I am not lying. And you asked me to read the manual on how to operate the snowblower when you taught me how to use it which is why I knew about the torque and the effect it can have after the engine has been turned off. But … I am responsible for the machine getting clogged up. I knew there was a bad storm forecast today and thought if the chute were to get clogged up, then I might not have to finish it all. So, last night I left some large rocks and sticks at the far end of the lane and … and, well you know the rest. But I never, ever meant for you to get hurt, I just thought we'd call it a day with it being blocked and with the storm and all … " I see his face is now crimson, he is about to explode so, without thinking, shamefully, it's out there; "It was Caroline; it was Caroline, father! She made me do it! It was her idea!"

What had I done? I'd dropped her right in it; put her right in the firing line. There had been no thought involved, I was just straight out with it. The only thought I did have prior to my outburst was that I had to show some accountability. To simply say I'd cut the engine off and nothing more, that it was a freak accident I didn't think would wash with him. He wanted someone to blame so saying I had purposefully clogged the chute up was, in my eyes, definitely the lesser of the two evils. He would be more lenient if he thought I was trying to shirk out of finishing a chore as opposed to being out to intentionally injure him. But, bringing Caroline into it, how had that happened? I felt guilt and shame in bucketloads. All the time I've spent contemplating about how to protect them all and at the first opportunity I use her as my fall guy. Well, there was no going back now, it was out there so I'd just have to see this one through.

Because we had been looking directly at one other during my confession, I'd had the misfortune of watching his face throughout.

This, I realise, is why I had dropped her in it – I was terrified, I didn't like what I saw one bit. He was fit to burst and had mother not been tending to his wound, I imagine he would have been off his seat in a flash, pinning me against the wall. Blaming Caroline, it appeared, was a colossal mistake. Not only did I feel beyond guilty, but I could see the impact of my words and it seemed to make him even madder, if that was possible.

Mother finished dressing the wound and I braced myself. "So that's your version of events then, is it? Caroline was the mastermind behind all this? It was her idea to clog the chute up and you happily went along with it, wanting to get out of doing your chores? This is beginning to be a recurring theme now, Thomas, shifting the blame towards Caroline, is it not? But, if that's what we're going with, then you're both to blame, is that not right, Mary?" We simultaneously turn to look at mother and she appears to be in a state of fugue, staring off into space. "Mary; MARY!" Nothing rouses her. "What the fuck? Stupid cow, she's on another planet that one. At least I know she's not involved, she's not capable of breaking her way out of a cardboard box!"

He turns his attention back to me. "Well, if what you're saying is true, you'd better get her in here right now, prove it to me. You claim you didn't set out to hurt me but hurt me you did as a result of your stupidity and laziness." He stares intently at me, waiting for me to make a move, but I can't, I'm frozen to the spot, not sure what to do. He starts to shout, "Caroline, oh Caroline, where are you? Get in here – *now!*" We wait, but nothing.

"Piss off out of my sight now, lad! And Caroline or no Caroline, you'd best get yourself back here within the next hour or so help me God … and be prepared to get what's coming to you! Go on! Shift it will you! Can a man no get some peace? I need to rest up and have a wee dram whilst I think up your punishment."

When we had been discussing how to execute our plan, Caroline had said all along she'd be watching the proceedings as they played out. I knew with certainty that she would have heard all the drama unfold when we arrived back in the croft, she would have been lying in wait. Now the real panic sets in with me. She knows my betrayal and she knows he is looking for her. I feel my heart breaking – what had I done? OK, yes, she was involved, but why had I implicated her in such a direct fashion? If she knows he's after her, she'll be in a panic too. Think Thomas, THINK! There's no way she'd hang about here. She will have fled, and it hits me straight away in that moment, I know where she'll be headed to. I have to go; I have to get to her before he does.

I'm off, I flee as fast as I can out into the snowy wilderness once more.

Bert

I let him take off out the door. I let him think I am going to remain here patiently waiting on his return – with Caroline in tow. But I have other plans, I'm going after him to find out what he's up to. He is off in search of her and when he finds her, I asked him to bring her back to the croft for a little showdown. He has pushed me to breaking point this time. I shudder as I imagine how much worse my injuries could have been. The storm was so intense, it was impossible to tell whether that damn snowblower had been turned off or not but why did I leave it to chance? Perhaps I'm starting to lose my touch? No! I dismiss that thought straight away before it takes root. Why did I trust that snivelling pathetic excuse of a son of mine? And he keeps blaming Caroline for his mishaps. He needs that knocked right out of him!

Turns out Mary is good for something after all! She has made a decent job of patching my thumb up. No point in going to the hospital now, there's nothing they could do for it. I am not giving the bitch credit though, don't want the glory going straight to her stupid little head now, do we? That's the last thing we need right now, her getting too big for her boots! I say nothing to her, she might as well be invisible. I don all the winter woollens and head outside.

The storm is fierce, and I curse him again. I should be tucked up indoors right now getting cosy and steadily merrier. But instead, I am out here braving the elements, breathing quickly and shallowly as my thumb throbs painfully all the while. Where is he? Where the fuck is he? I scan the surroundings, but he is nowhere to be seen. I continue down the path towards the barn but, nothing. I reach the barn itself and peer in but again, nothing. "Thomas, *THOMAS!*" Hopeless and futile. There's no way he'd hear me over the noise of the wind. What was he doing out here in this? Exactly where does he expect to find her?

I spend the next short while pacing around the perimeter of the croft, but he is nowhere to be seen. What is he playing at? Well, he has certainly succeeded in one thing – making me more pissed off! Wait until I get my hands on him! If there's one thing I will not tolerate, it's disobedience. I gave him a direct order to get back to the croft and now he is A.W.O.L.

With no other option, I head back indoors to see if the delectable Mary can shed any light on his whereabouts. The two of them are always conspiring, she's bound to know what he's up to. Isn't it funny how the sight of someone can make you feel physically sick? Well, that's how I feel every time I see the wench. No wonder I've been drinking more these days when that's what is waiting for me at the end of a hard day's work. Nice little touch too dearest, feigning concern when I came in earlier dripping blood. You almost pulled it off too but we both know that was purely to save your own skin. I imagine you were blissful inside, glowing at the thought of me getting injured. Well, I can soon knock that out of you too and make no mistake.

Rather than address her by name, I choose to slam my (uninjured) fist down in front of her; a good way to get her attention and scare her witless at the same time. That is how I like to keep her – teetering on the edge. Expect the unexpected, Mary, that is just how I roll. It wouldn't do to have you too comfortable and at ease for any length of time now, would it? Where's the fun in that?

"Where is he then?" She stutters a response and it makes her seem even more pathetic, adding fuel to the fire of rage I can feel smouldering away in the pit of my stomach.

"I ... I ... d-don't know, Sir."

"Like hell you don't! You and I both know you two are as thick as thieves so out with it; spit it out, woman!"

"Honestly, I don't know!"

"OK, I'm a patient man, let's look at it from a different angle then, shall we? He's gone to fetch Caroline, so enlighten me, where would the wonderful Caroline be, pray tell?"

There is a lengthy pause before she answers, this had better be good. "I'm sorry, I honestly can't think." She is lying to me; it is blatantly obvious. Something inside of me snaps. No more Mr Nice Guy. I'm on top of her in a flash, the weight of my body pinning her down. There is no way she can break free. She doesn't even resist; she knows that would be pointless.

I position my forearm across her throat, pressing my upper body weight down onto her, restricting her airways. "Maybe this will help jog your memory, Mary!" She makes a few involuntary choking noises but doesn't try to speak. "Aah, I'm being too lenient with you, am I? Well, we can easily fix that!" I bear all my weight down onto her and watch fascinated as the veins bulge in her neck and her face swells up, turning a lovely shade of purple. But hey presto, it has done the trick – she waves her arms, flailing them about – and reading the expression on her face, she has something to say so I back off slightly.

It takes a while for her to gather herself and I am all ears. She looks as though she's ready to speak. "Well, spit it out then!" But nothing! She genuinely looked as though she was going to speak but thought better of it. "Oh, you need a little more coaxing, do you? Not a problem." This time I go in for the kill, pressing my full weight on top of her with force. She makes some strange noises then everything goes eerily quiet. Did I push too far? I back off entirely and for a few moments there's nothing, she's just lying there limply. Then she bucks upwards, gasping for breath. I look at her eyes and I can tell she is utterly terrified – she thought she was going to meet her maker.

I watch as she slowly gathers herself. She tries to speak but nothing comes out. She is really pushing my buttons. I place a glass of water in front of her and she gingerly lifts it up. Her hand is shaking so violently there is no way the water is going to make it anywhere near her mouth. "You useless piece of shit! I'll need to do it for you, will I! Open wide Mary – do it!" She opens her mouth and I take it in – she looks like a lifeless fish; mouth gaped open wide, and it is a sorry sight to behold. Let's get this over with. I let a good measure pour down her throat. She gargles, chokes, and splutters then finally something is uttered but it's so faint I have to ask her to repeat it – "Neist Point."

"Neist Point? Seriously, Neist Point! What the fuck would they be doing there and in this storm? That makes no sense!"

"I believe it is Caroline's favourite place. I overheard a conversation Thomas had with her a while ago and they had been discussing the matter," she mumbles.

"You're telling me he's taken the bus all the way out there in this weather?" She simply shrugs, looking absolutely beaten.

This day is going from bad to worse. Well, if that's where he is headed, I might as well get a head start and get out there. I can lie in wait; that will be a lovely surprise for him when his bus pulls up. I can't wait to see the look on his face.

Thomas

I called out to her again and again but there was no sign of her. I had to get to her to warn her father was on the warpath. I had to find her to confess and put everything right (if she will entertain me that is, after my betrayal). I don't waste much time searching for her at the croft. In my heart of hearts, I know where to find her – her special place; her happy place – Neist Point.

It is now mid-afternoon and there won't be many more hours of daylight. With the storm still raging on, it was madness to be venturing out and especially somewhere as exposed as Neist Point. But madness aside, I was on a mission; I had to get to her.

I find myself torn in two. I have to make this journey to reach out to her, but I know he'll be sat in the croft growing evermore furious by the minute. What was he going to do to me when I return? He will be at boiling point ready to explode by the time I get back. He will have to wait though, I tell myself, trying to trick my brain into a false sense of security. If I have to deal with another punishment, then so be it. I deserve it after dropping Caroline in it in such a royal fashion.

There is something else though. It feels like an impending sense of doom unrelated to father and I can't seem to shake it off. Call it intuition but there was something just out of kilter about the whole situation and I couldn't put my finger on it. It had left me visibly shaken up. The bus pulls up. We have arrived at Neist Point …

CHAPTER 16

I see the car parked there in the carpark as we draw up. How could I not for it was the only one there. Father and I would probably be the only people here today setting foot on one of Skye's most famous tourist hotspots in the midst of this unrelenting storm. The whole island has been battered and blown to pieces with the fierce wind and blizzard-like conditions.

The bus conductor is reluctant to drop me off. "Son, it's not a good idea to get out. There won't be another bus out here today, lad, not in this storm. You're gonna be stuck, mark my words. Just go back to your seat and I'll drop you back off where I collected you."

"It's OK, I am meeting someone here." His face says it all, he is unconvinced but opens the doors anyway.

I dash out as fast as I can. I have to get to Caroline before he does. I can't even look back. If I see him giving chase, I fear my panic will reach new levels and I won't be able to continue. A little voice in my head questions whether he will leave the confines of his warm cosy car at all since the storm is wild now. But, even through the wind, I hear the unmistakable sound of a car door being slammed shut.

"Thomas. *THOMAS!*" How did he know to come out here?! He is hot on my tail and shouting to get my attention, but I have a sole focus and that is to get to Caroline. His calls ease off (perhaps tailing off in the wind) and I wonder whether he has given up; choosing instead to go back to his car. I mustn't be complacent though and I dig deep and carry on, all the while scanning for any sight or sound of her.

The focal point of Neist Point is the lighthouse standing 62 feet high and 142 feet above sea level. It is visible from the carpark. But not so today. I have been running in the direction of the lighthouse for the past ten minutes and have yet to catch a glimpse of it. The blizzard conditions are making it impossible to see anything. I look in the direction of where I imagine the lighthouse is situated and sense a vague outline of its structure but, like a nomad in the desert glimpsing an oasis, I can't tell if it's real or a mirage. Must plough on I tell myself. But what if she's not here? What if I've came all the way out here and there is no sign or her? And to top it off, I have infuriated father beyond measure. If he has been led here on a wild goose chase, I dread to think what will be in store for me.

It takes all my strength to battle through and keep the momentum going. My cheeks are bright red, and my face is sore to touch; a result of the snow and wind battering my exposed skin. I heard no further call from father so whether he has given up or is just keeping his distance for now remains to be seen. Still too frightened; I daren't turn around to check. If I see him in close proximity, I fear all my resolve will disappear instantly.

Some respite. The wind dies down, and the snow eases off slightly as a result. With the brute force of the wind tamed for the time being, the falling snow takes on more uniformity in its trajectory towards Earth. Then I see it – the lighthouse in all its glory. And, if I am not mistaken, a figure, a solitary figure.

The figure (if that is indeed what I see, and my eyes are not deceiving me) is some distance away. But it is enough to spur me on. I call on energy reserves I didn't know existed within me and I race towards my goal. Even if he is still tailing me, I feel with certainty there is no way he'll be able to catch up with me now, such is the pace I have attained. The closer I get, the more certain I am that it is Caroline. I run past the lighthouse cottages and there she stands, taking shelter at the foot of the lighthouse itself.

I stop in my tracks and I am bent double as I catch my breath. "Caroline," I manage, but nothing else. I need to pause and really get my breathing back to a normal rate before I continue. Part of me is concerned she will just take off in the wake of my colossal betrayal. Would she really want to hear what I had to say? She remains steadfast and attempts to communicate. "Why Thomas? Why? After all we've been through! We were supposed to be in this together. It was us against him! Remember?!"

It is the question I knew she would ask but the one I struggle to answer without making myself sound pathetic because, ultimately, I used her as a scapegoat to save my own skin. I decide to open with an apology. "I am so sorry. There is no excuse for what I have done. Truthfully, I don't know why I did it; it just came out. He had me properly scared and backed into a corner … the look on his face, Caroline, if you'd seen it!"

"Can't you see, Thomas, that only makes it a hundred times worse! You knew how mad he was, and you tried to wriggle out of it by shifting the blame my way!"

Rather cowardly I respond, "Well, it was more like sharing the blame rather than shifting it. You were involved too." Oops!

"Here I am thinking you came out here to apologise to me! I should have known! I've had it, Thomas! I've had it with him, and I've had it with you!"

I watch in horror as her eyes widen and she bolts off. Without even so much as a turn of my head I know the reason for her haste. He has caught up with us. This time I can't help myself. I look back and there he is. It puts me in mind of a raging bull charging towards us. And like a bull, his head is down, nostrils flaring, and his sights are set on me. "Thomas! Thomas! Wait there, boy!" Not a chance. I set off in pursuit of Caroline. Where is she headed? There is nowhere to go! She can't head backwards with father blocking the route. There is only one place she can go – the cliff edge; the tip of Neist Point.

We have been here before and not so long ago. The weather conditions were poor then and we were close to having an accident so I dread to think about what could happen today. I race on regardless; I can't let him harm her. It is wild again; we no longer have the luxury of the lighthouse to shelter us. I see her standing there at the very tip of Neist Point, nowhere else for her to go, her body being flung this way and that in the wind. She looks so vulnerable. If only I could turn the clocks back.

I go to her and outstretch my arms, gesturing for an embrace. I don't expect her to reciprocate but she surprises me when she does. "We can do this, Caroline, if we stand together, we can hold our nerve." She breaks our embrace.

"I can't trust you though, Thomas, I don't know what to think anymore."

"You can! It was a moment of madness; I wasn't thinking straight. We need to join forces or there's no way we will get through any of this. Please say you're with me on this! Please Caroline! He's coming!"

"I'm with you, Thomas, I always have been."

I make a foolish mistake. I peer over the edge. The jagged, stepped rock formations akin to those of the Giant's Causeway in Northern Ireland are barely visible under a blanket of snow but I know they are there. It puts me in mind of the vision I had the last time when we came here – of mother's tiny body being tossed from one of those stepped rock formations to the next on her way to her watery grave below. It would take nothing for him to push us over the edge, especially in these conditions. We still have light, but it is starting to become dusky, sunset will not be too far away. Then I feel it again, that impending sense of doom. We three are locked in this frozen nightmare. I have never relished any of the punishments he has dished out to us up at the croft but suddenly out here being battered by the wind and snow, so terribly exposed, I wish we were back there (and I never thought I would ever say that!).

Then he is on us. There is no escape. There is nowhere for us to go for taking only a few steps backwards would mean certain death. Like a raging bull his blood is boiling. "Thomas, you have pushed me to the limit this time! You are to blame for my injury today and no one else. You have had me chase you out here – in this! It's time you took responsibility for your actions and stop blaming other people!" He takes a step towards us as he says this and, with no alternative, we are forced to take a tentative step backwards.

I didn't expect it and I am surprised as Caroline takes centre stage. "We have had enough of you bullying us! You spend all of your time dreaming up punishments for us. We decided it was time to turn the tables and give you a taste of your own medicine!" Caroline has always been volatile, but she has seriously overstepped the mark this time. What was she thinking! I feel myself have an almost out of body experience, floating above the scene watching it unfold as though I were watching a movie. There is no way to take those words back now, the admission of culpability is out there. All that remains to be seen is what he will do with it. Caroline is on a roll, without waiting for his response she ploughs on; "Well, come on then, cat got your tongue?!" I can't believe it; she is goading him! Should I say something? What would be the point? There is nothing I can say to undo what has just been said. We are well and truly at his mercy now.

I still feel detached from the scene as though this is my body's coping mechanism, escaping the reality. I am watching a movie of three characters in turmoil, the landscape raw, beautiful, and dangerous all at once. The wind comes howling along the length and breadth of the stage, whirling the snow around in every direction, threatening to knock any one of the characters off their feet and send them plummeting to their death over the cliff edge.

His voice loaded with fury still somehow manages to cut through the wind. "Enough! I don't want to hear another word!" I move to position myself in front of Caroline to protect her, but I am not quick enough. I watch in horror as he plants both hands firmly on her shoulders and proceeds to start shaking her violently.

"No; No!" I protest but there is no stopping him, he is blinded with rage.

"No more talking, you hear! That's what got you into this mess in the first place!"

Caroline breaks down. "Father please, please stop! You are hurting me! Thomas, help me! Help me!" She is buckling under the strain and has already edged backwards since he is pushing her in the direction of the cliff edge.

Her pleas go unanswered. He is undeterred but I have to help her. With all my might I give him an almighty shove and it takes him by surprise. "My God lad, I didn't think you had it in you! Come on then, let's see what you've got!" I try again but of course this time I don't have the element of surprise working in my favour and at fourteen years old I am hardly a match for a grown man. He brushes me off as if it were nothing, as if he were merely shooing a pesky fly away.

"Leave my big brother alone you brute!" No Caroline! She is trying to get his attention to save my skin.

"What did you say?!" He is furious and he grabs her again and I feel so helpless. There is no-one here. No-one to hear my calls, to save us. We are at his mercy and he is only too aware of this fact. "I will teach you a lesson you won't forget!"

It was a moment that would be etched in my memory forever, one of those times where time stands still. You can vividly see what is about to happen and there is nothing you can do to stop it. He only lands one strike but it's fatal. With all his might, fury, and force, using his left hand he wields it skyward and at an unbelievable pace it comes crashing down towards me. As it makes contact with my skull all I see is his ugly, contorted face. My body simply collapses, surrendering to earth with no resistance, all of my limbs jelly-like. My delicate skull hits a rock on impact with the ground and I am knocked unconscious but not before I witness something so profoundly shocking it shatters me to my core. The strike father used to knock me out takes Caroline out too. He applied such force after sending me reeling, his fatal blow manages to knock her right off her feet, with dire consequences.

Caroline! My beautiful angel! I am helpless, there is not a thing I can do. With my whole being I try to summon the strength to move, to haul my battered body up but it is futile. The look on her face as he makes contact will haunt me in my dreams forevermore. She knows this is it. There is nowhere for her to go other than right off the edge of the cliff. Even the wind seems to be conspiring against us – his strike given extra weight with its blustery force. She was there one minute then in the next second gone, her life snuffed out in the blink of an eye. Then there is nothing. She is gone and I cannot contemplate what has just happened for there is only black, endless, impenetrable black.

It is true there was no-one there. Outside anyway. However, a young girl witnessed the whole scene unfold from the window of one of the lighthouse cottages. She watched in disbelief as the older man had delivered that fatal blow and continued to watch as he left the young teenager all alone in the midst of a snowstorm, fearful that he had been seriously injured. She ran to the kitchen to fetch her aunt. It took quite some time for her aunt to calm her down enough to be able to ascertain what she was saying. They notified the authorities immediately.

CHAPTER 17

The noise of machines beeping begins to register somewhere in my mind. I am being pulled in two directions. I want to remain in the comfort and silence of the black deep depths of unconsciousness but part of me is being pulled towards consciousness, curious about the beep, beep noise pervading my slumber. Reluctantly the curious part is the victor and I feel myself slowly, ever so slowly, come to life. Groggily I open my eyes and immediately shut them, the light is so bright! And the pain, it is so intense! The source I realise is the left side of my head. It is a blinding, stabbing pain and instincts make me want to lift my hand up to the afflicted area to soothe it but I can't seem to summon the strength to move either arm let alone a hand.

Think, Thomas. Think! What is going on and where am I? The it hits me with unbelievable force – Caroline! I see her petrified stricken face as she is catapulted over the cliff edge. I scream for her, "Caroline, CAROLINE!" What happened next was a blur but two ladies in white uniforms were at my bedside and, before I knew it, I was back swimming again in the black murky depths.

There was no sense of time or reality, but I experienced the same thing again. I woke to pain in my head and the earth-shattering truth that my sister was no longer a part of my life. I screamed and screamed until there wasn't anything left and those strange little figures in their white uniforms administered another shot of something into my arm and once again, there was only black.

I slipped in and out of consciousness for who knows how many hours or days even. But what did it matter, for I had lost my precious Caroline. I favoured those periods when I was out cold because they at least provided some solace where it was eternal nothing and there was no pain to be had, be it physical or emotional. I wasn't ready to face the harsh stark reality of life on this new plane.

It was during a lucid phase that I came to realise where I was – in hospital. The name tags and faces changed periodically as they worked different shifts, but the same white uniforms remained throughout. There seemed to be no end to the cycle of slipping in and out of the black nothingness for each time I came to life, I was gripped with an unshakeable fear and horror over losing her. The nurse's reaction to this seemed to be to keep giving me another shot of something which temporarily blocked all the pain and sent me diving deep down again. I could often hear them speaking in whispered tones about me, but nothing was ever tangible and with no real care for my own wellbeing, I was yet to quiz them on anything to do with my health, so all consumed I was over what had happened to Caroline.

He was clearly walking about Scot-free without a care in the world. With no-one there to witness what had happened, he will think he has got away with it. This fact is also sending me slowly insane too. The combination of those two things – losing Caroline and father committing his heinous crimes – has rendered me helpless, unable to cope with any form of reality. I oscillate from being out cold and numb to being lucid and a screaming shaking wreck.

I sense I have been here for some time because the snowstorm has long gone. In fact, gazing out of my window, I see very little snow left. It clings on to only the tip of a far distant hill.

There are more hushed conversations and staff with different coloured uniforms have come to check on me. I am starting to question if they are trying to figure out how to treat me. Perhaps they think I am a lost cause? The wound on my head has become more of a dull throb rather than a sharp piercing pain and, as I run my fingertips over the injury, I can feel all the perfect little stiches in a neat row holding everything in place.

So, if my wound is healing up and I am not in as much pain why am I still being held here? I consider the consequences of raising this question with them and fast-tracking my release i.e. a ticket straight back to the croft, then think better of it!

The following day it starts to become clearer. On waking I am inconsolable as usual and as usual a nurse administers a shot into my arm. I expect to float away into the black murky depths again but this time I remain awake and feel slightly calmer than I did before so I deduce that she must have given me a mild sedative. I watch with curiosity as a stranger walks into my room and makes himself comfortable in the chair in the far corner.

He has my attention. He doesn't appear to look as though he is a member of the hospital staff as he isn't wearing any kind of uniform but, if not, then who was he this first visitor I have encountered since my admission? He is also the first person to have come into my room, happy to just sit there in silence, not fuss over me or attend to my care. It was un-nerving just having someone sit there in stony silence observing me. How to react?

Eventually he broke the silence. "Good morning, Thomas, it is lovely to meet you. My name is George, George Traynor. I have been asked to come and see you as the hospital staff are concerned that you aren't coping well at the moment." Ah ha! He wants to poke his nose in and ask lots of probing questions. There is no way I am ready for that. I feel the four walls of my room closing in on me and a pressure that wasn't there before starts to pulsate all across my skull. The sedative works to counteract the likely increased heartrate but even still, I can feel myself going into meltdown again. I scream, "No!

No! No! Go away!" In no time, the people in their white uniforms appear again and George is politely ushered out of the room.

I assume that will be the end of George Traynor, so I am most surprised when he darkens my door again the following day. He selects the same chair in the corner of the room and once again adopts a silent but observatory stance. Again, I feel myself on edge, ready to lash out in a heartbeat. He knows this and appears to be playing it cautiously. "Thomas, I am very sorry if we started off on the wrong foot yesterday, the last thing I wanted to do was upset you. I do believe, however, it is important if you are feeling troubled that you get your worries out there. I fully understand that you might not be ready to voice your concerns yet so I thought it might be a good idea if you were able to write them down." He takes time to let his words sink in then he gets up off the chair and places a notebook and pen at my bedside table. "I will leave you for now, Thomas. If you are able, please jot a few notes down and we can chat again tomorrow." A warm smile forms on his face then he turns and walks out. I am surprised I managed to entertain him whilst keeping my cool and realise that I am more than slightly curious about this George fellow. He didn't push and prod me; he has left the ball firmly in my court and it is up to me to decide whether or not I am ready to open up.

The notebook and pen lie there untouched at my bedside for the remainder of the morning and well into the afternoon. I am very much aware of their presence but not sure whether I want to pick them up. After dinner it is almost an involuntary action, I reach over for them, deciding that where is the harm in writing a few things down? George doesn't even have to see it I reason with myself; it could simply be for my benefit.

I start by writing snippets about my siblings then become incredibly upset when I see Caroline's name there in black and white. I rip the pages out, scrunch them up, and hurl the balled-up paper across the room in the general direction of the wastepaper bin. It takes some time for me to gather myself again, a large part of me is thinking what the point of all this is? No amount of words written down in a notebook are going to bring my sister back. Then I think of him, his cruel blow ending in her demise and my subsequent hospital admission. It is enough for me to get motivated to put pen to paper again.

I am simply amazed at how the words are flowing. From seemingly nowhere all of my worries and concerns are out there, laid bare for anyone to read. And it was true what George said, it was cathartic – it felt so good to let it all out. I realised I had lost track of time for the dinner trolley arrived with my evening meal. I made short work of polishing off my food and went straight back to my writing. The words on those pages had never been uttered to a soul outside of the confines of the croft. My siblings were obviously well aware of everything which had happened over the years and we had many conversations about how we could bring father to justice. But we never quite knew how to go about it and were fearful of the consequences if we did talk and it then backfired. I pause mid-sentence and let myself fantasise for a minute about handing this notebook to George who then notifies the Police and, finally, father faces his reckoning. George was an adult. Surely, they would listen to him more than they would listen to me? There was absolutely no chance mother would speak out against him and George seemed to want to listen to what I had to say. Should I place my trust in him?

It is clear to me that it is not only father who should face up to his crimes. I blame myself wholeheartedly for what happened to Caroline. If I hadn't dropped her in it with father then led him to her, she would still be with us. She should still be here. It should be me dead and gone, a suitable punishment for my treachery. Why did they rescue me? They should have left me for dead at Neist Point!

I write on and on until it gets dark outside, motivated by the feeling that it was at least having some positive impact getting all this emotion down onto paper and by the prospect that perhaps something may come of it if I chose to hand it over to the authorities. Perhaps both father and I would have our day in court?

Then came the really awkward part – writing about the events at Neist Point. I wanted to get it right and didn't want to miss anything out, so I tapped into my memory and took myself back to that fateful day. The pain and anguish were palpable as I relived it all again, but my pen flowed freely, all the events captured now in written word.

I did a fairly good job of holding everything together until I clearly saw her face again teetering on the cliff edge. Then it all became a blur as I broke down, becoming completely undone and torn apart again. I was beyond hysterical and only began to slowly focus again when I heard my name being called …

I opened my eyes and found the source – it was Juliet and, by her side, a concerned-looking James. From the depths of despair, the tide turned in a heartbeat and I wept tears of joy and happiness. I had no idea how they had managed to sneak out to visit me in hospital, but I was elated to see them. We embraced for a long time, so overwhelmed to be reunited together. The feeling was one of unity in our love for one another but also in our shared loss of our dear sister.

I am relieved. There is no blame there. Clearly mother has given them an edited version of events which doesn't implicate me. I see no judgement in their eyes. They are as happy to see me as I am to see them. Whilst still feeling guilty about this, I am temporarily relieved.

Once we gathered ourselves, Juliet was the first to speak: "Thomas, we have been so worried about you! He wouldn't let us come. Or mother, that's why she's not been to see you."

"It's OK, I knew that would be the case, but I hope you've not taken a risk coming here, I'd hate for anything to happen to either of you for sneaking out to visit me."

James this time; "No danger of that, the old lush is seven sheets to the wind right now!"

"Well, all the same, as much as I'd love for you both to stay, you shouldn't stay too long in case he comes out of his stupor and starts asking questions."

"How are you feeling now?" asks an anxious Juliet.

"Much better thanks. The pain in my head has eased somewhat so that's good." I decide to keep my new friend Mr Traynor a secret for now. I haven't decided yet whether to show him my notebook, so I see no sense in delving into any of that with Juliet and James at the moment.

James wastes no time. "Right, what are we going to do about him? He can't get away with this!"

"That's enough, James. Thomas is still lying in a hospital bed, I'm sure that's the last thing on his mind right now!" (Actually, it is at the forefront of my mind – that and my own accountability in all of this – but I also keep that to myself).

"Sorry Thomas, she's right. I just can't believe Caroline has gone and he's still swanning about like an arrogant son of a—"

"Right James! Really, that is quite enough! Thomas is starting to feel better and you are going to make him unwell again with all this chat."

"It's alright, honestly, Juliet. I am well aware he should be held accountable but I am also only too well aware pursuing him is what landed me in here in the first place and ... well ... sorry, I can't find the words but you know what I am trying to say ... our beautiful Caroline." The strain is etched across all of our faces.

Juliet, always the optimist, leads us out of our gloomy descent. "Changing the subject, Thomas, do you think you will be kept much longer in hospital?"

"That's a good question and I need to find out what's happening. I feel well enough physically but I'm not sure."

"Well hopefully you can come home soon." She doesn't realise the gravitas and weight those simple words have on me; 'come home soon.' How on earth would I even contemplate going back there? My stomach lurches and I can feel the dinner I consumed earlier trying to make its way back upwards, so I hastily swallow it back down. Thankfully, I am saved by the bell and don't have to furnish her with a response for one of the nurses appears at the door. "What's all the commotion in here? It's time for you to get some rest, Thomas. Lights out please in the next half hour."

I turn my attention to Juliet and James. "OK I hate to do this, but you better make tracks before I get into trouble. We'll come up with something, don't worry." As I watch them leave, I am once again reminded of the weight of responsibility resting heavily on my shoulders. It all becomes too much, and my mind gives in when my body surrenders to sleep.

On waking the next morning instinctively, I reach out straight away for the notebook and read through its contents. I realise I have come to the decision to hand it over to George. I don't know him well at all, but I am going to have to put my trust in someone. He has already shown care and compassion towards me, so I am going to take a chance on him. Like clockwork he appears again at the same time and sits in his usual chair. A positive thought seeps unwittingly into my psyche – since his visits, other than the breakdown I had experienced when writing about Caroline, I had managed to hold it together. This reassures me somewhat and cements the fact that hopefully I am making the right decision in trusting him.

The positivity continues to shine through as I address him first without waiting on him to take the lead,

"Morning Mr Traynor."

"Morning Thomas and, please, call me George."

"OK, morning George."

"You seem to be in a good mood this morning, that is wonderful, Thomas. Now I am not putting any pressure on you whatsoever, but did you manage to jot any of your feelings down?" I answer his question by simply raising the notebook which I had held in my lap at the ready. "That's excellent. Do you mind if I come over and collect it from you?"

"Be my guest."

For an indeterminable period of time, George pours over its contents. I try to gauge his reaction from his facial expression, but he is giving nothing away. Eventually he raises his head, shutting the notebook simultaneously. He is quiet, obviously taking his time to choose his words carefully. "I can see you have been through a very traumatic time, Thomas." It is a rhetorical statement. I bow my head in silent acknowledgement. "We have work to do, and I don't think the hospital is the best place for you." His words set off a blind panic within me and what happens next is a blur but I can feel myself being physically restrained until yet another shot is administered.

When I eventually come back to life, I get a shock – George is still here. He sees the panic start to rise in me all over again and he is quick to act. "Thomas, no, it's OK, you are not going to come to any harm, I promise you that. Please, relax." Something about his tone and demeanour have the desired effect, I believe him. "I hope I am not over-stepping the mark here but the panic you experienced earlier, was that brought on by the prospect of going back to the croft?"

I have never admitted this to a living sole and I find myself nodding in agreement. "Given what you've been through, that's completely understandable. Please can we start again? I need to firstly make it clear; I don't mean a return to the croft, Thomas, but do you feel that you should still be in hospital?" I simply shrug. Where else would I go? "If I could find somewhere for you to stay, somewhere safe, what would you say?"

"I can't leave mother, Juliet, and James with him but … I can't go back."

At this, I start weeping, my whole body shaking and shuddering as the tears come unbounded, flowing freely. I know there is no way I can go back there, but leave my loved ones to his mercy? There is no stopping the torrent of emotion which pours out and George moves from his seat and holds me, squeezing me tightly. If anything, it has the impact of making the tears come on even stronger in waves. Being held like that felt so good but this simple act of kindness tipped me over the edge, and I stayed like that weeping in his arms until there was nothing left.

"Leave it with me, son. I will speak to the staff here and see what we can do. You may have to undergo a psychiatric evaluation so the specialists can assess your mental state before we move forwards. But please, most importantly, do not worry. My priority is with your safety, first and foremost. Rest up and I'll see you again tomorrow." From this encounter it was evident I now had a confidante, someone with whom I could share my problems with. He has read about my deepest, darkest moments and hasn't ran away. It gives me a small glimmer of hope.

But I am also left somewhat confused. He knows from my confessions in my notebook that I am partly to blame for Caroline's death. Why is he being caring and compassionate towards me? Perhaps this is just a smokescreen? Perhaps he plans to hand the notebook over to the Police as evidence. Then my mind starts to conjure up all kinds of scenarios. I imagine the Police will appear at my hospital bed sometime soon to read me my rights …

CHAPTER 18

Present Day

George

As we take off on our journey, I glance over at Thomas in my rear-view mirror sitting next to his wife and I cast my mind back to our first meetings all those years ago when he was in hospital. It was highly unusual for me to be called upon to visit a client who was still being treated in a hospital. In fact, highly unusual doesn't cover it, I have simply never been asked to do it before in all the years I have been practicing as a counsellor. However, this was no ordinary case.

The medical staff simply did not know what to do with Thomas. The trauma he was experiencing on a daily basis was unlike anything they had encountered before. They had been managing his outbursts by administering shots of sedative at varying degrees of strength but that could only ever continue in the short term. Seriously concerned for his welfare and unable to send him back home at this point, they searched for a local counsellor who specialised in dealing with children affected by trauma, hence my involvement. He needed an extensive psychiatric evaluation, but he was so traumatised at the time, they figured it might help to bring me in to calm things down in the meantime.

What I didn't see coming was the way he moved me. It is at the very core of your training not to become involved with any of your clients. Be sympathetic, yes; compassionate, definitely, but always, always remain objective. Something about the boy called out to me and I knew from that first visit I had to help him. Years of pain and trauma had left their mark. He wore that pain like a suit of armour, and it was going to take time to get him to fully trust in me to be able to work with him. In those early days, however, I think he was just grateful to see a friendly face.

I felt encouraged when staff had told me that my visits were having a positive impact. His uncontrollable and incoherent outbursts were happening less and less frequently. I remember on one of those early visits passing him a notebook and pen, unsure whether he would be able to transfer some of his pain and anguish trapped within onto paper. What I read chilled me to the core.

What Thomas had endured at the hands of his father was abhorrent. But it became evident as I read on why he was experiencing all these outbursts in hospital. He blamed himself entirely for what had happened to Caroline. Some of the writing was illegible as you could see it had been scrawled and written with haste but there was no mistaking the overall sentiment – he had laid the entirety of the blame firmly with himself.

I have kept the notebook and his file. They are still housed in my office. This morning I leafed through the pages of the notebook again, remembering how raw and vulnerable Thomas was at that time. The writing would flow well, then there would be scribblings and ranting phrases in the margin of the page or whole sections scored out. Some of the phrases where he has tried to emphasise a point are written with a very heavy hand. So much so, there are pages which are torn where the pen has ripped right through. And some pages were ripped out entirely.

Some of the legible rants included *THE BLOOD IS ON MY HANDS!', 'She is an angel, I am the DEVIL', 'No-one will love you now,*

Thomas! (This one in particular gave me cause for concern as he was writing about himself in third person). And worryingly, *'You might as well end it all now.'* He was only fourteen years old, way too young to be having suicidal thoughts.

Throughout his description of the events at Neist Point on the day he ended up being admitted to hospital, he never once held his father accountable for anything. Even his own injuries – he believed it was what he deserved, and more. He describes losing his sister Caroline and that her demise was entirely his fault. We had a lot of work to do. Once he had been through a thorough psychiatric evaluation, I remember reading the report (a copy of which is also still kept in my office) which gave me a better understanding on how to work with him.

Looking in my rear-view mirror again, I see that same troubled, lost soul looking back at me now. I had to bring him back, it was obvious he had never worked through everything. His case has haunted me over the years. I had to step in again and help Thomas find closure once and for all.

I was well aware he had created a good life for himself but, at the same time, was also well aware that he had never fully dealt with all the demons from his past. To this day I know he still blames himself and we have to put an end to this. He has to be made aware of the full facts, revisiting it as an adult and facing it all over again. I only hope he is strong enough to deal with it all now. We shall soon find out …

CHAPTER 19

Present Day

Janey

I can see George occasionally glancing back at Thomas in his rear-view mirror and realise that he is as nervous as I am. Riding in the back of the car I end up turning my attention out of the window, not wanting Thomas to see the beads of sweat popping up on my forehead. I have been periodically squeezing his hand in a gesture of reassuring support but had to loosen my grip as I felt my hands starting to go clammy too.

I was anxious for what lay ahead for him but, at the same time, anxious for the future of our relationship. The thing is, I had known Thomas for longer than he realised. I remember that day like it was yesterday, seeing his fragile limp body lying there, left for dead in the middle of a fierce snowstorm. I watched in horror as his father delivered that fatal blow. He then paused to look around, obviously checking that there were no witnesses, then he took off without so much as a backwards glance. It was then I screamed for my aunt and we phoned the Police.

It has pained me over the years when Thomas had tried to discuss his father with me and his upbringing in the croft. I think he has tried to shield me from the truth, not wanting to admit to me what a monster he truly is. How do I tell him I already know all of this? That I have witnessed it for myself with my own eyes? He doesn't even know I have a connection to Skye myself; that I had an aunt and cousins living here. (My aunt has since passed away, but I believe my cousins are still living here.)

More importantly, his biggest question is bound to be how did we end up together? If he knew I was that little girl staring out of the window that day and that I notified the authorities, it would shake the very foundations of our relationship and potentially tear us apart.

I was having recurring nightmares, the horrid scene playing over and over in my mind. Yes, I had called for help but a huge part of me wished I could have done more. I had helped the Police with their enquiries, giving them all the information I could, but then it all went quiet, and I wasn't ready to just close the door and move on.

It was at this point that George Traynor contacted me. He informed me that he was working with Thomas in a counselling capacity and was keen to build up a full picture of Thomas' background and crucially what happened at Neist Point on February 12th, 1998. I was only too happy to help, still traumatised myself from what I had witnessed that day and full of concern for Thomas' welfare. Thomas was a virtual stranger to me, yet our paths had collided, and I was willing to do all I could to help. Seeing him there lying limp and lifeless had had a profound effect on me. Little did I know then that the poor lost soul left for dead at Neist Point would one day become my husband and father of my only child.

I had been staying at the lighthouse keepers' cottages on holiday with my aunt. We had various activities planned but I recall our plans changed when (as is customary on Skye) the weather took a turn for the worse. I have always had a fascination with wild weather, so I remember, on that fateful day, I had been transfixed, staring out of the window when the snowstorm hit. I had hoped I would've been able to get out to explore in the snow, but it was far too wild, especially once the wind picked up speed. Imagine my surprise then when I saw lone figures appearing and heading in the direction of the tip of Neist Point. I knew there was something decidedly wrong about the scene. No-one in their right mind would have been out in that storm! They seemed to be almost oblivious of the conditions, so wrapped up they were in their ensuing altercation.

When I saw the older gentleman (now my father-in-law) deliver that vicious blow, I remember being in complete shock. I had been brought up in a close-knit, loving family and had never witnessed any violence. It shook me to the core. The callous nature with which the blow was delivered then him taking off like that, clearly the only thought in his mind being to save his own skin. In that moment I wanted to wrap my arms around poor Thomas, lying there, left for dead.

It was too wild, and he was too far away for me to see his face, but I can picture it in my mind's eye for I often see it in my now husband's face. When he has a dark day, I see that little boy lost look and I imagine this is what was etched on his face that day just before he was struck down and lost consciousness.

It has been so hard over the years keeping this secret from him. I can see he has wrestled with his demons from the past and, although he tries to hide it, I know him only too well. That pain is still there and is still very raw. There have been so many occasions I have been sorely tempted to just blurt it out, 'I know all about what happened, Thomas! I was there!' But each time my head has ruled over my heart and rendered me mute. To tell the truth would mean opening a Pandora's Box and I truly don't know whether our relationship could withstand the ramifications of that happening.

When I initially responded to George's request to see me it was of course in the capacity as someone who witnessed everything unfold at Neist Point. George was keen to hear about what happened that day from someone who saw it all first-hand. I can remember sheepishly entering his offices with my aunt, quite unsure what to expect. She waited for me outside.

He put me at ease immediately and didn't push for information. He seemed quite happy to sit back and take things at a pace I was comfortable with. Part way through as I was recalling the story, he could hear my voice falter and saw the tears begin to well up in my eyes, so he kindly pushed the box of tissues in my direction. At this point I went to pieces. Everything came out. I told George about my recurring nightmares and about how I kept seeing the image of Thomas' body lying there. It was haunting me in the waking hours too.

He remained calm and sympathetic. We talked for around an hour and he suggested I come and see him again before the end of my holidays. I only had a few days left and with this incident hanging over me I reasoned what harm could it do?

In the end I saw him twice before I left Skye. During these visits he counselled me (at no cost) to try to help me recover from what I had witnessed that day. It did help. When I left Skye, I still thought about Thomas, but the nightmares became less and less frequent. That being said, I never forgot about him. Periodically I would ask after him when I contacted my aunt and cousins. My aunt knew of Mary, Thomas' mother, through a friend of hers and was able to keep me informed (to a degree) about how he was getting on.

I am so grateful George didn't act over familiar with me when we met up again the other day. He recognised me immediately, as I did him, but he didn't allude to it. I was able to give a slight shake of my head to warn him to keep quiet when Thomas turned around to him to introduce us. Thankfully, he seemed to pick up on this and my body language and I think Thomas was none the wiser. Really, why on earth would he think we would know each other? That would make no sense in Thomas' head so I am quite sure if he did see any flicker of recognition or something just not quite right that he would simply brush it off. However, it had been difficult keeping my cool.

When I saw George, I couldn't quite believe it. It felt as though we had taken a step back in time, the three of us, reliving the past. And when George said it would be OK for me to stay at his house with Thomas, well it was all too much! I want to be there for my husband yes, but shacked up in George's house, I would feel completely suffocated and on edge. Would he be able to keep the pretence going if I stayed there? Mercifully, he didn't pursue it and both George and Thomas seemed to respect the fact I was happy to stay at the apartment.

I have kept this secret throughout our relationship and, in the recent years, have convinced myself there was no chance he would ever find out. In truth, I put it to the back of my mind. But when he took off back up here and then I discovered he was staying with George … well I could really feel myself sitting on shaky ground. However, it appears as though George too has kept things quiet at his end. I have no other option than to hope and pray he will continue to maintain his silence.

I reminisce about the first time Thomas and I 'officially' met. I left secondary school with decent grades and had my pick of colleges or universities. I ended up opting to study English at Edinburgh University. I was well into my first semester when a friend suggested I join the debating team. At the time I was quite outspoken and passionate about environmental issues, so this friend thought it'd be a great idea to channel this enthusiasm. Imagine my surprise when I attended for the first time fashionably late (as usual) only to find Thomas Taylor in full flow, fervidly stating his case on why the death penalty should be abolished.

There was no denying it was him. He was older yes, but it was still clearly Thomas. It was very fortunate he had been in full flow because otherwise he would have noticed me standing there open-mouthed in abject shock. And, also fortunate no-one else had been with me at the time as there was no way I was ready to talk about how I knew of him.

I took a seat in the wings, happy to sit and watch. He was mesmerising. He had clearly done a lot of preparation because his argument was compelling, and he wiped the floor with his opponent. I was intrigued and captivated in equal measure. It was truly amazing how that poor lifeless boy from years ago who had been treated so cruelly at the hands of the one person who was supposed to love and nurture him, had turned into this confident, articulate man who stood before me today.

Initially there was no physical attraction there, but I was inexplicably drawn towards him. I wanted to spend as much time as I could in his company. At this point, I am quite sure he didn't even know I existed! He was very serious, spending lots of time studying and had very little down time. If being a constant fixture in the debating team was the only way I was going to get to spend time around him, then so be it. It had forced me (for once) to get serious about something and I remember the day he first really saw me for the first time …

I was passionate about campaigning on any environmental issues so had been thrilled when, finally, a topic came up for debate which I could really get stuck in to – 'Climate change is the greatest threat facing humanity today.' I threw my heart and soul into it and it was evident from the start my opponent only had a couple of good points to make whereas I could have talked all day and night on the subject. I was completely in the zone and, at this point, unaware of Thomas' presence in the room. It was only when we were leaving, he approached me and I can't recall the exact words he used but it was something along the lines of doing an excellent job and yes, that was it, he was 'inspired.'

The lines of communication were now open, and we had a mutual respect for one another. After my impressive argument, he said he was keen to know more so I seized the opportunity and suggested we go out for coffee. This became a regular thing once a week and I said a silent prayer of thanks to my friend for putting me forwards to join. The romantic feelings I had for Thomas were not instantaneous, they developed over time. Initially, I was just so intrigued with how accomplished he was and how well he had done for himself given the unbelievably rocky start in life he had endured. He was studying towards his master's in finance and had a clear plan on what he wanted to do when he left university – he wanted to be a financial adviser with a view one day of owning his own practice.

I admired how driven and focussed he was and owe a lot to him as it had the effect of rubbing off on me. I was well aware I was more aloof and flightier and there was always the danger that I might not have made it to the end of the course but, with Thomas' encouragement, I stayed on track.

We graduated at the same time and by this point there was a strong bond between us. Neither one of us was ready to admit there were romantic feelings involved but it was clear to all of our friends and us, had we only been more open with one another. It took the graduation party and copious amounts of alcohol for the truth and the depth of our feelings to be revealed. Once those words were spoken and we both knew where we stood, we became inseparable. We were young yes but very much in love and decided to make a go of it and the rest as they say is history! When Michael came along that was just the icing on the cake.

I have toyed with the idea of confessing to Thomas over the years that I knew him before we met at university. In fact, I have played out full conversations in my head but each time it falls apart. The whole situation is too weird. How could he possibly accept that I witnessed his darkest moment as a young teenager then recognised him later in life and pursued a romantic relationship with him at university? What on earth would he think? And all those occasions over the years when I have had to listen to his edited version of events when he has talked about his upbringing, the pain visible to see. He has tried so hard to shield me from it, either not wanting to go there or too ashamed about how dysfunctional and traumatic it all was. And all the while I knew exactly what he had endured and was unable to say anything. It has been the elephant in the room. We both knew what he went through and neither one of us has been able to talk about it.

There were moments at the start of the relationship I did think I should tell him. It felt like a heavy weight I was carrying around on my shoulders. However, each time I considered talking about it, I talked myself out of it – how would our fledgling romance survive a confession of that magnitude? I was equally concerned about what effect talking about his past would have on him. I knew he had been counselled by George and he had clearly done a great job, otherwise I'm quite sure Thomas wouldn't have been mentally ready to undertake any further education. But even still, maybe his way of coping with everything was to forget about it and move forwards? It was not my place to go digging and cause him untold hurt and pain.

These past few weeks, however, the tide has turned. I had let myself believe his past was dead and buried. After all, he has established a great financial advisory practice and everything has been going so well in our lives, including Michael, who has become such a confident young man and a joy to be around. However, I was wrong. George has reappeared and, in his presence, my husband has started to fall apart. It is completely out of character for him to just take off in the way he has done. It is obvious he hasn't dealt with all his problems from years ago.

But, the fact remains, I haven't been completely honest with him; I have maintained a secret from him for all these years. I glance in his direction and he acknowledges me with a lukewarm smile, his face woeful. I reciprocate and feign the brightest smile I can muster. The car rumbles on, our destination yet to be revealed.

CHAPTER 20

Thomas

I gaze upon the faces seated in the car and realise I have much to thank each and every one of them for. I didn't expect Janey to accompany me on my trip up north and by a twist of fate here she is, and it hits me all at once how grateful I am for that fact. My sister Juliet flanks me on the other side and equally it feels so reassuring to have here with me too. And then there is George.

It occurs to me that we have been through a lot together, George and I. Whilst I did not appreciate him turning up so unceremoniously in the middle of the night not so long ago, without his poking and prodding, it is highly unlikely I would have contemplated taking the trip up here. I had been beyond shocked when we stood face to face that night but if I am honest with myself, I always knew that this day was coming. I have once again put my trust in him as I did all those years ago when I was just a boy. He has stressed that there is unfinished business for me here on Skye which I must face up to and I will once again be led by him.

George really came through for me when I hit my lowest ebb. He knew all those years ago when I was due to leave the hospital (whilst I felt torn about leaving mother, Juliet, and James), that I could never go back to the croft. He liaised with all the relevant authorities on my behalf and, with my agreement, placed me in foster care.

It was very strange to begin with, starting all over again in a strange environment with people I didn't know. However, in time I began to think of it as my home. My foster parents were Paul and Rachael Sands; a young couple who sadly were unable to have children of their own. They provided a safe haven and were very encouraging when it came to pursuing my education. They would tell me to 'aim high' and that 'anything was possible if I put my mind to it.' This, of course, was in stark contrast to the upbringing I'd experienced on the croft, so it was hard for those words to sink in initially. I had a very skewed and poor opinion of myself and it took a long time before the tide began to turn.

With the ongoing support my foster parents showed me and with George's help too (as I continued to work with him), my grades started to improve. So much so, at the end of high school I was being encouraged to apply for university. So, I have much to be thankful for. My education has allowed me to pursue a successful career in the financial sector and, more importantly, I met the love of my life at university.

I am still in contact with Paul and Rachael, and we meet up occasionally. They continue to foster kids and, as far as I am concerned, they deserve recognition in this life and the next for they don't take on the babies and the cute little kids everyone wants; they ask for the problem teenagers (exactly like I had been). They are determined to make a difference in that teenager's life and set them on a new trajectory. It is a calling with them to want to help and I will be eternally grateful to them.

Janey has just glanced over in my direction and has given me a reassuring smile, but I find it impossible to reciprocate, managing only a half-hearted smile in return. This is because we are traversing roads which are all too familiar to me and our destination needs no explanation, for I know where we are headed – Neist Point.

I am puzzled. Why is he bringing me out here? What good could it possibly do and what is he hoping to achieve by this?

"Stop the car!" It's out before I even think about it. George clocks me in the rear-view mirror but continues to drive on. "Stop the car I said!" I emphasise the words and this time they have the desired effect – he slows the car down and pulls over when it's safe to do so.

"Are you OK?" he asks.

"Am I OK? Hmm let's think about that for a moment. What do you think, George? You are clearly headed towards Neist Point and I can't for the life of me think why! What good could it possibly do, going out there?"

"Remember when I told you to put your trust in me? Well, this is one of those occasions. Please, trust me, Thomas."

Janey gives my hand a squeeze. With her other hand, she places it on my chest and gently pushes and it registers with me that I am sat on the edge of the seat, so I shift backwards.

"Thomas," Juliet whispers in my direction, "it's OK, we are all here for you." I release my hand from Janey's grip as it has gone decidedly clammy. I ignore both Janey and Juliet's advances.

"George, you are seriously wasting everyone's time here."

"Thomas really, just calm down, please. We have both agreed you have to face up to your past. Neist Point is the location where you experienced a very traumatic event, so it seems as good a place as any to start your journey. It's time, Thomas." 'It's time.' There are those two little words again. He appears to take my silence for an unspoken agreement and the car revs up once more.

'I can do this,' I silently tell myself. There's no need to get panicked. We are only going to a local beauty spot; an innocuous landmark, nothing to get worked up about. Yes, it was the site where I lost my beautiful Caroline and where father struck me with that ferocious blow, but it is just a place, nothing more, nothing less.

Then why do I feel so on edge? I feel Janey's hand guiding me back once more and I realise that I have been sitting stiff as a board on the edge of my seat once again.

This is silly! I am a grown man now and I have the support of everyone around me. Come on, Thomas, I will myself, dig deep. The car slows as we become snarled in the queue of traffic looking for parking spaces. In the distance I can see Neist Point Lighthouse and the sea beyond. My stomach lurches.

I feel as though I have shifted into autopilot mode. There is no synchronicity between my mind and body. I have left my seat and joined the others as they exit the car, having now found a parking space. It feels as though my body is going through the motions. But I fear if I over-think it, there is no way I would have left the car. My legs and feet feel like they are made of lead, but I lift them anyway, ignoring the resistance. I am vaguely aware of George giving me a pat on the back. It seems oddly ridiculous given the circumstances. As though a pat on the back from my old therapist is going to somehow lift the years of pain and anguish. I refrain from telling him so and trudge on anyway.

The last time I was here was as a fourteen-year-old boy, but I know the route and the landscape well. As I walk on this well-trodden path, I find myself switching back and forth between fourteen-year-old Thomas and present-day Thomas. It comes flooding back to me, the wild snowstorm and menacing winds. And then the feeling of being chased washes over me. All at once I am almost convinced father is behind me, hot on my tail. My consciousness switches and I am back to present day and I take in my surroundings and my companions. No need to panic, I tell myself. This is bound to happen. I haven't been back here since that day. Of course painful emotions will rise to the surface, it's to be expected.

I am quietly amused as I notice I am being monitored. George is the most brazen of the three, not even trying to hide the backwards glances. We cover more ground, and I can't help but keep on switching back and forth, back and forth. Today we have cool, crisp weather with very little wind (in stark contrast to 12th February 1998); the kind of weather which draws people out and, as I look around, I see this is very much the case. It is nothing like the hordes of tourists which descend in the summer months but there are quite a number of people out today. They all appear connected in a fashion — they are out for a nice jaunt to take in the splendour of this beauty spot. Yet here I am, nervously treading the path I walked some twenty years ago, only too well aware of what occurred at the end of the path. My heart feels blackened and once again I am aware of how weighted my feet feel. I pause for a moment then gaze ahead.

CHAPTER 21

All at once my throat constricts; it feels as though there is no air circulating and I simply cannot breathe. I grasp at my chest area as though this very action will breathe life back into my lungs but with nothing left in me, I slump to my knees.

The cause of my temporary paralysis – Caroline. She stands there as she did all those years ago, leaning against the lighthouse for support. I try to call to her, but nothing comes out. Janey is by my side and with her help I manage to stand erect once more, but I am oddly unaware of anyone's presence apart from Caroline's. It feels as though everyone else has melted away into the background and the only two people left on earth are her and I. The scene has a dream-like quality to it and I feel detached from my body as if sensing everything around me is unreal. Then she calls out to me.

Now my feet no longer feel like lead, quite the opposite in fact. Life is pulsing in my heart and lungs once more and I have a spring in my step as I respond to her call. She needs me. My little sister needs me again and, as I did all those years ago, I rush to be by her side. It doesn't seem to register with me that this is futile, that Caroline is dead. She has appeared before me and I have an overpowering urge to go to her and to protect her as I had failed to do so before in such spectacular fashion.

"Caroline!" I yell, stumbling as I go, oblivious to the terrain underfoot, my only focus being to get to her. "Is it really you?"

"Of course it is! Who else would it be?" In no time I am by her side and I hold her in a tight embrace. I am vaguely aware of a faint voice in my deep subconscious telling me that this is not real, it can't be real, but I smother that voice, not wanting anything to destroy this moment of happiness. Tears of joy and elation roll freely down my cheeks. I wipe them away and take a good look at my beautiful sister. She meets my stare and melts my heart with her kind words. "I have missed you so much, Thomas, I have missed you all. Please, don't leave me again."

"Never, Caroline, you have my word, I will never let anything bad happen to you ever again."

"Oh Thomas!" This time it is Caroline who goes to hug me, and I am only too willing to be held. Space and time have dissolved and all that remains are Caroline and I in our own little private universe. I have my old Caroline back, not the Caroline with a stricken face full of fear before she was so savagely pushed over the cliff edge. Standing before me is the happy-go-lucky, carefree Caroline.

A firm hand presses down onto my shoulder. That alone was not enough to rouse me, but it was shortly accompanied by someone repeating my name over and over and it was becoming louder and louder. More than slightly perturbed, I turn in search of its source. I find George hovering just inches away from me.

"What is it?" I say very abruptly.

"I need to speak to you, Thomas."

"Not right now, can't you see I'm busy?"

"It's about that."

"What do you mean 'it's about that?' For God sake, man, give me some space. Can't you see what is happening here? Caroline is back, so forgive me for not jumping at your beck and call!"

George is having none of it. He grabs me quite forcefully this time, ensuring that there is nowhere for me to escape to. *"Thomas, please listen to me. There is no Caroline and there is no Juliet. They are figments of your imagination; characters created by your subconscious mind!!"*

I freeze on the spot, his words echoing through me: 'There is no Caroline and there is no Juliet.' What is he talking about? How can this be? What is he trying to say? For reassurance I gaze ahead again and there are my beautiful sisters, as plain as day. Janey will back me up. I plead to her; "Janey, please tell him he's making this up! They are real. Please!" She walks towards me and holds me.

When she lets go her words shatter me. "Thomas, he is not lying to you. Caroline and Juliet are not real. They do not exist. I'm sorry, sweetheart."

I lose all ability to stand erect and crumple into a heap on the concrete path. "No, NO! NO!" I yell to no-one in particular. This is so far beyond my field of comprehension. It is completely unbearable. These two people whom I trust implicitly are telling me I am mentally unstable and have crafted siblings who do not exist? I cannot take it in, it is inconceivable. They are telling me that, what, my whole life has been built on fantasy? Impossible!

Unwilling to face reality, I decide to ignore him and turn once more to face Caroline. But just as I start to re-engage with her, Janey interjects, obviously aware I am choosing to ignore George's words. "Please Thomas, you have to listen to him! She is not real. She is not here, Thomas! Neither Caroline nor Juliet are real."

Try as I might, I am unable to simply ignore Janey. "Can't you see her? Or hear her? I have just had a full conversation with her!! She is stood with us, leaning onto the side of the lighthouse! Please tell me you can see her?" But sadly, I am met with silence.

"Janey, we had a chat only this morning about Caroline. I told you father had killed her and you were full of sympathy. What was all that about if you don't even believe that she is real?"

"The truth is, Thomas, I have only just discovered that they don't exist myself. Throughout the years, you have often talked about your siblings but since we have never visited Skye, I have never had cause to question their existence. That was until this morning. You were openly conversing with Juliet and the only people at the breakfast table were you, George, and me. I have never seen you do anything like that before. There have been occasions in the past when I've thought I heard you speaking to someone but when I approach you, it always stops. Also Thomas, please remember when you told me about Caroline being killed, at this point I didn't know the truth about your 'siblings'. You have always talked about them so why wouldn't I believe in their existence?

"However, I had a quick word with George before we set off today because I had been so alarmed about you chatting with Juliet at breakfast. He explained everything to me. I am so sorry, Thomas, but they simply do not exist." I hear her words, but nothing sinks in. It feels as though I am in shock and floundering, unsure where to turn next.

George takes over proceedings. "I feared this might happen and this is why I brought you out here. What you perceive to be true and real and what is actually real are two quite different things. Thomas, I have something to tell you and you are going to find it very difficult to hear. Please, let's take a seat." He motions towards a bench just metres away from us.

"No, I'm not leaving them! You can't make me!"

Janey this time; "No Thomas, we can't make you do anything you don't want to do but don't you want to hear what George has to say? You came all the way up here to find out as much as you can about your past, please, just hear him out."

An inner battle ensues between my head and my heart as I wrestle with what to do next. I see George and Janey walking towards the bench. They sit down and both look in my direction, waiting on me to make a move. I feel torn in two. I don't want to leave Caroline's side in particular (since I've just been reunited with her) but the truth is whatever George has to say, Janey is right, I need to hear it.

Still in denial about what George and Janey are telling me, I address my sister – "Caroline, would you mind if I left you with Juliet for a minute? I just need to go and see what George wants. I won't be long."

"Of course, why would I mind being left with Juliet? She's my sister after all."

"I know, of course … it's just that I didn't want you to think I was leaving you again."

"Thomas, I didn't think that for one minute. Now please go, they are waiting on you!"

As I glance in George's direction, I notice the solemn look on his face, and I brace myself. Whatever he has to say, I can deal with it. As I draw closer, the two of them shuffle up, leaving a space for me. Janey is sat next to me and places a protective hand on my thigh when I settle down.

We sit in a brief silence as we wait for George to gather himself. Eventually, he starts: "Thomas, did you never wonder why your father didn't go to prison for what he did that day?"

"Of course I wondered. But he was so clever, and manipulative, I guess I just assumed he had somehow wormed his way out of it. Maybe he made it seem like an accident or perhaps he lied about being there in the first place. I never got to find out what happened because when I recovered in hospital I went from there straight into foster care (as you know), and never heard from mother or father at all. I wouldn't put it past him to have put me in the frame for Caroline's death though. That would have sewn it up nice and neatly for him. There was no-one else there that day so with no witnesses it would be easy for him to lie about what happened. I was classed as a minor at fourteen years old so he knew I couldn't go to prison for it."

"Thomas, you do realise you have just mentioned Caroline's death. So, you know she is no longer with us?" A sharp pain like an electric current starts to trace across my skull with the impact of those words as I am desperately confused. I gaze in front of me and as clear as a bell I see Caroline and Juliet standing there, both looking directly at me. My hands move involuntary in the direction of my head to cradle the afflicted areas. This provides only temporary relief before another current tracks right over the crown of my head and a single word escapes from my lips, barely audible: "No."

"Sorry Thomas, what did you say?" Despite the pain I am more determined this time.

"No, I said! I don't know what's going on here. Maybe you are trying to trick me? What's your game, George?"

"I am not playing any games, Thomas; I simply want you to learn and understand the truth. And on that note, Thomas, there was a witness at the scene. Had there not been, it is unlikely you would have made it to hospital." I am momentarily distracted by Janey who is shifting around in her seat, clearly feeling uncomfortable. George too seems distracted with Janey's movements so we both wait for her to settle down.

"Do I know this witness? This really makes no sense, George. There was no-one else out there that day. It was wild. We were the only ones there."

"That is not the case because the authorities were notified, and an ambulance came to the scene to take you to hospital." He pauses and I wait for him to fill in the blanks, to tell me who the witness was. "And I am sorry, I am unsure who witnessed it, but to be honest, Thomas, that is all pretty irrelevant. I need to speak to you about what happened next that day and what has happened out here today."

"Go on then!"

"Firstly Thomas, I have tried to explain all this to you before but perhaps you just weren't ready to hear it at the time. And Janey, it is good you are here too because Thomas will need all the love and support you can give him." I can feel the colour draining from my face as I mentally brace myself. What is he going to hit me with? Surely it can't be that bad?

"You were clinically evaluated by specialists before you left the hospital all those years ago and it was their professional opinion and findings that you were suffering from Psychosis. They deduced the psychosis manifested itself as a result of the trauma you endured at the hands of your father as a young boy. It is my belief that you have had psychotic episodes throughout your life, likely starting well before the incident with your father at Neist Point."

His words start to sink in, but nothing makes sense. "George, I don't understand! Psychosis? Psychotic episodes? Are you saying I am a psychopath, George?"

"Not at all, Thomas! The two should not be confused. A psychopath is someone who is unable to feel for others and may act in reckless and antisocial ways. Psychosis, however, is when you lose some contact with reality. It can involve seeing or hearing things which other people cannot see or hear, hallucinations if you like. This can result in seeing people who aren't actually there or even feeling you've been touched by someone who isn't there. I fully appreciate this is a lot to take in but, if it helps, I still have a copy of the psychiatric report at home. You are welcome to have a look later."

"You've got that right at least. It is a lot to take in and pardon me if I am not fully on board with it! I mean come on; I am not mentally unstable! If I were, I would be the first to knock on my G.P.'s door."

"That's just it, Thomas, someone with Psychosis may not be able to recognise their symptoms and therefore it's quite feasible that you wouldn't seek medical help if you believed there was nothing wrong with you."

"It makes no sense, George. Growing up, I remember all the times I shared with my siblings and all the antics we used to get up to when father wasn't around. There were loads of high jinks. I recall James fashioning a saddle out of an old tractor seat then fixing it onto our tup Bruno then taking off at high speed up the hill. Then there were all the jobs they used to help me with around the croft. How could I have imagined all that? Please tell me – how? I have literally years of memories!

"And then there's Caroline. I cannot explain it, why she is here with me now because you are correct, father killed her! He planted his hands on her shoulders and shook her. Then he struck her, and she was sent flying off the cliff edge. How could I have made that up? I saw it all plain as day!"

"I don't know what to tell you, Thomas, other than I am afraid it wasn't real. And that wasn't 'James' riding that tup, it was you. You expertly created a fictional world, with you as the central character. It helped you cope with the day-to-day living under such traumatic circumstances. And, as for the scene at the cliff edge – it was you he shook so violently; it was you he struck, Thomas!"

Thoroughly fed up and exasperated with the way this conversation was going, I move to get up from the bench and head back to my sisters. George stops me in my tracks. "Where are you going?"

"Where do you think I'm going? Back to my sisters, Caroline and Juliet. This conversation is now over."

However, a feeling of blind rage starts to set in, and I turn around to address them both. "If what you are telling me is true, why have you waited until now to tell me? Juliet joined us in the car, George, when we were en route to Skye. If she doesn't exist, why didn't you tell me then?"

"I have to apologise for that, Thomas, but I had to see how it was going to play out. Juliet appeared to you I believe because you were already feeling anxious after being involved in a car accident and then I am guessing subconscious old trauma started to re-surface as we drove closer to Skye, hence Juliet was manifested.

"I had to bring you here to Neist Point to see if it brought any pent-up emotions back for you. I confess I was hoping you would see Caroline today then I would potentially be able to reason with your rational mind. If you believed she had been killed years ago, then how could she possibly appear before you today? But, the truth of the matter, Thomas, is that she never existed in the first place."

I have nothing. I have no response to give. I am utterly speechless and spent. The magnitude of what he has told me weighs heavy on my heart. As far back as my memory goes Caroline and Juliet have been in my life and he is telling me that what, my sisters whom I love dearly are not even real? They are a manifestation of a supposed mental illness? What did he say I had? Psychosis? And that I had suffered Psychotic episodes? Then it hits me, what about James! "James?" I simply utter and he answers with a simple shake of his head. I slump forwards, broken. It feels as though my heart has been shattered into a thousand tiny little pieces and my head is pounding terribly, unable to process this devastating news.

However, devastation soon turns to denial as I gaze forwards and see my sisters once again, still standing before me. "George it can't be true! It simply can't! I feel absolutely sane, and I can still see them! Even after what you have told me, they are still stood there. It makes no sense!"

"Thomas please, try to calm down. This is going to take a long time to process, and it is completely understandable that you can still see them. You have lived with this altered state of reality for most of your life. As I said, the Psychiatrist who evaluated you believed that your mental illness was brought about by severe trauma experienced during your early childhood. In some cases (and I know it was recommended in your case, Thomas), medication has to be taken for a lifetime and, if not taken, episodes of psychosis can re-occur."

Episodes? Episodes? "George, I don't experience *episodes!* This is my reality, not an episode!"

"Yes, I am quite sure it must seem like that, but I can assure you what you have witnessed today is not real and these experiences you have whilst they seem very real and life like, they are simply a creation of your subconscious mind. You created these characters, Thomas, because you have been mentally unwell. It is not your fault, and it is out-with your control. It provided you with a coping mechanism, a way to deal with day-to-day life to get you through it."

His use of the word 'characters' cuts like a knife through my heart. They may be 'characters' to George but to me they are my flesh and blood, my siblings. Janey has been unusually quiet. I need to hear what she makes of all this. I plead to her; "Janey, we have been together since we were in university. If I had a mental illness, don't you think I would be aware of it or at least surely you would have seen something?" She locks eyes with me, and I can tell she is struggling to form the words.

She takes a moment to compose herself then formulates her response. "I can't imagine what you must be feeling right now, sweetheart. It is a lot for me to take in too, so it must be so incredibly hard for you to hear all that. I cannot lie, there have been several occasions over the years when I have been concerned about your mental health. You have often gone into a fugue-like state where you are not fully present. You lose your train of thought mid-sentence. I never wanted to probe too much – I know you had a terrible childhood – so I just tried to be there for you, best I could."

She can see the shocked look on my face, and she moves towards me, presumably to initiate a hug, but I instinctively back off, hurt with her admission.

"Let me get this straight, Janey ... you suspected I was mentally ill, and you decided to do nothing about it? In all this time, you didn't think there was one opportune moment you could have discussed it with me?"

"Thomas, I am sorry. I am so genuinely sorry, but I thought it was for the best. You have moved on amazingly well with your life and you have so many positive things going on with your family life and your business that I guess I thought it might do more harm than good." I mull this over and remain unconvinced.

"Well perhaps you should have given me the chance to decide what I wanted to do about it. Instead, the decision was taken out of my hands and the 'problem', it appears, has just been 'brushed under the carpet.' This is my life, Janey; you can't do that! If you wanted to be there for me, you should have been upfront from the start if you suspected something wasn't right! And you mentioned earlier that you had supposedly heard me talking to someone when there was no-one there then stopping when you came near? You should've been honest with me, Janey."

George this time (providing Janey with what I am quite sure will be a momentary welcome reprieve); "Thomas, you must be aware that you take medication for this illness?"

"No!"

"According to your medical records dating back to when you were evaluated on leaving hospital, you were prescribed anti-psychotic medication and it was the recommendation of the Psychiatrist that you remain on this long-term."

"George, I am not lying to you, I am not aware of any anti-psychotic medication."

"Well, let me put this another way, are there any medications you take on a regular basis?"

Now I can feel the worry start to creep in. "There is something but I'm sure it's not what you are referring to." I take a deep breath and summon the courage. "My foster parents told me to take medication for my anxiety. I started taking it when I left the hospital and have been on it ever since. I was too frightened to come off it in case all the feelings from the past came back."

"That will be the anti-psychotic medication, Thomas. It sounds as though they were only too well aware of what you'd been through and were trying to shield you from the truth. I imagine they didn't want you to suffer any more than you already had done."

"OK George but if that is true then why have I seen Juliet and Caroline since I've been in Skye? I am still taking the medication, yet I can see them!"

"It is more than likely that you being back here has brought all the childhood trauma you experienced to the surface and, even under the influence of the medication, it's entirely possible that you could have another episode."

This is all way too much! I need some space! I head off blindly in the direction of the tip of Neist Point. Caroline and Juliet are still clearly visible and present, but my head is too swamped, I can't even entertain a conversation with either of them right now, so I march right on past them. I can hear my name being called but I have no intention of turning around or acknowledging it. I find a spot and sit down. Unwittingly, I choose a space right on the cliff edge. With feet dangling precariously, I peer downwards and lose all sense of time and space as I sit mesmerised with the waves crashing up against the side of the cliff. There is a deafening sound when contact is made, and it provides a welcome distraction from the churning thoughts of my mind. For a few precious moments I am not Thomas the husband; the father; the mentally ill person with a disturbing childhood. I am simply 'being' and witnessing mother nature in all her glory.

As with all good things, however, they inevitably have to come to an end. I can hear the footsteps directly behind me and the familiar voice of George which manages somehow to penetrate the noise of the waves. "It's time to go now, Thomas. Let me help you up." Like a little puppet on strings, I let my puppet master hook his hands under my armpits and guide me upwards.

CHAPTER 22

Utterly crestfallen and heartbroken I ride up front with George, our journey home sure to be a long one as we all sit in a stony silence. Every so often I hear George mutter something under his breath. He clearly has something to say but is too frightened to voice it. No doubt he has thought twice before bombarding me with anything else. Janey too remains silent. She will still be licking her wounds after our confrontation earlier. It dumfounds me that she has suspected I have been suffering with a mental illness for years and has said nothing about it.

I need this time. I need this silence to gather my thoughts. This has well and truly blown my mind. If I were to ask my companions how many people were in the car just now, I know the answer they would give but it doesn't match mine for I am only too well aware of the presence of Caroline and Juliet in the backseats. I do my best to block this out for now and focus on the conversation with George instead.

Nothing adds up. If I have been mentally ill and experienced 'psychotic episodes' then how was I able to excel at university, rise up through the ranks in my profession, and have a stable family life all the while being completely unaware I was ill? Surely the cracks would have been evident to myself and everyone else around me? How have I been able to live with this unknowingly for over twenty years?

However, the pills do concern me. They give me pause for thought and make me question what I believe to be true versus George's rendition of the truth. I can recall the conversation with my foster parents all those years ago. The grave looks on their faces. They made me vow to take my medication daily. They said it was vitally important to help with my recovery and to stop any anxiety setting in. I was only too willing to oblige, fearful of the repercussions of opening the floodgates to the well of emotions bubbling away under the surface. Then it just became habitual. I never questioned it. I simply kept taking the medication year on year on year. I reasoned that it kept all the panic and anxiety under wraps, helping me lead a normal life. But what if what it was actually doing was keeping psychotic episodes at bay? I need to see that psychiatric report. I don't want to see it, but I need to see it.

I break the silence as we pull up to George's house and I can almost feel the collective sigh of relief in the car.

"Let me see the report, George."

He brings the car to a complete stop and addresses me, "Of course." When we enter, he motions me to follow him through to his study. I take a seat as he fumbles through his filing cabinet. In no time he produces a bulky folder which I assume are my case notes. He leafs through it then locates what he is looking for and hands it over to me. "Everything you need to know is in here. I will give you some peace to look through it."

I sit with the report on my lap for some time as I summon the courage to open it. It feels like a heavy weight crushing my thighs and burning its way through the denim of my jeans, penetrating the flesh underneath. The words I feel sure I am about to read permanently branding my skin with 'psychosis' and 'psychotic episodes.'

My sisters are nowhere to be seen. Instead, joining me now in the room is James. It doesn't occur to me to even question how he came to be here. It just feels as natural as the air I breathe seeing him stood there.

"You know you don't have to open that file if you don't want to. They are all saying you are crazy but what if the opposite is true? What do you really know about this George character? Do you not believe in me? Do you not trust in Caroline, Juliet, and I?! We have been a part of your life for a lot longer than he has. We were here long before what happened at Neist Point!"

"Of course I do. At the same time, I simply have to read this report."

I turn my attention downwards to the neatly typed report. Its heading – 'Psychiatric Evaluation: Master Thomas James Taylor of Fair Isle Croft, Dunvegan, Isle of Skye.' At the foot of the front page – 'Compiled by Edward F. Morton (M.D.); Rowantree Clinic, Glasgow.'

I quickly scan my way through the document which is fairly extensive. At first glance, there appears to be contributions from a psychologist, social worker, occupational therapist, some of the nursing staff from my time in hospital, and several extracts from George detailing our chats during my hospital stay and beyond. However, most of the analysis is from this Edward Morton chap.

I am relieved to find he has provided a summary of his findings at the end of the report, negating the need to read it in its entirety.

"It is my professional opinion, having liaised with many other specialists on the matter and having spent quite some time with Thomas himself, that he is suffering with Psychosis. He is an articulate, intelligent young man but is hallucinating and delusional on a regular basis. He believes he has siblings called Caroline, Juliet, and James. He regularly converses and interacts with these characters, wholeheartedly believing them to be real.

Thomas has had a very traumatic childhood. He had a very difficult relationship with his father (who is currently being investigated by the Police and the Local Authority). To ensure Thomas' safety he is being placed in foster care whilst investigations are on-going into whether Thomas' father (Robert Taylor) was in any way responsible for the injuries which Thomas sustained leading to a lengthy hospital stay commencing on 12/02/1998. It is my belief that the trauma he has endured from a very young age and throughout adolescence has caused the Psychosis to manifest.

Whilst in hospital, he experienced a number of psychotic episodes. Hospital staff struggled to deal with the mental health crisis Thomas was enduring and they sought the help of Mr George Traynor, a counsellor specialising in helping children and teenagers with mental health problems. Thomas responded well and has continued to work with Mr Traynor but that alone is not enough to treat his condition. I have prescribed anti-psychotic medication and recommend that he takes this long-term, potentially for the rest of his life."

I close the file. I guess there was nothing there which surprised me since George had already prepared me. But, seeing it there written in black and white in the form of an official document made it seem all the more real somehow. It literally knocked the stuffing right out of me.

I had to sit with this reality I was being confronted with and consider its validity. Perhaps George was correct. Perhaps everything in this report was correct. Perhaps I am crazy. I made the journey to Skye to revisit my past and deal with, as George so aptly put it, 'unfinished business.' There certainly was unfinished business. The world as I previously knew it had literally been blown apart. I felt lost and vulnerable, floundering in unchartered waters.

I raise my head and take in my surroundings. There is no James. This is worrying. Have I really just had a hallucinogenic experience? If I were to stop taking my 'anxiety pills' what would the repercussions be? Would I sink further into a deep Psychosis? I shudder at the thought. The words of Mr Morton still ringing in my ears: 'I recommend he takes the anti-psychotic medication potentially for the rest of his life.'

My feelings of being lost and vulnerable are quickly replaced by a red-hot fury. The hatred I feel for the man who was supposed to be my protector and carer are as raw today as they were on the day he so savagely struck me to the ground at Neist Point. He is the cause of all of it! If what George and the Psychiatrist are saying is true, I created an imaginary world to cope with the daily abuse I suffered at his hands.

The floodgates open. It feels like my soul has been laid bare. A tidal wave of pent-up rage, sadness, and bitterness burst forth. I cry with wild abandon for the poor boy I was, living through that hellish nightmare. I cry for what could have been. What a sad, sad twisted excuse for a human being my father was and still is. Since the day Michael was placed in my arms, it has been my life's work to love and nurture him. The thought of Michael having to endure even a fraction of what I went through makes me feel physically sick to the stomach.

Even after all this time he is unrepentant and still playing his sick little games. As if mother isn't going through enough right now, he tormented her by visiting her in her care home and said God only knows what to her. I wish I had been there! I will have my day with him. Man to man. Will he still be so sure of himself then? I am no longer the little boy he so easily dominated.

I am distracted by a persistent knock at the door.

"Who is it?"

"It's Janey, please can I come in?" I mumble a feeble "OK." She bursts into the room. "Thomas, I am so sorry, but I could hear you crying from the other side of the house. I couldn't just leave you on your own. Come here." She holds me tightly and I melt into her warm embrace. "Is it the report, darling? Is that what has got you so upset?"

"That and the fact that it feels as though none of my life makes any sense anymore! It has all been based on fantasy. I am upset but I am so angry at the same time. None of this would be happening if it wasn't for that pathetic, sadistic father of mine."

"That is very true, sweetheart. No-one should have to go through what you went through."

We sit in silence for several minutes then Janey looks at me square in the face. "Do you think you will go and see him whilst you are here?" It is a fair question and one I have wrestled with.

"On the one hand, I could do to put an ocean-sized distance between us. But, on the other hand, part of me desperately wants to confront him, to ask him things I wasn't able to as a young boy. The main one being 'why?' Why did you put mother and I through it all? Why didn't you get me the help I clearly needed when I was mentally ill?'"

"That makes sense, and it might give you some closure on everything."

Janey goes quiet again then starts fidgeting and shifting about in her seat.

"What is it? Is everything OK?" I hear her take a couple of deep breaths before she answers me.

"No, not really. There is something which has been playing on my mind too, Thomas. Please know that I have wanted to tell you this before. There have been many occasions when I thought about it, but it genuinely never seemed like the right time. That is not a cliché. I just felt before that it might do more harm than good."

I interject, I can't help it. "God Janey, you've got me worried! What is it? The last thing I need right now is more bad news."

"I know, I know. But I have thought about this long and hard, and I can't think of a better time to tell you. You are here to learn the truth about your past and I can't keep this from you any longer … When your father struck you at Neist Point, I witnessed it. It was me who phoned for the ambulance."

CHAPTER 23

I am flabbergasted, thoroughly dumfounded. I look at my wife as though she is a stranger. How could this be? I started this journey not knowing what to expect and I have now learned that I have a mental illness and my wife (my soulmate and confidant whom I thought I knew everything about) hits me with this – 'when your father struck you at Neist Point, I witnessed it.'

I turn to her to form some words but nothing tangible comes out, only garbled noises. "Oh Thomas, I am so sorry. Please, please believe me I have wanted to tell you – long before now! I know you are going to be in shock, you have every right to be. Do you want me to give you some space or do you want me to explain what happened?" This time there is no hesitation or any garbled words.

"You better explain it and it had better be good."

"OK, I will tell you everything. I don't know if I have mentioned it before or not, but I too have some relatives on Skye."

"No Janey, I can't say you have! Another revelation!" She ignores my jibe and carries on.

"I have lost contact with family here. The main contact I had was with an aunt, but she has since passed away, leaving two cousins who I never hear from. My aunt had a small flat in Portree but when my visit was arranged back in 1998, she thought it might be fun for us to rent accommodation at the lighthouse keepers' cottages at Neist Point."

She pauses. Reality dawns. She saw it all from the window of the lighthouse keepers' cottage. "Go on."

"I remember how wild it was that day. I heard voices outside and that's why I went to the window to look out. I was shocked anyone would be out there in those conditions. The wind and snow were fierce. I could see something wasn't right. There were raised voices. At first, I could see you race to the tip of Neist Point, engaged in a conversation. Then an older man joined you. And, well, you know the rest."

"That's just it, Janey, I don't! Who did you see out there that day? Did you see Caroline?"

"No, there was no-one there apart from you and the man I now know to be Bert."

"So, what are you saying? You saw me conversing with an imaginary figure before father joined me?"

She hangs her head, "Yes." Like a jigsaw puzzle, all the little pieces were starting to come together. There was more and more undeniably compelling evidence affirming that Caroline, Juliet, and James were not real.

"So, let me just get this straight ... when father struck me down, he didn't hit anyone else with that blow?"

"No, that would have been impossible, there was no-one else out there apart from you and him. And what you said earlier was correct. Bert did shake someone violently before he landed that blow, only it wasn't Caroline. As George explained, it was you."

The walls are closing in. "You have blown my mind, Janey. I have so many questions! All this time, all these years which have gone by and you expect me to believe that you couldn't find the right time to tell me? What was it you said? Something along the lines of 'it doing more harm than good.' Surely keeping this to yourself is doing more harm than good – for our relationship! Also, there is the small matter of how the fuck did we end up in a relationship in the first place? Did you pursue me? Did you take pity on poor little Thomas? And then what, when the time was right, you swooped in and made your move?" She tries to speak but I silence her, I am on a roll and will not be interrupted. "And I have shared moments with you when I have opened up and told you I had a difficult upbringing. I held back! I held back, Janey, because I didn't want to put any of this on you but all the while you must have been sat there thinking 'yes I know only too well what it was like for you!'"

"I can explain! The reason I didn't tell you when we had chats about your childhood was because I could see how painful it was for you. And I was terrified that it would drive a wedge between us. That might seem selfish keeping it to myself, being worried about 'rocking the boat' but up until now you seemed so happy in your life. Yes, there were times when I was concerned (we had a chat about that earlier), but you always seemed to pull yourself out of it. Having Michael and raising him brought so much joy to our lives it just didn't seem right to hit you with this.

"As you can imagine, I was understandably concerned when you said you were coming here. It was all very mysterious at the start – you had me thinking (briefly) that you were maybe having an affair."

"An affair?"

"Well, I kept trying to reach you on the phone and there was no answer. So, I phoned your Inverness branch since you said this is where you were going to be based but they had no record of you arriving and they weren't expecting you either. Not only that, I managed to locate the accommodation you had booked in Skye only to discover there was no Thomas there so I told the proprietor I would take your place and that's where I have been staying ever since I got here. I was more than relieved to find out you were staying with George and there was no other woman involved! When I realised the truth about why you came here, I was so relieved I could be here to support you. Now that you are learning about what really happened here, it just seemed like the right time."

"OK, assuming I can digest what you have just told me, please tell me how we came to be together. I am all ears, truly!"

"First of all, Thomas, I may be many things but I am not a predator. I never 'pursued' you. Seeing you lying there that day left for dead in that violent storm, it really affected me too. In that respect I could not get you out of my head for a long time. I couldn't shake the vision of Bert lashing out so savagely at you like that either. Then racing off as if he'd just tossed a piece of rubbish to the ground. It was horrific. So yes, at that time to a degree I did pursue you because I periodically checked in with my aunt to see how you were doing. She knew an acquaintance of your mother's. I learned you had moved in with foster parents and I was so pleased to hear you weren't going back home.

"That was the extent of it, just the odd question to my aunt now and again. And it was born out of genuine concern for your wellbeing and nothing more. There was no subterfuge, no masterplan to find out where you were and to dig my claws in. Surely you know me well enough now to know that is not how I operate.

"When we first met it was entirely coincidental and I don't regret it, I bless that day. I started at Edinburgh University completely unaware that you were on the same campus. I am not lying to you. I swear I had no idea. I first saw you (as you know) when I joined the debating team. I recognised you immediately but kept my distance. If I am honest, I was completely in awe of you. The way you had turned your life around and how accomplished you were when you put your argument forwards … Things only progressed when you asked me out for coffee and well, you know the rest of the story. I am sure you can appreciate at that point there was no way I could tell you what I know. You were clearly well on the road to recovery. The last thing I wanted to do was to set you back. Then when we became close, it just never seemed like the right time to tell you. I am sorry though, sweetheart, truly sorry. I hope you can find it in your heart to accept that and we can move on from this."

She looks at me for some reassurance, but I have nothing to give. I am completely spent. I cannot remember a day like it. My mind has shut down involuntarily and is incapable of taking any more in. I make my excuses and head in the direction of the bedroom to lie down.

With my mind in utter turmoil, there is no chance of any sleep coming my way but sitting alone with my thoughts still seems preferable than engaging in any further conversation. I do not want to run the risk of hearing any more revelations today thank you very much! It is all too much to process. My heart attempts to reason with my head, affirming that I simply need time to sit with it, to digest it all. Then my head catapults into orbit, darting this way and that, spinning out of control. What I have heard today has shaken me to the very core of my being and I question whether I will ever be at ease with it all.

George knocks on my door a couple of hours later to tell me dinner is served. Like a robot I mechanically go through the motions of eating what has been put down for me. It could have been haute cuisine or prison gruel for all I cared. I could sense Janey desperately trying to read me for any sign that I was coming around and processing what she divulged earlier. But there was no way I was ready to play happy families just yet.

After dinner I head out alone onto the deck. It is a blessing. A combination of the fresh air and the noise of the water gently lapping up against the rocks has a soporific effect, taking me out of my head and making me feel drowsy. Unfortunately, it doesn't last long. George pulls up a chair next to me.

"Apologies Thomas, I know it was a hell of a lot for you to take on board today. There really was no easy way to tell you and it was impossible to sugar-coat it. You need (and deserve) to know the truth. Anyway, I don't want to bombard you any further. I just came out to check on you." He gets us to leave. I must be a glutton for punishment. It's out before I remember the vow I made to myself earlier in the evening not to engage in any more conversation.

"Whilst you are here, there is something which has been niggling away at me."

"Go on, ask away."

"It doesn't quite add up, George. Your crusade to bring me back to confront my demons. The 'unfinished business.' I mean, I understand it from my perspective, but what is in it for you? Why go to the bother of tracking me down all these years later and put me up in your house etc.? What do you gain from all of this?"

"It's not about gaining anything. Your case has haunted me over the years. I know you had gone on to lead by all intents and purposes a 'normal life', but I also knew until you knew the truth and faced up to it, you were living a lie and it would all completely unravel. That is part of it. The other part is harder to explain. From the minute I spent time with you in that hospital, I felt a connection with you. What your father did was wicked and callous, and his mark is still being felt today. You were so lost and vulnerable and for whatever reason, it became my mission to help you; to heal you and set you on the right path. The professional code of conduct of not getting attached went right out of the window. For me, you became the son I never had."

I turn to him and not for the first time today I am once again rendered speechless.

CHAPTER 24

The Following Day

After a fitful night's sleep, I wake to a new dawn, to a new reality. I consider that which is within my control – my relationship with Janey and where we go from here. She is still staying in the apartment I had originally rented and that is a blessing. It has given me some much-needed breathing space overnight and this morning. I was bowled over with her confession. To say I was shocked was a gross underestimate. Entering a serious relationship with someone whom she knew from such a shocking encounter is unconventional to say the least.

However, we have had many happy years together and there is Michael to consider too. I did briefly imagine what life would be like without Janey in the picture and it felt bleak. Did I want to split our family unit up? Not a chance. Had this revelation come at the start of the relationship would I have carried things further? Unlikely. Janey was right on that count. There wouldn't have been a good time to tell me at the start. When we met at university yes, I had moved on to a certain extent, but it was all still quite raw. I certainly couldn't have contemplated having someone in my life with the knowledge of my past which Janey possessed. It would have been a link to a time I wanted dead and buried.

I waste no time and put her out of her misery as I know she will be agonising about where things stand. I text her. "Make your way over. We will be heading out shortly. Love you loads. T xxx"

As for everything else, that is not so easily resolved. I researched the usage of the pills I take for my 'anxiety' and sure enough they are widely prescribed to people suffering with psychosis. Everything I have been told and everything I have read points to the only logical conclusion there is – the report was correct, I have a mental illness attributed to the trauma I experienced during childhood. However, my heart still aches for my siblings and I still don't feel ready or equipped to just let them go.

At least George and I agree on one thing – our itinerary for today which involves going to see mother. She is very much battling her own demons held within the fierce grip of dementia. But she is still my mum at the end of the day and, when I am feeling as low, I know just being in her company will lift my mood.

I have already rung ahead to find out how she is doing today. Happily, I was told she would be able to see visitors as she is having 'one of her better days.' It is a welcome relief. I resolve to put all my worries to one side for the time being, focussing instead on my visit. It has been so long since I saw her last. Would she even recognise me? We have chatted often on the phone, but it is not the same as seeing her in the flesh.

That being said, I must set my expectations low. Yes, she might well be having 'one of her better days', but the reality is she is battling a serious brain disease. She might recognise me but equally she might not have a clue who I am. George and Janey are accompanying me to the home, and I don't know how I feel about that. I reason that she is used to people going in and out of her room so it should be fine. One sniff of mother getting upset or feeling crowded though and I will give them their marching orders!

A rather sheepish-looking Janey arrives shortly after I end the call to the care home. I know in my heart I have to put my faith in her. We have so much history together, so many shared memories. I can't help it; I need to draw a line in the sand. I need her support and love way more than I need to make an enemy of her right now. I hold my arms outstretched. "Come here, love." The tentative look she had melts instantly into a wide beaming smile and she willingly moves towards me and surrenders into my arms.

We waste no time in setting off. The general consensus is that it is best to go and see her as soon as possible if she is feeling well. Just the very thought of seeing mother in the flesh after all these years has lifted my mood tremendously. Janey too appears to have a spring in her step. No doubt she feels lighter after shifting the weight of the burden she has carried around with her all those years. "No more secrets," is what I whispered to her just before we left and she matched my plea, "No more secrets," being her response.

There was no question what I was going through since the night George turned up on my doorstep was gruelling. But at the same time, it was cathartic. Even the news which Janey divulged last night. It felt good, almost in a cleansing sense. Everything was out in the open. Nowhere left to hide. "No more secrets."

It felt courageous 'coming home' to Skye. I had never been truly honest with myself for although I have remained living in Scotland, it was blatantly obvious I was in a sense on the run, fleeing from my past. Without George's constant cajoling there was no way I would have returned here. I had smothered down feelings of guilt when I thought about mother, reasoning what could I feasibly do to help her now and that she was in the best place. Regular phone calls to the home had helped to quash these feelings somewhat but it is no substitute for seeing her in the flesh. This felt right. To be able to visit her, to see her, not just a voice at the end of the phone. Perhaps it might even be good for her mental health to see me, to help her memory come back even if only temporarily. Or perhaps I am expecting too much, I must keep reminding myself she could just as easily be locked into her own little world.

When we arrive at the care home a 'Beatrice' is there to greet us. She doesn't even need to speak. She needs no introduction. She looks exactly how I pictured she would following the many conversations we have had over the years.

"Thomas! It is so good to finally meet you! Mary will be thrilled, I'm sure."

"The feeling is mutual. I am so looking forward to seeing her but before we go through please, I need to extend my heartfelt thanks to you and your team for all the work you do with mother. It is so greatly appreciated."

"Oh no, not at all, we are just doing our jobs."

"I understand that, but it can't be easy at times and it is a great comfort to know she is being well looked after." I pause and take a sharp intake of breath. "One more thing, Beatrice ..."

"Yes?"

"She hasn't had any more unwanted visitors?"

"Aah, your father?" I nod in acknowledgement. "No don't you worry, Thomas. He hasn't shown his face and if he did, believe me the Police would be notified. All our staff members here are well aware of the situation and trust me, there will not be a repeat performance." I release an audible sigh of relief and Janey reassuringly squeezes my hand.

Beatrice senses my nervousness. "Are you ready to see her, Thomas?"

"Of course, lead the way." We dutifully fall in line with Beatrice at the helm and eventually reach her room. She asks us to wait outside for a minute as she lets mother know we are here. I can only hear muffled voices but after a short time we are ushered through.

It feels surreal. I do a quick mental calculation and realise it has been some twenty years since I was last in the same room as mother. I am a 34-year-old man, and I was just a 14-year-old boy when she saw me last. Even without her illness I am quite sure it'd be difficult for her to recognise me.

All at once I feel a great wave of protection wash over me and I motion to George and Janey to hang back for a minute. Just until I am sure she is OK with having me in the room. I am only too well aware she could take fright, especially after her recent nasty visit from father.

I take tiny little tentative baby steps in her direction. She hasn't seen me yet since the back of her chair faces the door, and she is positioned looking out of the window. I am momentarily distracted as I take in the view. Another silent prayer of thanks to Beatrice and her team. The view mother has out of her window is nothing short of spectacular. In the forefront are the well-tended gardens of the home. Not so much colour at this time of year but beautiful none the less. There is a large holly bush off to the right teaming with red berries. And, directly in front of her window sits a bird bath and bird feeder so no doubt she will see plenty of wildlife. However, it is the view beyond this which captivates me. Loch Portree is visible in all its splendour. The morning sun causes sparkles and shimmering light like a blanket of stars right all along its surface. And, if I am not mistaken, off in the distance sits the Isle of Raasay.

I snap back to reality as I realise I have reached her chair. My heart is hammering in my chest. I continue my slow inch forwards then start to walk around the side of the chair. This is it. I am now stood face to face with mother. Only she hasn't looked up yet, seemingly unaware of who might've come to see her, so I take the opportunity to sit down in front of her, not wanting to intimidate her by standing towering over her. Her eyes are still cast downwards, fixated on the action of rubbing one palm and then the other. She is thoroughly engaged in the action.

I pluck up the courage to speak and it comes out as a very weak "Mother." The hand rubbing ceases and she slowly raises her head. Eventually we lock eyes, and I am immediately despondent. There is nothing there. She is completely vacant as though a ghostly presence is inhabiting the frail body of my mother. Although twenty years have passed, she is instantly recognisable. She hasn't changed much at all. What she suffered at father's hands aged her I'm sure, but she almost looks as though since she's moved here, she has been frozen in time, still very much like I remember her. All the anxiety and stress having left long ago. She no longer has to fear for her life or for mine. All her needs are being taken care of here and for once she is being property cared for.

The tension in the room is palpable. I sense George and Janey eagerly anticipating my reaction – has she recognised me? I put them out of their misery with a shake of the head and signal for them to come and sit down beside me. Mother looks quite at peace. I feel sure she won't be too concerned if they come over. They flank either side of me and I can't help but hang my head in disappointment. I absolutely knew this could be the case, that she might not recognise me. I thought I had mentally prepared myself for this eventuality, but it still came as a disappointment.

Then I felt it. Janey frantically rubbing my thigh to get my attention. "Thomas; Thomas! Look!" she said animatedly. I looked up and again directly towards mother. The ghost had vanished, and my mother's beautiful features were illuminated in a beaming smile.

"Thomas? Thomas? Is that you?"

I wanted to leap towards her, to hold her so tightly, but refrained myself from doing so. The last thing I wanted to do was scare her witless, so I opted instead for a calmer approach. "Yes mother, it is me! It's your Thomas!" I held my hands out towards her and she reciprocated, placing both of her hands in mine. The joyful tears flowed freely. We had an unshakable bond unbroken by time or her illness. I could feel the years melting away in that short time.

Internally I cursed myself for never coming back.

I have built a life for myself, yes. But at the same time, I have been in denial about a lot. When I think about what mother and I have been through together I am utterly ashamed of myself for leaving her alone. Never visiting. Appeasing myself with the thought that a few regular phone calls to check in on her were enough. Clearly that's not the case. She has recognition. She has recognised me, and I have felt that closeness to her once again. Things can never go back to how they were before. Seeing mother – this has to become a part of my life and undoubtedly Michael's life too. It is only right that he should know about his heritage and he needs to meet his grandmother too.

She averts her gaze. It lands upon George and she extends to him the same radiant smile. He beams back. Then like a thief in the night she quickly steals her hands out of my grasp, clutching them anxiously close to her chest. The veil of confusion has descended. Her eyes glaze over, the eyes of a stranger. I know in that instant when she's looking at me, she is looking right through me. She doesn't have a clue who I am. Breathe, Thomas. You knew this could happen. To even have that fleeting moment of recognition was simply something to be treasured.

I sit back in my seat to try to give her some breathing space too. It is blatantly obvious she has retreated into her shell. But, at the same time, she is as timid as a new-born lamb and needs to be treated as such. Seeing her look so fragile makes me want to reach out to her all the more. There is nothing else to do but sit tight and wait to see if she comes out of it. At the very least I pray she doesn't take fright and start screaming for one of the carers.

It gives me the opportunity to scan around the room. This is mother's world. A place I know very little about, but it has been her home for many years now. How cruel that she has finally found a place to be at peace but at the same time, thwarted with such a debilitating illness. This first thing I notice (and it would be impossible not to notice since there were so many) are all the framed pictures of me when I was a young boy. They adorn the walls and sit proudly on her table. Curious. There are none of Caroline, Juliet, and James.

This is yet another clear indication staring me literally square in the face. It screams at me – they are not real, you have made them up. They are figments of your imagination. George has been silently watching me take all this in and I can tell he knows what I am thinking but at least he shows some decorum and refrains from saying so. Janey has also remained silent throughout the visit but then her reasons are slightly different. She is terrified to knock the status quo any further by putting a foot out of line so is instead waiting on a cue from me.

We sit like this in silence, all tentatively waiting to see if mother is able to free herself from her fugue but to no avail. After twenty minutes or so I put the other two out of their misery. "Come on, let's leave her in peace." We rise and I resist the urge to get too close to her still fearful that she might take fright.

George and Janey reach the door before me and it is barely audible but even still, I am sure she said it. As quick as a flash I reposition myself in front of mother, but she is back to being thoroughly engrossed in rubbing her palms again. Eyes downcast, not wanting to entertain anyone. The other two sense the commotion and want to know what's happening but I want to give her a little bit more time. Nothing. She is lost in her solitary world. Did I imagine it, or did she really say what I think she said?

I wait until we are outside in the carpark. "Look at your birth certificate … that's what she just said to me." Two blank unbelieving faces stare back at me. "Well, come on then, what are you both waiting for? Let's do it! And while we're at it, I'd like to see if there are any records on Caroline, Juliet, and James." Neither of them heard her utter a word, but I heard it. I believe mother was trying to communicate with me, to convey an important message and it simply cannot be ignored.

CHAPTER 25

When we settle into the car, I waste no time. I type 'births, marriages, and deaths – Isle of Skye' into a search engine and bingo, a telephone number is produced. Without hesitation, I hit the button to make the call then end it abruptly before it is answered by the recipient – George was frantically making a gesture for me to cut the call by slicing his hand back and forth across his throat.

"What? Why can't I make the call, George?"

"There is no need for you to arrange an appointment to see anyone. You will only be able to arrange a replacement birth certificate which will take Lord knows how many weeks to arrive. And in any case, I have a copy at home in your file."

"OK perfect! What about checking to see if my siblings' births are registered?"

"Again Thomas, there is no point in discussing that with a registrar. They cannot divulge confidential information. I think we both know you are not going to find anything anyway. However, if you insist and if it goes some way towards further cementing in your head that they do not exist, why don't you have a look online? There are many websites where you can get information on family trees."

I consider this and decide that it is sound advice. I also consider that fact that I haven't seen hide nor hair of either Caroline, Juliet, or James all day. I allow myself to imagine that they do not exist. Will this help my mental state? Will it help me on the road to recovery from this psychosis I am apparently blighted with? It seems inconceivable not to have them in my life.

Yet, as I open the internet browser on my phone and select the first website which appears, boasting it is 'the UK's No.1 go-to website for researching family trees,' it hits me like a brick. Alongside asking for their full names, undoubtedly the next question I will be asked is to provide their dates of birth. What are their dates of birth? I do not have an earthly clue. How could I not know my own siblings' dates of birth?

I involuntarily drop my phone and it hits the footwell of the seat with a loud thud, causing George to stir.

"Everything OK back there?"

"You are right, George."

"Right about what, Thomas?"

"They don't exist. Caroline, Juliet, and James – I don't know their dates of birth! I'd never considered it before, but *I don't know their dates of birth!*"

I collapse into Janey's arms, sobbing uncontrollably like a small child. She doesn't say anything, content to hold me tightly, patiently waiting until there are no more tears left to cry.

It is almost laughable (well if it didn't hurt so much!). All the evidence I have been presented with since I arrived here and all the time I knew the answer myself. The brain is both truly a marvel and a torturous beast at the same time. All the visual interactions I have had with my siblings over the years and all of the conversations, they were so real, so lifelike. To think that my brain conjured all that up is unbelievable.

Obviously, as George said, the medication has kept the psychosis at bay in my adulthood. I can't recall having many conversations with my siblings since I left Skye and went to university. I had put this down to us losing contact with one another when I was placed into foster care then subsequently moved on to university, but I see the reality of the situation now. The medication was working its magic and allowing me to lead a normal life. But now that I have returned, old wounds have opened up and it has clearly lost its potency.

The absence of Caroline, Juliet, and James will leave a gaping hole in my life. But it gives me solace knowing that Janey and Michael will be there for me. And George – possibly? There is no denying we have known each other for a very long time now and he knows me perhaps even better than I know myself.

George too just let me cry it out. Like Janey he didn't utter a word. I imagine he was more than relieved that I had (finally) figured it all out. And, he had the decency not to point this out to me.

Like a weary soldier, I heave my carcass up and out of the car when we arrive back at his house. Even though I am all consumed with my emotions, I can't help but notice that George seems somewhat distracted.

We have been in the door a matter of a couple of minutes, and he is like a cat on a hot tin roof. I collapse, absolutely spent, onto the sofa and Janey slumps down next to me. George disappears for a few minutes then reappears in the living room not looking like himself at all.

"Thomas, I have located your birth certificate." Of course! I'd forgotten all about that with all the drama over my siblings. "I have left it on the desk in the office."

"OK thanks." I manage. He bows his head and shuffles off Lord knows where. I remain seated. The anticipation it appears is all too much for Janey.

"Well, aren't you just a little bit curious? Go and take a look!"

It is true. I had been more than a little bit curious following the visit to mother but finding out about my siblings had literally knocked the stuffing right out of me.

"OK, you are right, sweetheart, I'll go take a look." With heavy hands and a heavy heart, I heave myself off the sofa and head in the direction of the office.

On entering, I move into position to sit at the desk. Surely there can't be any more surprises? Without scanning it whatsoever, I decide to read it in its entirety from top to bottom.

I start by raising it to eye level. As I slowly, cautiously, scroll down, I notice nothing out of the ordinary. None the less, my palms have started sweating and my pulse has quickened. Deep breaths, Thomas. All looks in order. Until, that is, I read 'Father's Name' – 'Traynor, George.' Time stands still as the revelatory document flutters its merry little way to the ground.

CHAPTER 26

I thought the tidal wave of emotions I had experienced since I set out on this journey had reached their climax. How wrong could I be! This sets my mind spinning in a whole new direction. Yet again life as I know it has turned upside down and inside out. George – my father? Not George the counsellor, George, my father!

On so many levels now it all makes sense. It didn't quite add up in my head the story he'd spun about bringing me here. What was it? Something about my case bothering him as it was the one case in his career he had never brought to a satisfactory conclusion – there were 'loose ends.' He talked about how I had never faced up to the truth and needed to come back to confront it all. A part of me had questioned this lame reasoning from the start but his persistency combined with the guilt I felt over never going to see mother were what led me to start this journey. He needed to reach out to me – I am after all his son! All his talk of 'thinking of me like a son.' I am his son!

This raises so many questions. Exactly how long has George known about this? How long has he held my birth certificate in his possession? Please God tell me he has only found out about this recently. If he knew when I was younger, he could have removed mother and I from father's torturous grasp. There I go, referring to Bert as father. He is not 'father,' he is Bert. He is nothing to me. What I endured at his hands and he's not even my father! The red-hot fury explodes in my head and throughout my body, firing me into action. That bastard! What he put us through and all the while he was nothing to me!

I leap off my seat, ready to storm out, but I am stopped in my tracks. A very sheepish-looking George peers around the door of the office. Neither one of us knows how to act. There are so many questions buzzing around in my head, but he needs to explain himself first. I grit my teeth and clench my fists in an attempt to stem the torrent of questions I'm ready to fire in his direction. It works and I manage a simple "Well?"

"Let's take a seat."

"I'd rather stand if it's all the same with you." My body is so fired up, sitting down at the moment seems inconceivable.

"First of all, Thomas, I need you to know that I only recently found out." Some of the tightness in my chest loosens its grip. "When I saw the birth certificate, it was only shortly afterwards that I contacted you. I am as bowled over by this as you are. I truly had no idea."

"You'd better take me back to the start, George! I need to know what happened!"

"Of course you do. The truth is I loved your mother deeply, Thomas. We knew each other as far back as our school days. It all started after a chance encounter at a mutual friend's wedding. We both knew there was something there, but she was with Bert at the time. Nevertheless, we exchanged numbers discreetly. Over time we met up and became inseparable. We knew it was wrong, but we couldn't help ourselves. It was very difficult to carve out time to see one another but whenever we could, we would meet up.

"It was your mother who ended our affair. She was terrified of your father. Err sorry, Bert. Truth be told, I was too. It was probably a blessing things ended when they did because I dread to think what would've happened to Mary if he had found out. She didn't love him. She stayed because she was too frightened to leave him. Frightened of what he would do to her and to me if he found out. In all honesty though, I think he knew about us. Bert's fury and outbursts only escalated and intensified with time. Culminating of course in your hospital admission. But I never stopped loving her, never stopped thinking about her. It is the sole reason why I have never looked at another woman since."

"Ok, ok, but what about when she was pregnant with me? Surely you must've suspected that I could be yours?"

"That is true, Thomas, I can't deny it, I did wonder. However, I didn't know she was pregnant, not at first. All contact had been severed and Bert was very controlling by this stage. Gone were the days when your mother would even get the chance to attend a social event of any kind. I heard on the grapevine that he was drinking excessively and that no one had seen hide nor hair of Mary. I was desperately worried about her but equally, I didn't want to jeopardise her safety any further by intervening. I truthfully didn't know what to do for the best.

"Life moved on in the inevitable way it does. Days and weeks then months merged into one another. I had no idea of your existence. That was until one day I bumped into her at the Post Office, buggy in tow. She saw the look of shock in my face and immediately shook her head. If there was any chance you were mine, there was no way she was going to entertain the possibility. I tried to offer help and support as a friend, nothing more, but she wouldn't hear of it. She was utterly terrified of Bert's wrath and therefore, needed to keep me at arm's length.

"Believe me, Thomas, there wasn't a day which went by when I didn't think about the two of you. I have kept as close an eye on you as was feasibly possible. However, I had to keep reminding myself that it was equally possible Bert could be your father.

"I finally got the opportunity to go to your side when you ended up being admitted to hospital. When I got the call to come to have a chat with you in a professional capacity, there was no way I could turn it down. My heart shattered when I saw how broken you were. Bert had abused you terribly, both physically and mentally. The wounds and bruises would heal up, but I feared the mental damage would leave its permanent mark. I did everything in my power to get you out of that house. I know what that would've done to your mother, but I couldn't see you suffer at his hands any longer. I knew Mary would never leave him but at least I could do something positive to help you.

"You thrived after that. We have your foster parents to thank for that. They helped you see what a bright future lay ahead. You secured a place at Edinburgh University where you met Janey and the two of you went on to build a life together. It gave me solace and reassured me that I had done the right thing. I was unsure if your mother would ever forgive me for playing my part in having you placed in foster care, but I had to hope that she saw I was acting in your best interests."

"George, I need to stop you there. So, at this point, you had no idea that I was your son, correct?"

"That's right."

"OK, but you profess to loving my mother, yet you were instrumental in re-homing me and your relationship with mother never became romantic again? So, she was bereft, childless, and back in Bert's merciless hands!?"

"Thomas, when you put it like that, it makes it sound callous. There was no black and white, no right and wrong. It was a very difficult situation. I had the opportunity to do something right by you, to play a part in helping you have a brighter future and I grabbed that with both hands. I had no idea whether you were my son or not at this time and Mary was unwilling to entertain the possibility. Bert had systematically worn her down over the years until there was nothing left. My name was mud in that household, and I had to steer well clear. Whether he knew your mother and I had been involved, I remain uncertain, but he certainly knew I had recommended that you be transferred into foster care. Perhaps he has mellowed somewhat over the years but at the time let's just say he wasn't my number one fan!"

"Please, can we get to how and when you found out I was your son, how you came to be in possession of my birth certificate."

"Yes, of course. I don't know if you recall but when we visited Mary, she looked over in my direction and gave me a beaming smile." I nod my head and shrug my shoulders at the same time, gesturing for him to continue. "Well, that was no coincidence. She was smiling at me because she recognised me too. When she was placed in the care home, for the first time in years I was able to have regular contact with her again. There was no longer any threat of Bert intervening. He washed his hands of her the minute she was admitted.

"I visited her at least once a week and I have kept that up over the years. It was wonderful to see her face light up when she saw you. Those precious moments of recognition are few and far between now as her illness has progressed. I talk to her a lot about the past, about times we have shared, about you and how well you are doing. It is all in an attempt to rouse her into the present, to get her to focus.

"On one such visit, she was locked into her little world so I thought it might help to show her some old photographs. She had a shoebox under her bed filled with photographs, so I started leafing through them, showing her them one by one. I talked and talked, trying to be as engaging as possible, but I got no response so left to my own devices, I started delving further into the box. There were a few old letters, but I kept digging until I reached the bottom of the box where I found an official-looking document. My instinct was to just replace the photographs and put the box back under the bed. It felt like snooping and I wasn't comfortable with it. As I started replacing a couple of the photographs, it caused the document to dislodge, revealing its title – 'birth certificate.'

"It could have been Mary's birth certificate. But I knew there was a chance that it was yours and I had to find out. When I saw my name printed there, I couldn't believe it. And sadly, I couldn't share the moment with your mother for, at the time, she was lost in some distant world. I am not ashamed to say I wept. I wept and wept for all the years we lost that we could have shared together. But I also wept joyous tears, I was elated. The news I had so wanted to hear was finally affirmed. And then, I wept tears of sadness for what might've been between your mother and I. She had known all along I was the father, she had me named on your birth certificate after all. If only she had taken a leap of faith and tried to leave Bert, things might've been very different … for all of us.

"When did I find out this information? Only recently I assure you, just shortly before I made contact with you. I must, however, apologise for turning up in the middle of the night like that. You looked at me like you had seen a ghost and I am not surprised. I wasn't thinking straight. I had to see you and, frankly, I was not in the right frame of mind. It was foolish and I can see how it could've alarmed you, so I apologise sincerely for that."

I take a seat once more at the desk, letting it all sink in. I wanted to be angry at mother because she could have changed our lives for the better, but how could I be? Bert had utterly dominated her; she saw no way out. She had been well and truly trapped. And now she is battling a serious brain disease. All I feel is a mixture of love and pity. She really had been dealt a dreadful hand of cards in the game of life.

I lock eyes with my 'new father.' "One thing is puzzling me, George." He raises his eyebrows in anticipation. "It's the birth certificate. You claim to have only found out about it and that, when you did, you immediately contacted me?" He nods in agreement. "But it wasn't you who brought it to my attention, was it? It was mother. Exactly when were you going to enlighten me?"

"Yes, I can see why that might concern you, Thomas, but truly, you have to believe that I was going to tell you. It was always my plan. I was so shocked when Mary said what she did to you. It has given me such hope. Her dementia has already done so much damage, but she clearly hasn't fully succumbed to it, not yet. It certainly wasn't how I planned on you finding out, but in a strange way I am delighted. I am sure it will have given your mother great joy to be the one to finally tell you the truth, to point you in the right direction. A special gift from her to you.

"It was so important for you to come back to find out the truth about your mental state. But equally important was you finding out about your parentage. I didn't want to hit you with everything all at once so I thought you finding out about me could wait until you had processed the fact that your 'siblings' didn't exist. I know this is huge. It is so much for you to take in and it is a blessing indeed that Janey has come. You two have a fabulously strong relationship and I know she is absolutely there for you. She will be next door waiting on tenterhooks for you to let her know what the birth certificate says. And Thomas, please know that I too am 100% here for you. I know it will take a long time for you to wrap your head around all this, but I mean what I say, please know that. It would be wonderful if we could build a relationship but no rush, we can take things nice and slowly."

He is right. Baby steps is what is called for. I imagine that if were watching this on a movie, the son would fling his arms around his newfound father. But this wasn't the movies, and I wasn't yet ready for such an outpouring of emotion. I could already feel a sense of curiosity about what the future would hold. My life had taken a new trajectory and what did this mean for me and my family? Yes, there was a definite sense of curiosity but equally, we weren't at the happily ever after stage either! I found myself in unchartered waters. I was floundering and wasn't entirely sure how to feel or act. Two things immediately came to mind. I had to let my wife know who her real father-in-law was and, secondly, I needed to pay a certain someone a long overdue visit.

CHAPTER 27

I make my excuses – about needing to talk things through with Janey – and leave George standing in the office. Janey, as I had suspected, wasn't far away. She was eager to know what I had found out, but I discovered that I wasn't quite ready to divulge anything just yet. I had something I needed to do first and it had to be alone. I simply shook my head at her to indicate that the birth certificate hadn't yielded anything of interest and made up a story about having to nip out to collect some bits and pieces for dinner. From the look on her face, she wasn't wholly convinced but she didn't stop me from leaving either.

It was surprising that twenty years had passed but I still knew my way around Skye. In particular, the way back to the croft. Another surprise (and initially I couldn't decide whether it was a pleasant one or not), were my siblings' presence in the car. All three were accompanying me. I was not alone. Even after all the evidence I had been presented with, it seemed that the mind literally had a mind of its own! Deep down I knew they weren't real and the sane, logical part of me questioned how they could possibly have just appeared out of nowhere. But, at the same time, it was undoubtedly comforting to know they were there. I reasoned that I could tackle my demons and confront my mental health issues when I returned to the Scottish Borders. For now, I decided that I was happy to entertain each and every one of them.

They were chatting amongst themselves and I was picking up snippets of conversation here and there … "he's not going back there" … "we'll turn off soon" … "nope, it doesn't look good." Until, eventually, James plucked up the courage to speak to me directly. "Thomas please, turn the car around! You can't go back there!"

I went to answer him but was addressing all three when I said; "There will be no turning back. I am going to the croft. I need to confront him and nothing any of you say can change my mind."

Juliet this time, showing her usual concern for my welfare; "But Thomas, look how far you've come. You don't need to go back there. He might be twenty years older but he's still more than capable of inflicting damage. Maybe not so much so physically but mentally – he is wicked! Please, think about what you are doing. Don't do it, Thomas, please."

She is only voicing her concern; I am well aware of that but with more than a little agitation I respond, "Look here, I found out something today which has quite literally blown my mind. George Traynor, who I know to be my counsellor, it turns out we have a more intimate relationship than that – he is my father! So, that godforsaken piece of shite festering away in that croft up there is absolutely nothing to me! And he needs to know that I know. This can only be done face to face, man to man. I am no longer the little lost boy he once terrorised. I need to do this for me. I need retribution; to confront that beast. This day has been a long time in coming! I will give him a piece of my mind and for once, he will have to listen to me." They are temporarily silenced after my passionate outburst.

George

Now he knows. The enormity of the situation starts to settle in. I could sense that, all of a sudden, he no longer knew how to act around me. Our roles had shifted exponentially and neither of us knew what to do next. I wanted to embrace him, my long-lost son, my broken boy. But this is not the time. I can't force a relationship and he has many emotional wounds which run deep and need to be addressed before he can move on in his life. I know one thing for sure though, I will be there for him whenever, period.

In time, it is my hope that he can trust me and lean on me. To trust me enough to let me fully into his life and potentially forge a relationship with the grandson I have never met too. At the same time, I cannot let my mind run away with itself too much, fantasising about what might be. All I ever wanted was to meet someone, fall in love, and start a family. It was a cruel twist of fate that the only woman I ever wanted was already taken and that she was married to such a brute.

Then it occurs to me, I have a daughter-in-law sat through there I need to reacquaint myself with in my new role as her father-in-law. But slowly does it. Undoubtedly Thomas will be with her now, informing her about the new status quo. The best thing to do I deduce, is to keep a low profile until either of them approach me first.

I don't want to barge in when they are in the midst of conversation, so I give it some time then cautiously, I edge towards the door and exit the office towards the living room. I take in the scene … no Thomas. Only Janey is present, sat with her head in her hands. She springs to her feet as I enter.

"George, tell me now, what did that birth certificate say?"

"Has Thomas not spoken with you?"

"No George, he upped and left, making an excuse about needing to go out to get something for dinner."

This was worrying. It was clear where Thomas was headed. "Janey, I fear I know where Thomas is going." I motion for her to sit back down. "I never envisioned being the one to tell you and it isn't right, but I have no choice. Hopefully, Thomas will understand that. I am pretty certain that he is going to the croft to confront Bert. Bert is not Thomas's father, Janey, I am."

I watch the whole range of emotions play out on her face. Shock gives way to confusion and, eventually, realisation dawns. This time, she launches herself upwards and towards the door at lightning speed.

"Well, are you coming or what?"

"Of course!" I say a silent prayer for Thomas' safety and hope that we get there in time before Bert has a chance to inflict any more damage.

Thomas has taken the BMW, leaving us with the Volkswagen Polo. Not a particularly fast vehicle but nevertheless, Janey still manages to take off at breakneck speed. Her foot is flat to the floor on the accelerator pedal, and I have to ask her to ease off slightly. If we are to be of any assistance to Thomas, we have to get there in one piece!

Janey has never been to the croft, so I navigate us there. The conversation is largely related to the giving and receiving of directions until she starts asking questions similar to those Thomas had recently posed: 'how long had I known?', 'for how long and when was I involved with Mary?' and 'does Bert know?'

Having answered all her questions to the best of my ability, she ends with one final question: 'does Thomas know that you and I had a connection after his accident in 1998?' I explain that no, we hadn't discussed that, and also that we met in a professional capacity. I am not at liberty to discuss who I am treating at work; it goes against my professional code of conduct. She seems satisfied with my response.

By the time I have finished answering all the questions and successfully navigated us to our destination, we find ourselves ambling up the long driveway towards the entrance of Bert Taylor's croft. I scan the grounds but can see no sign of my BMW 5-Series.

CHAPTER 28

The black veil of foreboding descends as I near my destination. The all too familiar bleak hopeless sense of dread consumes me as I close in. Some of my passionate resolve to confront him wanes as I fight to keep the demons at bay. Instead of the intended grandiose entrance full of bluster and noise, I find myself gently idling the car up the driveway and cutting the engine, happy to sit in the car a minute or two just gathering my thoughts.

This is not lost on my companions. "Are you OK, Thomas?"

"Yes thanks, just taking a little time out."

James again; "Well, if you turn around, that's OK, but if you choose to go in, remember, we have got your back."

"I know that, thanks everyone."

I had to go in. I had to do this. Even without the latest revelation that George was my father, this visit was long overdue. It is highly likely (given his character) that anything I have to say to him will fall on deaf ears, but it needs to be said. How could I ever fully heal and move on in my life without confronting him?

Just taking those few precious moments to collect myself has the desired effect. I find the much-needed strength to continue on. Unwilling to allow another negative thought to penetrate my brain and stop me in my tracks, I launch myself out of the car and march purposefully towards the front door.

A few loud thuds on the metal knocker is all the warning I give him before I pull the unlocked door towards me and land with both feet on the threshold. "Bert! BERT!" I holler and wait a couple of seconds. With no response, I advance further into the croft.

He has changed nothing. The place feels as though it has been frozen in time. I cast my eyes over the coats hanging in the hallway and notice an old coat of mother's still hanging there. Also immediately obvious is the stench of the place. It is filthy. This, however, is new and takes some adjusting to! It smells dank and mouldy and rotten. It was never sparkling when I lived here but nothing like this. As I pulled up to the croft, the grounds had a dilapidated, unkempt feel to them. But, on entering the croft itself, the sense of decay and neglect are visible everywhere.

The hallway leads directly to the kitchen and the aroma is nothing short of pungent. Rotting food and leftovers litter all the countertops. There are indeterminable spillages down every kitchen unit I cast my eyes over. Plates and crockery are piled high close to the sink in such a haphazard fashion, it seems unfathomable that they have maintained their precarious balance. How could anyone live like this? The cows in the barn are better accommodated! No doubt he is only concerned about where his next drink is coming from. 'Keeping house' would be of no interest to Bert. That leads me to the logical conclusion of his whereabouts …

I approach the door to the dining room and give it a good shove. There he is. There he is in all his glory, slumped in the same (now threadbare) chair I remember him sitting in. There is a bottle of Scotch at his side, three-quarters of its contents sunk. Scanning around, there are empty bottles of liquor discarded here, there, and everywhere. He appears to be blissfully unaware of my presence in the room. The alcohol has clearly numbed his senses. Well, let's see what we can do about that!

Looking at this pathetic excuse of a man wallowing in self-pity, it strengthens my resolve and this time I do my utmost to ensure he hears me. "Bert! BERT!!" Nothing. "Wake up, man!" Still nothing, he doesn't even stir. I venture further into the room and come to a standstill in front of his chair.

Unlike mother, Bert has aged, significantly, clearly a result of his unorthodox lifestyle. His face is weather-beaten and lined with deep furrows. His hair has changed colour and has thinned out drastically. Only a few patches of lank, greasy grey hair cling to his scalp. It appears as though he has tried to fashion this into something resembling some sort of a style, but he has failed miserably. His clothes are shabby, torn, and desperately in need of a good wash but by the look of them, they could fall apart going through a wash cycle. And his cheeks and nose are ruby red, tell-tale signs of an alcoholic.

There is a nasty aroma emanating from him and there is no mistaking it – stale urine. From the look and smell of him, he is drinking himself into a stupor and not bothering with any toilet breaks. Disgusting! None of this is lost on my companions. I can hear their chitter chatter as they take it all in. "Oh, the smell!", "This place is vile", "How can he live like this?" Indeed, indeed!

This wasn't how I expected things to play out. How can I possibly get any closure when I can't even get a conversation out of him? I try again, bellowing his name but nothing, only the sound of my voice echoing around the room. With no other option available, I lean forwards and grasp both of his shoulders in my hands and give them a good shake. The action doesn't wake him up. Instead, his body arches off to the left at an impossibly looking uncomfortable angle and his head lolls backwards with no support, causing his mouth to gape open. He was well and truly out for the count!

What now? I can't just leave! If I leave, there is a good chance I would never come back and I would never have my day of reckoning. At a loss, I look to my siblings for advice. James and Juliet come up with various suggestions which I consider in turn but then rule each one of them out. I then lift my head as I hear Caroline (who has thus far been silent) start to speak. "There is something which could work." She doesn't wait for any acknowledgement from me and carries on. "How about this. We get him out of the chair, bundle him into the car and drive around for a while. He might just sober up if we let some fresh air in and turn the music up?"

I consider this. It sickens me, the thought of sitting in such close proximity to this stinking putrid lump. But she could be right and without any other feasible idea I start to think that yes, this could work. The motion of lifting him up and dragging him out of the croft might be enough to rouse him and, if not, blasting his face with fresh air and noise from the stereo ought to do it. We jointly decide to give it a go.

I crouch down and angle my body in such a way that I manage to drape one of his arms around my neck. Gripping fiercely onto this appendage, I raise the dead-weight of his carcass to a stand. I am surprised. There is not much to him. He is a shadow of his former self and it takes far less exertion than I had anticipated to hold him upright. He can't weigh much at all; his frame is tiny. Perhaps he has succumbed so fully to his addiction, he has forgotten to nourish his body with food, preferring to simply quench his thirst for alcohol instead? Well, whatever, it was certainly going to make my task easier!

Even through all the effort of heaving him out of his seat, he remains in an impenetrable stupor. There is the odd grunt-like noise but no attempt to open his eyes or form any words. Perhaps he will come to life as I drag him out of the dining room? Only one way to find out.

I take it at an easy pace. Yes, he has a small frame, but it's still no mean feat dragging a lifeless body along. At first, all the effort is on my part. However, as we reach the far side of the kitchen, he applies a little weight onto his feet. On the face of it to look at him, it looks as though there is no cognitive function taking place. But there is some distant thought process is quietly at work of its own accord for the steps he is taking become more considered and pronounced. If I were to remove my grasp, he would simply crumple in a heap on the floor but aided along, he is somehow managing to work with me.

My siblings offer words of encouragement, but I need to stop for a minute to catch my breath. I lean for support against the wall in the hallway and try a last-ditch attempt to rouse him before exiting the croft. It would be far better if I didn't have to execute Caroline's plan. If I could only get him to come to life! We couldn't be any closer, he is draped around me but still no response when I shout his name. I give him another shake (whilst trying to maintain the positioning of his arm around my neck) but zilch, nothing, there is literally no-one at home!

I take a deep breath and dig deep as I negotiate the last section – moving him from the hallway to the car. I am silent now, focussed on this last task. However, my siblings are chatting animatedly amongst themselves; "What a state to get yourself in", "He is a lost cause" and worryingly, "Someone should put him out of his misery!"

I had hoped the blast of icy cold air when we ventured outside would be enough to engage his senses but, again, nothing coherent or determinable; only the grunts and groans of someone heavily intoxicated. I began to wonder if Caroline's plan would come to fruition.

Now for the hardest part, angling this lifeless body downwards and onto the passenger seat. There is now a fair old wind blowing and for the first time, he makes an attempt at communication – I hear something akin to "What?" I take full advantage of his newly found lucidity but reason that if I want him to co-operate with me, I should refrain from showing any signs of contempt. "Bert, help me out here, let's get you to a seat. I am going to count to three and on three, I need you to crouch down then lift your feet into the car and sit yourself down. Can you do that for me?" Nothing. I just have to hope he does what he's asked. Here goes nothing! "OK, one, two, three …" His eyes remain firmly shut and there is no sign of movement. Fabulous! "OK," I say, speaking to no-one in particular, since it is abundantly clear he is still very much 'under the influence.' "You leave me no option!" I unhook his arm from around my neck and immediately the bulk of him collapses to the earth with gravity, but I intercept this just before he hits the ground and manoeuvre him haphazardly into the seat.

Beads of sweat have formed on my forehead and I press both palms onto the roof of the car directly above the passenger door to steady myself, head bowed until I catch my breath. "Well done," I hear Juliet murmur. I pause for thought. There is no going back now. I have him in the car but where are we going exactly? Stick to the plan! As Caroline said, if we drive around with the window down and the music up, he should come to life – surely? "Come on, let's do this." (A reassuring prompt from James who I am quite sure is loving every minute of this. Any sniff of adventure and devilment – James is your man!)

I am only too happy to open all of the windows when I get into the car – the smell of stale urine and alcohol emanating from him in such an enclosed space is almost unbearable. It makes me gag. I am not alone. My companions are equally disgusted. We set off with the windows down and the radio up loud (that too provides a welcome distraction from the nauseating aroma circulating in the car).

With no destination in mind, I start off by driving the dirt tracks around the croft, ever hopeful that he will just come to life. If that were the case, it wouldn't take much to double-back to the croft. I did not relish the prospect of having a show-down with him in the car. I can hear noises every now and then, but he is still maintaining a lifeless slumped posture and his eyes remain sealed firmly shut.

Perhaps the only thing which is going to speed things along now is time. He clearly needs time to sober up. I give him a gentle shove to angle his head further in the direction of the window and the icy cold air which is filtering through the car. I am so angry with him that, for a fleeting moment, it occurs to me how easy it would be to unfasten his seatbelt, push the door open, and give him a jolly good shove. He is utterly defenceless. And that, I am quite sure, would send Bert Taylor off to meet his maker post haste.

However, that was not my intention. I am no killer. But I needed this, I deserved it. I needed my time to have it out with him once and for all. He will not deny me that! Lost in thought, I realise that we have left the grounds of the croft and adjoining properties. We are now traversing one of the main thoroughfares.

"Where are we going?" a slightly concerned Juliet pipes up. I have no answer for her as I am not entirely sure myself.

"Erm, nowhere in particular, just driving around!" Caroline has once again been unusually quiet, and I wonder if she is considering the merit of her plan.

I get lost in traffic. It doesn't seem to matter what time of year it is; the roads are now notoriously busy on Skye (so George informed me recently). My car seems to have been pulled and sucked into the throng of cars traversing along the long stretch of road.

We have progress. Bert is periodically uttering the odd word here and there. His eyes are still closed but it is some time now since he had his last tipple and I think the fresh air is starting to take effect. This brings Caroline out of her shell. "I told you this would work. We just have to be patient."

Where are we? I had momentarily lost my bearings, too distracted by listening to Bert. Wherever we were headed, there were a number of cars all headed in the same direction. I snap back to reality and take in the surroundings. I now see the reason for the influx of cars – we are nearing Dunvegan Castle. Sure enough, most of them indicate and pull over, having arrived at their destination. This will be the last of the tourists for the day, since I notice the sun is now hung low in the sky.

I continue on. My unwelcome passenger is now shaking his head from side to side. Things are starting to look promising. He is showing more signs of regaining consciousness. I keep the speed up and head west. It starts to become obvious pretty quickly where this westerly approach is taking us.

George

This was disconcerting. I had been certain Thomas was headed here to confront Bert. If not here, then where? Think! I scan the outside of the croft and see an old rusted up (but possibly still functional) pick-up parked right outside. I turn towards Janey and she looks as perplexed and worried as I am.

There is only one way to find out. "We have to go knock on the door, see if Bert is there."

"Yes, we do," she gingerly responds. We approach the door together, but I take the lead and give the knocker a couple of raps. Silence. I try again but nothing. Without waiting for Janey's authorisation, I push the door and find that it opens easily.

We search the croft thoroughly but with no sign of either Bert or Thomas, we are back outside a few minutes later. We are more than elated to be out in the fresh air. It was utterly putrid in there! But now, we are sadly stumped. Where were they?!

I motion to Janey to be quiet for a minute. I listen intently to see if there any voices close by, but I can only hear the noises of animals feeding and the occasional gust of wind. We need to check the barn and outhouses before leaving so we split up and search the grounds.

It doesn't take long. Around ten minutes later we meet up again at the front of the croft. Nothing. No sign of either of them. I rack my brain. Perhaps he has gone to the care home to see Mary, to tell her he knows about me? That would be a plausible explanation for Thomas' disappearance, but not for Bert's. I think we have to assume Bert is A.W.O.L. There is no sign of him, and his vehicle is parked outside. Why would they leave the croft? It made no sense.

Janey is the first to voice her opinion. "I think I know where they might have gone ... back to the beginning, back to where it all started." The penny drops.

"Neist Point!"

"Exactly."

"Come on then," I urge, desperate to get there as quickly as possible. My only son and the love of Janey's life could well be in grave danger.

CHAPTER 29

George

It doesn't take long to get to Neist Point. I can see in the distance only a few cars are parked up in the carpark as it is getting late in the day. We close in and it becomes immediately apparent that one of those cars looks very like mine. In no time at all, we pull up and I scan the registration plate – it is my car. "Bingo!"

Then Janey pipes up, "Why has he brought him here, George? I get it, this is where he experienced massive trauma (hence the reason I suggested coming here), but still, do you think Bert would willingly come out here?"

"No, I don't believe he would, but I am sure there is a logical explanation. We need to get out there to find out what's going on – and fast!"

"Agreed. I'm just worried about him. What if this has brought on another psychotic episode?"

"Yes, that is entirely possible. We should be prepared for anything. Most importantly though, let's get to Thomas as quickly as we can. His safety is paramount. Bert might be older and physically weaker than Thomas, but I do not trust him." From the look in Janey's eyes, I have just voiced her concerns.

We exit the car in tandem and set a brisk pace. From the carpark to the tip of Neist Point, it is approximately two kilometres which, at a reasonable walking speed, would take around forty-five minutes to traverse. There is, however, only one route so without doubt, we were going to come across them. Even if they had veered off the path, the landscape here is so open, you can see for miles around so I felt confident we would see them soon.

Thomas

It seemed fitting that this was where we had ended up. It hadn't been my intention to come back but the irony of the situation wasn't lost on me. Bert had become more lucid on the approach to Neist Point so the timing on arrival had been just right, coinciding with him starting to open his eyes. I had gone along with Caroline's plan without fully considering the consequences. It occurred to me that had Bert came to life whilst the car was being driven along, Lord only knows what could have happened. He could've taken fright, resulting in me crashing the car. Or, what if he had had the opposite reaction and lunged for me? The end result would have been the same – the car would have been run off the road. I shudder at the thought.

No, Caroline's plan had been executed perfectly. I cut the engine and scan the area. Good, there weren't many cars or tourists to be seen. I then turn my attention to Bert who is showing signs of regaining consciousness with the car being at a standstill. His words are now easily decipherable – "What?" Then I watch as he vigorously rubs his eyes. "Where am I?" he says, eyes now open and taking in the surrounds. He hasn't clocked me yet.

What happens next happens in an instant. He turns to his right and immediately spies me. I lock eyes with him. For a split second I wonder if he even has a clue who I am. Twenty years have passed. Would he recognise me? His actions give me an immediate answer.

His eyes widen in horror like a rabbit caught in the headlights and he bolts out of the car and takes off down the path. It is oddly fascinating and equally strangely amusing all at the same time. How could a person who was so heavily intoxicated simply spring to life with such velocity?

"Don't let him get away," cries a determined James.

"Don't worry, he can't get far, there's only one route." I launch myself out of the car and all four of us follow in hot pursuit. The tables had turned. The power had shifted. The last time I was here with him, he was in hot pursuit of me. This gave me a much-needed boost and I powered on.

He knew. I saw it in his eyes when he looked at me. It had come home to roost for him. He was the physically weaker of the two of us and he had taken fright. In addition to that, he would be all too aware that in my sober state I had an advantage over him. I had manipulated the situation by getting him into the car unawares and driving him out here. He knew I had the upper hand. Then, when he saw where we had parked up, that would be the nail in the coffin. He would know I was seeking retribution. (I hadn't intended to come here but it's unlikely Bert would think that).

The gap closes. Every so often, he turns around to see where I am. He isn't fully steady on his feet and every once in a while he trips and stumbles. It is uncanny, the similarity to twenty years ago. Only, the players have switched roles! Back then it was me listening out keenly for his fast-approaching steps behind me.

Then something distracts me. A noise coming from some distance away, barely audible. It sounds like someone is shouting my name. The wind dies down somewhat and at that point I hear it clearly – "Thomas!" And there is no mistaking who had shouted it for I knew that voice probably better than I knew the sound of my own voice – it was Janey.

CHAPTER 30

How did she know to come out here? I had been so fixated on getting to Bert to confront him, I hadn't even thought about Janey and George following me. Twenty years on and all the players are back out here (with the addition of George, my newly found father) – how fitting. I must remain focussed and so I plough on undeterred.

Bert is showing no signs of slowing down. If anything, he has quickened his pace. It is fortunate that we arrived late in the day for there are very few people here (I see the odd dog walker and straggler off in the distance). Otherwise, I am certain we would have aroused unwanted attention. I quicken my pace to match his.

We have now covered quite some ground. To my right, I run towards the lighthouse cottages and I picture a terrified young Janey gazing out all those years ago. He can't go much further, and he knows it. We are at the end of the road. Only the lighthouse itself and the cliff edge lie beyond this point.

He darts around the compound (which comprises the cottages; a courtyard and the lighthouse) and manages to find an opening. I follow. We arrive within seconds of each other. We are stood only a few feet apart, both now at a standstill in the open grounds of the courtyard. I watch as he slumps forwards, thoroughly spent. Then, he turns around to face me.

"What do you want from me?! Why have you dragged me all the way out here, and against my will?" He looks pitiful. It infuriates me all the more. That he (of all people) should be feeling sorry for himself after the years of torment he had mother and I endure. He can't bear it. "Well? Aren't you even going to say anything? You chase me all the way out here to this godforsaken place and you can't even have a conversation with me?!"

Then I see it in his face. His features contort. He turns in an instant from the frightened, pitiful creature I had encountered only moments ago, to the nasty, evil monster which haunted my childhood. "What is it, boy? Cat got your tongue? You always were useless. A low-down good-for-nothing waste of space." He pauses then twists the knife in deeper. "Just like that crazy bitch mother of yours!"

I cock my head from side to side, taking him all in, scrutinising him as if he were a new lifeform, beholding him for the first time under a microscopic lens. In that moment, it occurs to me he could say what he liked to me. The words did not hold the gravitas they once did for I see it now; they are only words. The choice is mine – whether I let those words sink in and cause irreversible damage. Or, whether I see them for what they really are – the rantings and ramblings of a bitter, old, twisted soul so pickled with liquor, it is quite possible he doesn't even have a clue what he is saying.

However, this does not mean he is off the hook. He needs to hear a few home truths. This is after all why I brought him out here. It is not only Bert who is growing impatient. James lets his feelings be known;

"Well, aren't you gonna give him chapter and verse?"

"I am getting to it, James, believe me!"

Bert launches in, "No fucking way! So, you haven't outgrown your little fantasy world then? You still speak to your *imaginary* friends?" (he emphasises the word 'imaginary' for maximum impact).

Indomitably, he carries on. "The thing I cannot quite understand is how you ever bagged a piece of skirt. What woman worth her salt would happily put up with that shite You were a complete waste of space years ago and nothing, it seems, has changed!"

He has now successfully pushed my buttons by bringing Janey into it. "I am a complete waste of space, am I? You bastard! If I am certified mentally ill and 'hear voices,' then it's your fault! All the abuse I suffered at your hands and witnessing how you treated mother, that's what caused me to start hearing voices in the first place!" He shakes his head, dismissing what I've said. "I have read the psychologists report which was carried out following our last encounter at Neist Point … after you attacked me, landing me in hospital. It is damming. It is all there in black and white; it confirms that my mental state was all your doing. What was it he said? 'Psychosis brought on by significant and sustained trauma inflicted by the boy's father during childhood, both physical and mental.' How you managed to worm your way out of a prison sentence for what you did, I do not know. You left me for dead out there in that storm."

I see he is taking his time to choose his words carefully, clearly fearful of implicating himself. "They couldn't prove nothing! It was your word against mine and let's be honest here, they're not gonna believe the ramblings of a psychotic, delusional lad! Oh, and your mother backed me up! She gave me an alibi; said I was with her when it happened." He is delighting in telling me this part, his face full of glee. "She took a little persuading (if you know what I mean – put in her place ya ken), but she soon came around. Then bingo, I killed two birdies with one stone! Got myself out of trouble with the law and got rid of you at the same time. George thought I was mad at him for meddling. Nothing could be further from the truth! His meddling secured you a home with foster parents and I was rid of you once and for all! Mary wasn't far behind you either! Crazy bitch totally lost her marbles, and the care home was only too happy to take her in. I got myself a sweet wee life after that, rid of the pair of you!"

He truly is a piece of work. There is no remorse whatsoever. He thinks himself marvellous for plotting and scheming to get rid of mother and I and for managing to evade being brought to justice. And all for what? So he can live a lonely existence in that now putrid, stinking croft where no doubt he will end his days having drunk himself to death!

By no means did he deserve it, but I decided to give him one last chance, one last chance to make amends. "If I was such a burden to you and you wanted rid of me, why didn't you get me the help I needed when I was living in the 'fantasy world' you described? Perhaps I'd have been taken off your hands then." He laughs out loud at this.

"What, and ruin all the fun I was having watching your pathetic little puppet show?! You didn't know the difference between fantasy and reality, your personalities were so intertwined. I never knew which one I was talking to!" He is bent double laughing as though this is the funniest thing he has ever heard.

It is too much. Caroline now has her say: "Are you really going to let him speak to you like that? Tell him the truth." Of course. I feel around in my coat pocket and come across it immediately. There is a chance he does know but he might be completely in the dark. I brandish my birth certificate in front of him. He might have been utterly cock-sure of himself only seconds ago, but self-preservation is high on his agenda and he doesn't inch any closer towards me to see what the document says. "Very well, if you are not prepared to come forwards to read it, I will happily share its contents with you. Bert, this is my birth certificate. I would like to draw your attention to the section where it says 'father's name.' You see, it's not your name in print there, it states 'George Traynor.'"

Now it is my turn to revel. His face says it all – he is in shock. And it is now my turn to twist the knife in. "Looks like she got one over on you!" I snigger now and my siblings join in with me. Just at that moment, my wife and father round the corner and join me, flanking me either side.

Bert once again dons the hard-faced exterior. "Oh, I might've guessed you pair would be in on it. No show without punch eh!" This time, he does start to move forwards – in George's direction. "You son of a bitch!" I waste no time and place myself squarely between my real father and the imposter.

"If you want to get to him, you will have to get past me first!"

"Oh, now he shows some balls! That's the kind of attitude a son of mine would have. But you are no son of mine, are you? Show me that birth certificate! Prove it to me!" I hold it only inches from his face. He scrunches his features up in an attempt to read it then backs off.

"I think you'll find George is not the 'son of a bitch' here. It's you! If this had all come out when I was younger, mother and I could have had the chance of a good life, a 'normal' life."

"Aye, would've saved me a lot of hassle too. Stupid bitch should've fessed up!"

"Really, really?! And what would you have done to her if she had? She was scared witless of you! You ruined my life and hers! All the torture I experienced and then the psychosis, it could all have been avoided! And for what? You aren't even my real dad!"

All the pent-up emotions I had sought to bury over the years came to the fore. At the same time, I could clearly hear the voices of my siblings offering various words of reassurance and encouragement. It had all been building up to this point. Instinctively, I lunge straight for him.

I push him with such force I was unaware I even possessed. He goes stumbling backwards and crash-lands on the concrete. He lets out a cry like an injured animal and attempts to get back onto his feet. But he is not quick enough. I am on top of him in an instant and I raise my arm heavenward, ready to bring my fist towards his face. At that moment, my intention is to pulverize his skull; to put him and us out of our misery once and for all but I am stopped in my tracks. Janey screams at me, her voice fever pitch: "No, NO Thomas! Don't do it! He's not worth it!" I snap back to reality in an instant. She is right, he's not worth it. If I follow through and kill him, then I potentially lose her and Michael and my chance at forging a relationship with my real father.

I roll over him and he wastes no time. He is on his feet now and running off blindly. With no sense of where to go and what to do, he looks like a pheasant darting here and there, his balance somewhat precarious. Janey and George rush to my side.

"Are you OK?" Janey asks.

"I'm fine thanks. Tell me, how did you know to come out here?"

"An educated guess."

I revert to the task in hand. "What are we going to do with him?"

George this time: "I think you've said what needed to be said. You can move on now, Thomas. Why don't we offer him a ride home and that will put an end to it once and for all? Janey and I can accompany you, make sure he doesn't pull any stunts. There's no reason for you to concern yourself with him anymore after that."

"Offer him a lift home? Really?"

"Thomas, it shows that you are the better man. It shows that he hasn't won, that no matter what he does or says, you will come out on top."

I consider this. My gut instinct was to leave him here, abandon him like he did me but there was a truth in George's words. If I did as he suggested, once again I had the upper hand and would be seen to be unaffected by Bert's wickedness. "OK, we can offer him a lift, but undoubtedly he will throw it back in our face."

"There's every chance, Thomas!"

We leave the courtyard and scan the surrounding area. Janey spots him straight away. "Over there," and she points him out. He is just off the path close to the edge of the cliff. Rather than raise the alarm and cause him to run off, we approach quietly. He isn't aware of our presence – yet.

I do my best to quell the unrest. My siblings are universally not in support of this plan. They think we should turn around and never look back. However, we are fairly close to him now. It is a wide-open vista of sky and sea beyond. Once again, I hear the noise of the waves crashing on impact with the cliffside and I am reminded of the scene twenty years ago.

George gives me the nod to start a conversation with him. No doubt Bert will think this is some sort of a trap, so I try to make it sound as sincere as possible (which believe me is no mean feat when all I feel like doing is wringing his bloody neck!).

"Come on, Bert, come with us, we will give you a ride back." His movements are jerky. He whips his head around and snaps it back. From the look in his eyes, he is terrified. He knows what I meant to do back in that courtyard and, if it hadn't been for Janey, he knows I would have followed it through. He says something but his words are lost on the wind and travel out to sea, so we advance further, closing the gap between us.

This time he initiates the conversation. He turns to face us, and it suddenly dawns on me how close we are to the cliff edge. "Do not take another step! Ya hear me? Any one of you takes another step in my direction and so help me God, I'll fling their carcass over the edge!"

I hear something and it scares me witless. It's Caroline. "Now's your chance, Thomas! You will never get another chance like it. Put that miserable bastard out of his misery once and for all! Push him,

Thomas! Do it for me and do it for you, for all the hurt he has inflicted. He thought nothing of tossing me over the edge, so why should you? They will try to talk you out of it, but don't listen to them, Thomas, do it for us!" I am momentarily conflicted, then come to my senses.

"No Caroline, I won't do it!"

Bert sneers and ridicules me in response to this. He mimics my voice, *"No Caroline, I won't do it …_*Hearing voices again, are we? You are a loon just like your crazy bitch mother. You've lost your marbles too you know. Mark my words, in no time, they will cart your ass off to that care home too. How fitting – you and her side by side, two crazies locked up together!" This time George interjects before I have a chance to say anything.

"Enough Bert. Don't you think you've done enough damage? Let's draw a line in the sand. It ends here today. You go your way, and we go ours. Forget about the offer of a lift home, just let it go, no more, Bert."

"Aah, it finally speaks, the wife-stealer and adulterer. Oh, and now, the prodigal father so I am led to believe! Do not for one minute lay all the blame at my door. You have more than played your part in all of this! Interfering and sticking your nose in where it wasn't wanted. After all, we wouldn't be stood here today if it wasn't for you as Thomas wouldn't exist now, would he? And the world as we know it would be all the better for it."

"Now look here, Bert, you've overstepped the mark one too many times!" I watch on in disbelief as everything which happens next unfolds. George takes a step towards Bert. He doesn't lash out at him. However, Bert instinctively takes a step backwards, feeling threatened by the advancing George.

There was nothing obvious jutting out of the earth, but Bert had stumbled on what we later discovered was uneven, rough ground.

His balance was completely off kilter. His arms were flailing, and you could see terror in his face. He was desperate to regain control over his motor function, to stabilise himself, but it was impossible. The chain of events was set in motion and the initial stumble sent him reeling backwards.

I reached forwards; arms outstretched. He made a vain attempt to reach for my arms, but it was hopeless, and he knew it. We all watched in astonishment and horror as Bert Taylor drew his last breath. He careered over the cliff edge, his body consumed by the furious waves below and his screams were sucked in by the prevailing winds.

We all dropped to our knees and peered over the edge. There was no sign of him, as though he had never existed in the first place. The watery depths had claimed him, and he would not be released from their grasp.

We sit like that, peering over the edge, for an indeterminable period of time, fully expecting to see his face appear at any moment. It didn't seem possible that such a formidable life-force such as Bert could be snuffed out in an instant like that. Eventually, with no sign of him re-appearing, we retreat and sit some distance away from the edge. We have no words so sit there in a mutual shocked silence. The only sounds to be heard are the perpetual gusting winds, crashing waves, and Caroline's summing up of the situation – "Good riddance to bad rubbish."

CHAPTER 31

Six months after Bert's passing

Life has a strange way of just easing back into a natural rhythm. No matter what trauma you endure, life simply ploughs on regardless. Days turn into weeks and weeks into months. You just get sucked along with it.

Leaving Skye was bittersweet. It felt as though a huge weight had been lifted off my shoulders. I was coming to terms with my reality and my mental state. I had faced the demons from my past head on and they hadn't destroyed me. I was no longer haunted by old ghosts.

However, leaving meant leaving George and leaving mother. I had only just discovered my new father then had to bid him farewell. But there was no way I could leave my financial advisory practice a minute longer – clients were starting to become impatient in my absence. There was also Michael. I yearned to be back home, to spend time with him.

When the time was right, Janey and I sat him down and explained that there was someone he needed to meet – his new grandfather. George had been patient with us and fully understood that we wanted to take things at a slow pace to begin with. This was not the case with Michael. As soon as he knew about George, he just had to meet him. So, arrangements were made, and he came to stay with us for a couple of weeks.

From the minute he arrived (a couple of days ago), there was an obvious bond between the two of them. George marvelled in the new experience of having a grandchild and Michael was only too happy to lap up all the attention. It was a joy to behold and, honestly, I could feel the start of a relationship forming between myself and George.

When I look back over the years, even although neither of us knew we were so intimately connected, he had looked out for me and shown genuine concern. It meant a lot. Wherever this was going, it felt as though our relationship was blossoming. There was even a connection between George and Janey. It was light-hearted. They shared a similar sense of humour and, it appeared, a deep affection for one another.

I had taken some much-needed time off work whilst he was here and set about planning what we would do with our time together. We were only a couple of days in when he asked if it would be possible to have a private chat. I could tell from his demeanour this was to be a serious discussion.

"Sorry son," (he had just taken to calling me son) "I need to speak to you about Bert." The heavy weight re-appeared across my shoulders. "There was an investigation into his disappearance." Of course there would be. I had been so preoccupied with work etc. that I hadn't given the matter too much thought. He carries on.

"I have a friend on the force and was able to get some inside information. Don't worry though, I haven't mentioned anything about you being my son. I don't want to arouse suspicion. The good news is they never found a body. The sea swallowed him up good and proper." I motion to him to hush and quieten his voice down. Michael was only upstairs, and God forbid should he hear a word of this. Newly silenced, I then give him a nod to carry on.

"You know what folks on the Islands are like for making up stories. All sorts of weird and wonderful tales have been told. But the truth is, no-one knows what happened to him. No-one has come forward to say they saw him or us out at Neist Point." At this, I breath a huge sigh of relief.

"It was a real mystery to the Police – his car being parked right outside but there being no sign of him. They have followed up on various lines of enquiry but each time, have hit the proverbial brick wall.

"Although a thorough investigation was carried out, by all accounts, Bert was somewhat the recluse. He could go for days or even several weeks without seeing a soul so there was no-one to raise the alarm straight away. The only time he mingled with people was when he needed to get his food or drink and he limited that contact, preferring instead to stock up for a month at a time. The only other contact he had was with the local vet if any of the animals needed tending to, but that contact was few and far between (he was tight with his money and animal welfare wasn't high on his list of priorities).

"With no body and no witnesses, they don't suspect any foul play. Their report concluded that it was completely out of character for him to just disappear. However, at the best of times now, his behaviour wasn't what you would classify as 'normal.' He has succumbed to alcohol and it was plain for anyone to see that he was no longer able to look after himself or the croft. You only need to spend a couple of minutes in the place to realise the magnitude of his mental decline and his addiction problems. You saw that for yourself, the state of the place and all the empty bottles of liquor strewn everywhere. They have parked their investigations for now. The only open line of enquiry is that he is a missing person, and should anyone have any information in relation to this, they should come forwards."

I sit back and take it all in. All things considered, we were extremely lucky. There were very few people out there that day (I can recall only seeing a couple). I had, however, been too preoccupied at the time with Bert to pay too much attention but, from memory, they had been dog walkers. Hopefully, the status quo remains intact and they don't go to the Police.

I try to picture the scene in my mind from a third-party viewpoint. You had Bert out front being chased by me then not too far behind were George and Janey. It is unlikely that George and Janey's presence would have aroused much suspicion (they had been quite far behind us). However, the worrying part was me chasing Bert. But could this be interpreted for something else other than a chase? Two people out on a run together only meters apart perhaps? After all, we had arrived in the same car … it is possible that this is what someone would see? I had to cling to the hope that that is what it looked like.

However, had there been any witnesses to the scene at the courtyard or the cliff edge afterwards, that was a different matter entirely. I chide myself for even contemplating this. There wasn't a soul in the courtyard (our own company aside). The cliff edge though, I couldn't be so sure. I had only become aware of external surroundings after Bert met his untimely death. At that point, I can say with certainty there was no-one there.

It is true, neither one of us was wholly to blame for his demise. But how would it look in a court of law? I had a physical and verbal altercation with him in the courtyard, causing him to run off. Then, at the cliffside, George had advanced towards him (when he had been provoked) causing him to stumble backwards and lose his footing and fall to his death. Yes, we hadn't pushed him but I was certain that a good lawyer worth his salt would find that we were both culpable.

I simply had to adopt George's perspective – no news was good news. I tell him so and he nods in agreement. We make a mutual decision at that point – nether one of us will speak of the matter again and we will move on with our lives. I take a mental note to relay everything he has told me to Janey so that she too is in the loop and hope that she will happily agree (as George has done) to never speak of it again.

We slip easily back into our new family life; this awful matter well and truly behind us. For the remainder of George's stay, we make the most of our time together – us showing him the beautiful Border countryside and what it has to offer and him helping to prepare sumptuous dinners and telling us tales about folklore from days gone by around the Highlands and Islands. Michael is engrossed, thoroughly engaged.

But, what of my siblings? I continue to take my medication but not the same dose I took before I travelled back to Skye. I cut the dose in half which means it is not as potent and, as a result, my siblings now appear to me occasionally. I had made the decision to work on my mental health but, I wasn't quite ready to let them go, not just yet. I didn't hide this from Janey. We talked about it at great length. Given what I had just been through, she fully understood that it would be very difficult to let go completely for now. We would take it one day at a time – together, as a family.

A couple of months later, I was sat at my desk in a rare moment of peace and contemplation. Caroline appeared to me. I immediately straightened my posture, receptive to what she had to say for I could see the grave look on her face.

"I have been waiting for the right time to tell you this, Thomas. It's about that day out at Neist Point with Bert. I saw someone … I saw a face … peering out of the window of one of the lighthouse keepers' cottages …"

THE END

ABOUT THE AUTHOR

This is my debut novel, so it would mean so much to me if you could take a minute or two of your time to leave a review. I plan to write a sequel to 'It's Time' so if the first book does well, this makes it all the more possible to write a follow up... with your help!

I would love to hear from you. Please find me on Facebook (Rachael Dytor Author) or at www.rachaeldytor.com where you can subscribe to my mailing list. Be the first to hear about forthcoming releases and promotions. (If you enjoyed this book, you will also be able to get a sneak peek at the first two chapters to the sequel to IT'S TIME when you subscribe!)

Printed in Great Britain
by Amazon

63631193R00153